The Interpreter

Suzanne Glass

D1115459

McArthur & Company
Toronto

First published in Canada in 2000 by:
McArthur & Company
322 King Street West, Suite 402
Toronto, On
M5V 1J2

Canadian Cataloguing in Publication Data

Glass, Suzanne
  The interpreter

ISBN 1-55278-130-5

I. Title.

PR6057.L37I57 2000   823'.92   C00-930257-3

ISBN 1-55278-130-5

Printed in Canada by Transcontinental Printing

10 9 8 7 6 5 4 3 2 1

For Ruth and Alick,
With my love always.

Acknowledgements

Amongst the many people to whom I am grateful for their help, I would particularly like to thank my agent, Jo Frank, and my editor, Kate Parkin, for believing in me from the very beginning.

Thanks also to Jerome Groopman, Professor of Medicine at Harvard Medical School, for his time and expertise.

Thanks to my wonderful friends Romana Agliati and Laura Ziv for bullying me to start writing, and to Lesley Piper, Franca Tranza, Nicky Zatland, Michelle Berman, Jane Stocker, Marion McCarthy, Kate Elton and my mother for lending me their ears on demand.

Thanks to Sarah Hartley, Miles Pulver, Eva Wollenberg, Hayley Wollenberg and Nicole Lever for their input.

And to my father. Without him, *The Interpreter* would quite simply have stayed in my mind.

Twice or thrice had I loved thee,
Before I knew thy face or name

John Donne
'Air and Angels'

ONE

Dominique

I was in the dark. Or at least in semi-darkness. I always worked best when the light in the booth was dim. So I was in this half-lit makeshift booth, in the semi-darkness except for a blue glow from my tiny reading-lamp. In the semi-darkness, in the makeshift booth in the grey conference hall on Lexington Avenue in New York City.

My colleague that day was a spotty Liverpudlian who had once put his hand on my thigh while I was in the middle of a piece of simultaneous translation. I had shifted my position and carried on translating from French to English, spouting forth about the size and hue of tomatoes, and managed after that to avoid his gaze for months. Other female interpreters had reacted more aggressively to his clammy paws and had complained to the International Interpreters' Association, but I had said nothing. These days, for fear of being struck off he picked at his skin and his cuticles rather than seeking out the thighs of his colleagues.

'You go first Dominique,' he said.

I nodded and pulled my headphones down over my ears. I looked at my watch. Four minutes to go. The delegates were filing back into the hall. Black, brown, red, grey-haired doctors and researchers, all of them sauntering back into the room. I pushed my hair off my face and took a few long deep breaths. Usually the intense concentration of the morning had calmed my nerves and by the afternoon I was raring to go, running closely behind the voice of the speaker, following his rhythm, his intonation, his speed, his tone. But on that Friday the adrenalin was still pumping at the start of the afternoon session. I put it down to stress. I put it down to the effects of my conversation with Anna the week before. Now sitting in the blue glow with three minutes to go before kick-off, through my headphones, I heard not the shuffling of the delegates' papers, but last week's conversation that had played itself over and over again in my head.

'He's bad,' she had said in her almost accentless English.

'How bad?' I had asked.

'He's bad,' she repeated. 'He has ulcers in his mouth. He's horribly thin. He can't concentrate. I'm trying to persuade him to take the medication now. He's told his father about it.'

'How are you?' I asked.

'I'm not so great, Dom,' she said. 'Not so great. I feel, you know, like you feel when it could be the beginning of the end for someone you love. I feel, I feel . . .'

The line had gone dead.

The receiver crackled. My headphones crackled. My colleague prodded me rather too close to my thigh. It was my turn to interpret. Through the glass of the booth I could make out the chairman of the conference limping up the steps. He turned his red fleshy face towards his audience. I swallowed. The chairman cleared his throat too loudly. It hurt my eardrums.

I reached for my control panel and adjusted the red volume button. The chairman began.

'*Bon après-midi mesdames et messieurs, je vous souhaite la bienvenue à la deuxième partie de notre conference.*'

Good afternoon, ladies and gentlemen, welcome back to the second part of our conference.

'*J'espère que vous n'êtes pas trop ensommeillés après tout cet alcool pour apprécier notre prochain orateur . . .*'

I hope you're not too sleepy after all that red wine, to appreciate our next speaker.

Dr Katz came up onto the podium. I looked at the watch Paul had bought me, so that I would 'feel' every second I was away from him. The light was too low to see the hands, but I knew I had about twenty-five minutes to go. We worked in half-hour sessions. That was about as far as the concentration would stretch in a stint of simultaneous interpreting. It was tough stuff. Interpreters are more prone to strokes and brain haemorrhages from stress than the rest of the population.

I felt the Liverpudlian staring. I closed my eyes and the words of the speaker kaleidoscoped in and out of mine. He talked of the need to find a cure for the common cold, the number of working days missed because of the virus, the amount of ineffectual medication on the market, the hunt, the chase to be the first to come up with something new, exciting, innovative. He spoke faster and faster. I ran faster and faster behind him. His breathing was shallow. Obviously a smoker. You could always tell when you were interpreting a smoker. The speaker took a sip of water. I weighed up whether there was time to take a sip of mine. I decided against it. I would have fallen a sentence behind him and it was always hard to catch up. The Liverpudlian prodded me again. I looked at him. He pointed to the control panel. It was his turn to take over. I nodded, all the while talking, finishing my sentence, finishing the speaker's sentence, talking about the advances in his research. I switched off my microphone a split second before he switched on his. A seamless transition from my voice to his. My colleague began to talk. I rolled my neck from side to side, unclenched my fists and vowed to get out of the habit of digging my nails into my palms till they bled while I translated. Some of the delegates turned round to stare at us, startled by the change of voice in their ears. At moments like this they suddenly remembered they were listening to human beings and not to machines. I stood up and carefully pushed open the cardboard door of the booth. I closed it silently and crept out of the back of the conference hall along the corridor to the bathrooms.

In the white tiled room I sat down on a low black stool in front of a huge mirror. I looked at myself without seeing, brushed my reddy-brown hair, applied my lipstick and just sat there. Words buzzed in my head, unstoppable as the threatening hum of a circling mosquito. Not the words of the speaker I had just translated, though that would hardly have been unusual. I often heard other people's words, other people's voices in my head for hours after I came out of the booth. The feeling is the same as when you have sat in front of a computer screen for hours and for some time afterwards the words dance in front of your eyes. But no, these were not the speaker's words. I just kept on hearing that line of Anna's, 'He has ulcers in his mouth. He's horribly thin . . . He can't concentrate.'

I found myself now translating the words into French. Sitting on the stool in the Ladies and whispering to myself, '*Il a des plaques dans la bouche, il est affreusement mince . . . il n'arrive pas à se concentrer.*' You idiot, I thought, what use is this?

Someone flushed a toilet. I realized I had been out of

4

the booth for more than ten minutes. You never did that to your colleague. You never stayed away for more than ten minutes. He might want you to look up a word. He might be having a coughing fit and need you to take over. I ran back down the corridor, tiptoed into the conference hall and slipped back into the booth.

It was lighter now. They had pulled back the heavy purple velvet curtains at the side of the hall. I could see the Liverpudlian clearly. He had been attacking his face viciously while he had been working. He turned and gave me a dirty look. I looked away and sat down.

I opened my medical dictionary. Reams and reams of medical vocabulary in four languages. I tried to read a page every night before I went to sleep. 'You ought to read something a little more steamy,' Anna said to me once and threw a copy of *9½ Weeks* onto my duvet. 'Read it,' she said. 'You might learn something.' I read it. I learnt and we laughed about it. That was before Mischa's ulcers.

The Liverpudlian was going at it fifty to the dozen, leaning back in his chair, his feet up against the desk, one toe poking through a hole in a grubby sock. He sounded to the untrained ear as if he were translating fluently. It was only the initiated who would have realized he was ill-prepared and making mistake after mistake.

I ran my eyes over the conference documentation. However well you prepared yourself, however many hundreds of words you learnt in readiness for a medical conference there was always a phrase that would trip you up. But I had a head start. My father was a doctor and the names of drugs and illnesses had been the vocabulary of my youth. 'Dad,' I had said, the night before on the phone from New York to London, 'Dad, can you explain to me a bit about viruses?'

He had laughed and said, 'That's like me asking you to teach me Italian in a phone call. Look, fax me the documents and I'll try to explain things to you in context.'

'I can't,' I said.

'You can't?'

'You know this stuff is always confidential.'

'I'm your father,' he said. 'If you want help you'll just have to trust me.'

'I'll think about it, Dad,' I said.

I didn't fax the documents. I stood in my apartment with my finger on the green start button of the fax machine, about to transmit, and changed my mind. 'Confidentiality,' screamed the Interpreting School director in my head. 'Confidentiality. Break your vow of confidentiality, get caught and you are out. Your vows are as solemn as the Hippocratic oath, as sacred as the nun's marriage to Jesus. What you learn in that booth must stay there or else your career is at an end.'

I could hear the Liverpudlian getting a little out of breath. I tapped lightly on the desk in front of me, caught his attention and raised my eyebrows. We interpreters quickly learned the non-verbal code, the language which we speak while we are talking. The raised eyebrows meant, 'Are you struggling? Shall I take over?' He shook his head. There was a certain shame in handing the microphone to a colleague before your stint was over. It was like ending a sprint before you reached the finishing line. He made it, panting to the last word. The audience applauded the speaker. The Liverpudlian switched off his microphone and spluttered into his grey handkerchief. I felt repulsed.

The chairman stood up to make the closing remarks for the day. I was on. Mike on. Headphones. 'Focus, Dominique, focus.' Miss a word and you have missed the train. It had been a long day. I was tense and tired. My colleague shoved a note under my nose. 'I'm off,' it read. Against the rules to leave me there alone, even if it was the last speech, but I didn't care. I gave him the thumbs-up sign and he was gone. I was more relaxed with him out of the way. The words tumbled out of me. I was spurred on by the finishing line. 'Ladies and gentlemen, I think you'll agree we should also say thank you to our team of interpreters. They've done an excellent job and it's been a gruelling day.'

I leant back exhausted. I always found it amusing and slightly embarrassing when I had to translate praise about my own work.

I should have felt nothing but relief. The day was over. Thousands of words had flowed through me into thin air. My grotty, spotty colleague was gone. I ought to have walked out of there with a spring in my step. I ought to have rushed out into the streets of Manhattan. Instead I sat very still in the corner of my booth and waited for the delegates to file out as they had filed in. I could see no-one but still I felt as though I were not alone in the room. My headphones were on the desk in front of me. I heard faint voices coming from them. I picked them up. There were clearly still two or more people in the room talking. They had forgotten to switch off their microphone. I could hear them speaking in hushed tones, but I couldn't see them. Part of the hall was out of my line of vision. I reached for the control panel. I turned up the volume and held the headset to one ear.

'. . . quite by chance,' said a deep male voice with a Southern drawl.

'You don't stumble on these things by chance,' said an older voice and coughed a smoker's cough.

'They did with penicillin.'

'Billions of dollars are invested . . .' for a moment my headphones crackled '. . . HIV every year, my young friend. No-one, not even he, could find a quasi-cure by chance. Anyway, what makes you think it could work?'

I stiffened.

'The other day. In his lab I saw it for myself. Cells that should have been riddled with the disease holding their own. Couldn't believe my eyes.'

'And he's told no-one?'

'No, just me. He's a loner. I think I'm his only confidante.'

'And you reckon he's credible? Worth backing?'

'I reckon he's a genius. But modest with it. Never brags. I can't say it's conclusive, but I'm damn sure he's onto something. I think he'll be persuaded to come with us.'

I started to shake, sitting there trapped in that booth. A little at first. Then harder. I was afraid they would feel the vibrations of my movements. Mischa, I thought. The ulcers. The swallowing. The wasting away. There's a way out. These voices in my ears, they have the answer.

I was thinking so loudly, I almost forgot to listen.

'Follow his progress,' said the older, smoker's voice. 'And for God's sake make sure he keeps it under wraps till we get our act together and we can bring him on board. Land me this one and I'll back you to the hilt.'

'Trust me,' said the deep Southern voice and laughed a deep and heavy laugh.

The conversation stopped abruptly. Someone had switched off the microphone. I dug my nails into my palms and waited. I heard movement. I shoved my papers into my briefcase. I crept out of the booth, I walked out of the side door, I burst into a run along Lexington Avenue.

I ran and I ran, past Fifty-Third Street, Fifty-Second, on to Fifty-First, left on to Third Avenue, Second, left into Beekman Place, shouting to myself, 'Anna, Anna, tell Mischa, there might be a way!' I rushed past the doorman and pounded up the stairs to my apartment. I went straight for the telephone on the kitchen wall beside the fridge. I dialled Anna's number from memory and suddenly I froze. A voice in my head was screaming at me. 'Your vows of confidentiality are as solemn as the Hippocratic oath. As sacred as the nun's marriage to Jesus.'

TWO

Nicholas

I knew Dominique's voice long before I knew Dominique. I knew all their voices, in fact, for some time before I considered them as human beings. During those long hours, sitting listening to them translating from languages of which I knew little, I was entirely reliant on the skills of the interpreters. And yet for weeks I thought of them as no more than translating machines. When one of them stuttered or stammered, floundered or faltered, I fiddled with my control panel as one would with the buttons on a radio. The superhuman efforts behind the sounds that entered my ears and those of the other doctors and researchers never crossed my mind. They were no more than groupings of English, French, Italian, Spanish or German sounds passing through channels one, two, three, four and five, providing a service and reverberating in my headphones. Sounds that could be summoned with a flick of a switch and dismissed with the same. Now that I can begin to understand the cerebral dexterity required to listen, to absorb, to speak and to convey meaning all at once, I still feel somewhat guilty at my one-time lack of appreciation of the interpreters.

These in-house international conferences organized by Landmark, my pharmaceutical company, though sometimes dull, provided relief from my otherwise solitary working life. At times I was happy to banter with colleagues during coffee breaks. At others I wished myself back in my white coat and mask in the laboratory poring over coloured liquids in test-tubes on white laminated surfaces, or peering at cells through microscopes. Within the sterile walls of my working environment I might have been anywhere. The buzz of Manhattan in no way penetrated the characterless Sixties building in which I worked, and I was so far removed from the reality of the outside world that often when I ventured out on to Lexington at the end of a day, squinting in the sunlight or bracing myself against the biting air, I felt as though, in those paces between the laboratory and the street, I had travelled between one country and another with no journey in between.

I had been in Manhattan for six months by the time I first heard Dominique's voice. It was some time after that that I first met Dominique. She and the words she spoke in the booth had little to do with one another.

I had been transferred from the Florence branch of Landmark to New York, to continue my research on paediatric leukaemia, surrounded by some of the world's leading scientists. I could pretend that my motives were entirely altruistic, but that would be a lie. And in all of this I would like to try at least to be honest with myself, though I am not sure quite how well I will succeed. Though I was driven by vocation, that of course was just a part of it. I was fired too by the passion of discovery in my field. At times I even felt a fraud being paid for this work, for lost in the world of experimentation I was little different from the gawky adolescent working on wooden benches in the school laboratory in Florence.

But though to experiment was the very essence of my

work, unlike Dominique I had never felt a burning need to travel, to experience different lifestyles or cultures. I did not seek adventure outside the laboratory, but adventure it seems, sought me. 'Manzini,' he called. 'Manzini come here a moment.' Grevi, my boss at Landmark, where I was working in Florence before my transfer to New York, had summoned me. 'Manzini,' he called through the open door of his office. 'I am waiting.'

I walked in and stood squarely in front of him. I had worked under Grevi for eighteen months, since I had changed my path from paediatrician to researcher, but all that I knew of him had been learnt from others. He had lost his wife to liver cancer. He had lost his child to some cult or other and he had grown ever more steely. Now he sat behind his chrome desk, fingering the silver moustache that he must surely have waxed at the tips, and he said, 'Manzini, I'm sending you to New York. You will continue your research there and you will meet eminent scientists from all over the world. How soon can you leave?'

I said nothing and he allowed me no time for his words to sink in. 'Manzini,' he said, 'you are wasting my time standing here mute and idle in my place of work. Kindly say something or leave.'

'I would like some time to think about it,' I said.

'You have till 8.30 tomorrow morning. And remember you are not irreplaceable. There are plenty of doctors who would die for this opportunity. And if you do deign to take this position, Nicholas, don't get big ideas about yourself. Remember to stick to the task in hand.'

I turned to leave, angered as ever by his autocratic ways. Grevi rarely offered either praise or criticism and it was only by dint of the fact that I remained his employee that

I could assume he was satisfied with my work. When I had proposed tracing the immune systems and the genetic backgrounds of a sample of newborn babies, to ascertain which were more prone to disease, he had immediately agreed to my suggestion. When the findings of my studies tracing the first six months of the lives of the infants had proved interesting and presented us with new hypotheses, he had registered them, logged them and spoken about them in public. But he had never openly acknowledged my achievements and I cannot pretend that this lack of recognition did not leave me feeling aggrieved.

Walking home that evening along the Arno, I felt a wave of resentment well up in me. Grevi was practically ordering my transfer to another continent. He had not so much as entertained the idea that I might have a private life in Florence that I was loath to leave behind. In my anger I did not stop to consider that he was vested with remarkable powers of intuition.

In all of our lives there is a before and an after. A time before which you would almost certainly have behaved in one way and after which you could never again react with such fluidity, such naïvety. My BC and my AD were before and after Dominique. Before decisions came with very little angst. Afterwards that changed.

And so on the way home from my encounter with Grevi that night, practically wading through the conkers and the autumn leaves, but still comfortably warm in my shirt-sleeves, I allowed my decision to come upon me. I loved Florence and I knew its every crumbly nook and cranny. And, dwarfed on either side by the sandy, rusty buildings of the Renaissance, their colours mirroring the leaves in the fading sunlight, I loved it with an added poignancy. I loved it as I had loved the newborn babies when I was about to take the decision to move from paediatrics to research. I loved it especially when summer was over and we, the Florentines, reclaimed its narrow pavements from the jostling tourists. Then, during the little spare time I had, I would stroll through the narrow back streets, dropping into a bar to drink an espresso at the counter and chat, or to sip a cappuccino in a dark corner, depending on my mood.

That evening I wandered for hours through Florence. If my wanderings were in search of a decision, it can have been no more than a subconscious one. I went first to the Red Bar on the corner of Via Tornabuoni. Everything was bright red. The high leather stools. The counters. The waitress's lipstick. '*Un doppio espresso,*' I said.

'*Certo, dottore,*' she said, and pouted her scarlet lips. Maria, since I had known her, had experienced all sorts of innocuous symptoms that necessitated an examination. Her chest was raw, the small of her back was aching, her ear was throbbing and all of her ailments appeared remarkably close to erogenous zones. Knowing that she was too short of cash to make frequent trips to the doctor and reluctant to acknowledge my suspicions as to the cause of her symptoms, I would examine her in the tiny dark office at the back of the bar, making sure that the door was ajar. '*Sei carino, dottore,*' she would repeat again and again. The word *carino* means both kind and sexually appealing.

When Maria's ailments became ever more frequent I made sure I slipped my 'friend' Carla into the conversation from time to time, and on occasions after work I asked Carla to join me at the Red Bar. Though Maria looked put out, her pains became increasingly infrequent.

'*Carla non viene stasera?*' . . . 'Carla is not coming tonight?'

she asked, looking hopeful. I explained to Maria that I was on my way to meet her. I watched her face fall, drank my espresso from the chunky little red cup and left. From there through the back streets, past the massive impressive red-roofed Duomo into a tiny crumbling piazza, where at the far end I pushed open a heavy wooden church door and crept to the altar in the darkness that was broken only by the flickering of three candles. I did not pray, for I am not religious and I think or at least I used to think that prayer was pointless if you didn't have belief, but I stood in contemplation in the stillness for a few moments. A woman in a pew a few rows behind me began to sob softly, breaking my reverie, and I turned to leave.

Out of the church into dusk, I walked past the stone carvings with their dead eyes, past shopkeepers closing their shutters and restaurateurs opening their doors. I walked and I walked, up the thin white marble steps of the Uffizi, through the revolving glass doors. At the entrance I showed my doctor's pass and handed over my 1000 lire. The woman behind the counter handed me a set of black headphones attached to a black box, and explained that I could listen to a guided tour in the language of my choice. Channel 1 English, Channel 2 French, Channel 3 Italian, Channel 4 German and for some strange reason I turned to the English. I wandered through the wide halls with their mosaic floors, listening to a posh man with a radio-style voice talking about the Uffizi Gallery and its treasures, about da Vinci and Donatello, about Titian and Tintoretto, and I stopped in front of a copy of Michelangelo's *Creation*, so that the posh man could explain the painting with those two cracked fingers straining to touch one another.

It was not high season and the corridors were unusually

quiet, but still a number of unmistakably American tourists were visiting the museum. Perhaps I had come to see how I would feel amongst them, to reach my decision, albeit subconsciously, about a change of country and of language. Only when an attendant tapped me on the arm, mouthing something at me, her voice drowned out by the taped voice of the guide, did I realize that the museum was about to close its doors.

Down the steps into the velvety blackness of the night, I made my way to Carla's house. I have mentioned her only briefly, because though we were friends and lovers I cannot honestly say we were soul mates or indispensable in each other's lives. And so on that evening I hurried through the narrow doorway, up the four flights of rotting steps to her front door. I knocked five times, the signal that it was me and it was safe to open up. She came to the door in her red kimono with her white-blonde hair loosely tied back. She kissed me distractedly on the lips and began immediately to talk and to talk, telling me about her day at the hospital, about the anaesthetic that had gone horribly wrong, the five-year-old child who had to be resuscitated and the panic in the theatre. On and on, reminding me why I had been unable to detach myself emotionally and had finally decided to take a break from paediatrics. On and on she went, her chin in her hands, her elbows propped on the kitchen table. Talking and talking, not really caring if I was listening, and when she had finished I said what I was unaware that I had come to say. 'Carla,' I said. 'I am leaving Florence. I'm moving to New York.'

THREE

Dominique

The word 'secret' lends itself to hushed tones, to excitement and to anticipation. The men I had overheard whispering excitedly about discovery were carrying a secret. I was not. I was burdened by suspicion too massive, too heavy, to label it a secret. The ancient Hebrew word for secret, *sod*, is weighty and numbing. The word *sod* far more accurately describes my load.

I was numbed. I allowed myself to be anaesthetized by the enormity of my insider information and as always when thought became too onerous, I threw myself body and soul into the world of work.

Pharmaceutical and general medical conferences were my field and during my first months in New York, the months when Paul and I were trying to keep our relationship alive through letters and phone calls, Landmark generated most of my assignments. But the Manhattan Translation Agency, with whom I was registered, occasionally asked me to attend conferences and meetings in other areas. 'Dominique darling, would you, could you, possibly consider giving up your Saturday for me and go and work down in SoHo? Someone's dropped out and I'm desperate. Please call me and all will be revealed. Thank you sweetie,' screeched the voice on my answerphone.

Deborah. Mad Deborah with different-coloured bows

in her hair to match each outfit. Mad Deborah who reminded me a little of Anna in her wackiness. I wanted to say no to her for two reasons. I wanted to say, 'No, no, I am tired, so tired, mentally weighed down by the shackles of confidentiality. Sorry, but I can't. I just can't do it.' I wanted to say no, because I knew exactly what a Saturday conference meant. It meant a smaller group of people and that in turn meant consecutive interpreting, and I just didn't think my nerves would take it. But I didn't say no, of course. I had never learnt how.

I should explain that the interpreter learns three different ways of working, of which consecutive translation is undoubtedly the most terrifying. The speaker makes his presentation and we, the interpreters, sit by his side, noting his every word in symbols, furiously flipping over the pages of our lined pads. We have to develop our own brand of shorthand. A faster, more accurate brand that leaves out nothing and that combined with arduous memory-training turns the interpreter into a regurgitator *par excellence*. We might draw a little umbrella symbol and depending on the context it could mean, 'We hope everyone will be well cared-for under this new system,' or it might mean 'Tropical rainstorms are frequent in this area.' Whatever the significance of the symbol it is up to us to make sure that, several minutes later, the little umbrella symbol conveys an accurate message which we can instantly regurgitate in another tongue. When the speaker has finished we stand, notepad in hand, at the front of the room and redeliver his speech verbatim in the required language. The audience, impatient and irritated at not yet having been able to understand anything, hangs on our every word.

I wanted to refuse, to say, 'I am just too exhausted to

give up my Saturday for a bunch of psychologists.' I wanted to say that but I couldn't. So I found myself on my way downtown in a yellow cab in my brown suit with the velvet collar. And suddenly in the back of that cab with the torn black plastic seats and the dodgy suspension, I began to feel nauseous. The nauseous six-year-old on the way to school in her murky green uniform in the back of someone's car. Nauseous, with black spots that threatened child migraine, dancing in front of my eyes. Because the night before, long after I was supposed to be in bed I had heard my mother shouting at him, yelling at him that he had been rude to our guests. 'You will be my ruination,' she yelled in her French accent. I didn't understand the word ruination, but I remembered how it sounded. I forced myself to memorize it, to recall the way it made my mouth move from a kiss to a smile and back to a kiss again, so that the next day I could ask my teacher what it meant.

And my father had said something then that I strained in vain to hear, and then he had added, 'Here we go again. I just hope Dominique's asleep.' My stomach had churned as I waited on the landing while their voices grew louder and louder. Her pitch rose higher and higher, until it was drowned out by the sounds of the man on the TV in the lounge. My father had stormed out of the kitchen and I could hear the angry clanging of pots coming from the sink. And when I was sure, absolutely sure that they weren't in the same room, I had crept down the stairs and into the kitchen and stood with my bare feet on the cold lino floor. I stood there till my mother turned round and jumped at the sight of me. Then I had explained that Daddy hadn't meant to say anything wrong, that maybe she hadn't understood it properly and that what he was actually trying to say just came out in the wrong way, that I hated it when they shouted and couldn't she please go and hold his hand and make up with him.

And my mother, weary at the sink in her plastic apron let me speak for a little, but I was only six or seven or eight and it was way past my bedtime and anyway what could I possibly understand of such things? And she said, 'Understand Dominique, always understand, *c'est le ton qui fait la musique* . . . it's not what you say, it's the way you say it.' Then she kissed me and shooed me up to bed, past the lounge door. And I ran up the stairs and stopped dead at the top. Because on those nights, on the fighting nights, I never went straight back into my bed. I would curl up on the landing on the scratchy carpet in my yellow pyjamas with green frogs on them or the blue ones with the white pandas, and I would listen for sounds of war or reconciliation. My ear to the floor, I would listen for movement. My heart would pound at the sound of words exchanged between them and I would try to hear not just what they were saying, but how they were saying it. Their pitch, their tone and their rhythm. The revving of my mother's car engine, though rare, was the scariest sound. The slamming of the kitchen or living-room doors shut me out and I was frightened to be left in ignorance. It was better to know. Better to know so that I could make it all right, so that the next day I could run backwards and forwards between them and explain things. But more often than not the exhaustion got the better of me there on the landing floor and I would fall asleep and lie there till one of them came and carried me back to my bed.

The morning after the fighting nights I often found myself staring up at the ceiling in the school medical room, with the black dots dancing in front of my eyes.

Actually I didn't mind that bit so much because the black dots often turned into coloured dots that wove themselves in and out of my vision. The clapping contractions in my head that followed were the worst, but by that time my mother had come to collect me in her dark grey Beetle, apologizing all the while to the school nurse for any inconvenience I might have caused. On the way home I didn't feel quite real. My fingers or my arm or my face went all tingly and I couldn't ask the questions I wanted to ask. Questions about the state of communication or lack of it between her and my father.

The being sick part would almost always wait till I got home and afterwards I would lie in my darkened bedroom, with my mother's long cool elegant fingers over my eyes to block out the vestiges of light and numb the pain. I still remember the feeling of her weight on the edge of my bed. The warmth of having her there in contrast to the coolness of her fingers. The warmth and the coolness summed her up and you never knew which you were going to get.

And then a shadow would appear in the doorway. A long thin shadow. The shadow of my father and he would say, 'How's my best patient?' And my mother would answer, telling him I had been sick twice or three or four times. United in their concern for me they had resumed communication. It was worth every retch.

So in the back of the Manhattan cab on my way down to SoHo I felt nauseous. I had to ask the driver to stop and let me out on Twentieth and First Avenue and walking past the diners and the tenement buildings on my way downtown, the polluted air did me some good and I began to feel a little more composed. Composed enough to hope that Deborah from the agency had made a mistake. Perhaps only one member of the group would require translation of the paper to be delivered in French on the theories of educationalist Pascal. And if so I would be spared that whole ghastly ordeal of consecutive inter-preting, where you had to stand up at the front of the room, where you were exposed for all the world to see, unprotected by the walls of the booth and by the darkness, terrified in case your tights had laddered or your mascara had smudged on your cheek. And if they didn't need me to do consecutive interpreting I would be able to do what they call *chuchotage*, which is literally whispering your translation simultaneously into the ear of your client. *Chuchotage* is a good deal less stressful than consecutive interpreting. You can stay seated and hide to the side and slightly behind your client.

On that day the gods must have heard me. When I arrived downtown and walked into the red brick building and through the glass doors into the seminar room, the faces that greeted me were friendly and informal and someone introduced me to a jolly round man called Steven Priory and he said, 'I'm the only ignoramus here. The only one who won't understand the paper in French. So it'll just be me needing your help.'

I pulled my plastic chair up close to his and explained the technicalities of *chuchotage*. A technique that my pro-fessors at interpreting school mistakenly thought that they had taught me. They were wrong, quite wrong, to take credit for it, for I had learnt *chuchotage* long before then, in the back of the car sitting next to my little sister on Sunday outings.

I would cup my hand around her ear while she whimpered and we sped past the different shades of green on the way out of London and I would say, 'What he really means is that he loves her.'

'You can never get it right,' my mother would hiss.

'She says it will all be all right soon,' I'd whisper to my sister.

And my father might say, 'Could you please, please just leave me alone for two minutes. Just two minutes.' And then in a lower voice, 'This cannot be good for the girls.'

My sister would start to cry loudly, sitting there next to me in her stiff pink cotton dress hiccuping with her thumb in her mouth and the fat tears streaming down her fat cheeks. And I would pull her to me and translate 'Daddy says it will all be OK in two minutes. It will all be fine in two minutes.'

The seminar leader, a tall lanky man in jeans, wandered over to me with a plate of digestive biscuits. 'Fortify yourself, Ms Green,' he said. 'We'll be starting in two minutes.'

I smiled, relaxed. This was as easy as it came. The lecturer started to speak. I turned to my client and began to whisper in his ear.

FOUR

Nicholas

Vox: the voice, according to the Oxford English Dictionary, is 'the sound uttered with the resonance of the vocal cords'.

It all started with her voice. Not her words, because they were not hers. In that sense she was but the sieve, the filter through which information passed. So it began not with what she said or how she said it, but with some quite intangible quality in her voice. In the same way as you can sit opposite a woman for months and not see her, I had listened to her for hours and not heard her. I had made no conscious distinction between her voice and the voices of the other interpreters who took over from her, picking up a new sentence where she had finished the old. I needed them and I used them. But quite suddenly, one day at the end of a long and winding speech, she laughed. A deep throaty laugh of relief that it was over. A miracle when I think about it, that she laughed, for I know now that she was not happy at the time. But she did laugh and the sounds, from the darkened booth at the back of the room, travelled through wires and boxes and rang in my ears. She realized quickly that she had pressed the pause button too late and that she had been caught out, and I heard her say, 'Oops,' before she disappeared.

I could tell you that her laugh sent electric currents

through me. It didn't. That came later. But it fascinated me. It woke me from my ignorance and in an instant she became a woman in my mind and not just a mechanical device.

Of course I turned round to look for her, straining to see the interpreters in the far right-hand corner of the room, but I saw only the grey silhouette of a man's figure leaving the end booth.

I listened for her after that. The next day and the next. For two days I flicked the switches of my control buttons between channels, hoping to find her there. I am ashamed to say I had no idea where I might locate her voice, because I had paid her no attention. I knew only that for some of the time at least, she must translate into English. I listened sometimes to the English and sometimes to the Italian translations during the sessions. But over the course of the days that followed, I heard only an animated male voice and a droning mature woman's voice. In the end I wondered if it might have been her. If the droning woman might have a deep throaty laugh quite dissimilar to the tone of her voice at all other times.

Smiling and nodding on matters of medical ethics I bluffed my way through the coffee breaks over these two days. These recent sessions had been dedicated to ethical issues but my concentration was somewhat lacking. I even managed to make fun of myself. Was I so desperate for female company that I could fall for a disembodied laugh?

On the third and last day of the sessions on ethics, an eminent French professor and friend of Dr Grevi's whom I had met in Florence came to talk and I thought I'd better pull myself together and listen. He might corner me and quiz me later and I pictured myself saying, 'Sorry sir, I was scanning channels searching for the voice of a woman. A woman with an incredible laugh and I didn't quite get what you said.' So I walked into the hall, determined that afternoon to concentrate. I sat down, behind the blue desks. I untangled the wire of the headphones in front of me and pulled them over my ears. I switched to the English channel and listened to the introductory speech and I focused on the voice of the male interpreter. The press, he was saying, were always out to catch us on matters of ethics and it was advisable to work out the answers before interviews so that should you find yourself in an uncomfortable situation you would know how to react.

How do they do it? How do the interpreters manage, with no more than a split second's delay, with such precision and such apparent nonchalance at one and the same time to pass the microphone to a colleague, to change as they did then from a man's voice to a woman's and to continue the flow of the translation as if they were one and the same person?

'*Je connaissais un docteur,*' said the speaker. 'I knew one doctor,' said the interpreter. '*Où la presse s'est rendue compte de ce qui ce passait,*' said the speaker. 'Where the press got wind of what was going on,' said the interpreter . . . '*Et la vie de tous les médecins dans la compagnie est devenue un cauchemar,*' . . . 'And they made the lives of all the doctors in the company a nightmare.'

Gliding over his words, fluently, softly. Close enough to touch them with hers. Moving with them as they move. Rising and falling. Tracing them closely with her tongue, enfolding them between her lips. Lingering when he does. Quickening her rhythm as he does, the sounds of her breathing audible now as she climbs with him to the peak, to the point where the rhythm fades and winds down, slowly, gently, to the end.

FIVE

Dominique

The *Uetliberg*, I have always thought, must have deprived Swiss therapists of thousands of francs in fees, for to climb it and to reach the cosy café at the top in winter or the mossy plateau in summer is as liberating and as cathartic as to sit and to pour out your heart.

We stood, the three of us, Anna, Mischa and I, at its foot, contemplating the uphill climb. Literally translated as the little mountain, the *Uetliberg* is exactly that. Neither a hill nor a fully-fledged mountain, it stands over Zurich beckoning, threatening, challenging or inviting, depending on the season.

On a Sunday morning in mid-November, Anna puffed a last smoke-ring into the cold air, stubbed out her cigarette with her shoe, reached out a hand in a red fingerless glove to each of us and yanked us upwards.

I had come here, alone, soon after I arrived in Zurich, and had puffed and panted my way up one of the gravel pathways. It was a warm day in late summer and as I walked, my heart beating fast, my eyes had begun to water. I thought at first that it was the exertion or perhaps a reaction to the fluffy white pollen with its spidery legs that floated ahead of me. 'Paul,' I thought, as I climbed. Paul, who had sat with me on my bedroom floor the night before I left London, surrounded by labelled cardboard boxes. Paul, who had grown with me through adolescence, yet somehow held me there. Who had slid with me learning between the beige sheets of a single bed at his parents' house. A house where no-one ever yelled, where voices were never raised. A house where arguments were whispered. A house with carpet whose pile was so thick that you never even heard a floorboard creak, and with walls so insulated that sounds never carried. Paul, who, in good faith, had taught me his way, assuming all the while that it would be mine. Paul, who had begged me to study in London and not in Zurich. And I had said yes. Yes, I would. It would be wrong of course for us to spend time away from each other and then somehow, strangely, unexpectedly, my words had fallen over each other at the entrance exam to the interpreters' school in London. But for the entrance test to the Masters programme in Zurich my mind had been crystal clear and sharp as a bell. So I had ended up here, climbing the mini-mountain with Paul on my mind, and realizing suddenly that pollen had lost its potency by the end of the summer and that these tears were no allergic reaction, but rather tears of guilt. And I wiped them away fiercely and braced myself. There was after all no need for guilt. This was but a brief interlude in our lives. A long-distance relationship would be just fine for eighteen months. I had promised him we would survive it. For there was, of course, no other path.

Now, some months later, Anna, Mischa and I had begun our ascent of the *Uetliberg*. Our starting-point was different from the one I had chosen on that late summer's day. The mountain's face, softened then by grassy slopes inviting you to come and rest awhile, now offered us no more than a frosty reception. Anna's grip of my hand, pulling me upwards, took me back to her fierce handshake on the first day of interpreting school. She had squeezed my fingers so tightly and unexpectedly in the cold designer waiting-room. Her handshake, like her friendship, was not offered. It was simply given. And she had said, with her accomplished Eliza Doolittle enunciation, 'You are nervous.'

Yes, I was nervous. Terribly so, sitting there waiting for my exam results. So nervous in fact that I had barely noticed her. I looked then at this incongruous figure sitting there in the sterile tidiness of chrome, glass and steel surroundings. Her jeans were ripped, her left forearm tattooed with a green butterfly, her silky light brown hair streaked with blonde and falling over green eyes that said, 'You name it and I have done it.'

'You are uptight,' she repeated, 'and you are English. I heard you speak before.'

I nodded.

'Where are you staying?' she asked.

'I'm still in a hotel, until I know whether I'm going to be accepted on to this programme.'

'Where?'

'The old town.'

'Ah,' she said, 'the place for ladies of the night.'

'I . . . I didn't know. I just booked myself into the first place I could find.' I felt myself turn scarlet.

'The red-light district,' she said and laughed.

We were interrupted by a booming voice behind me. 'Fräulein Green, Fräulein Dominique Green, a born inter-preter,' said the school's director. 'That's what the examiners think. Congratulations and welcome to our programme. I am sure Signorina Terni will show you the ropes.'

I could not help but detect the cynicism in his voice. It

was not Anna's conformity but her brilliance that had persuaded the examining board to allow her to continue into the second semester of the programme.

And yes, Anna showed me the ropes. Only now, looking back, do I understand how she and Mischa paved the way for what was to come. Only now do I understand that Anna, Mischa and I were the prologue without which I would have no story to tell. 'First,' she said, 'we must find you somewhere to live and guess what? I think I have just the place.'

I allowed myself to be led by Anna, as she walked ahead of me, cigarette in hand, up the steep tree-lined streets behind the university, alongside the tramlines, up the three flights of steps to a yellow door. And it wasn't until she had rung the bell that she said, 'Oh by the way, if you take this place your three flatmates will be men.'

'Men,' Paul had shouted, when I told him. 'Three men. I suppose they are all after you. This is ridiculous. It's crazy. You can't possibly live with three men.'

But I felt oddly comfortable sharing an apartment with them. They were medical students, all of them, and given that my father was a doctor, I was perturbed neither by the blow-up plastic heart in the sitting-room, nor by Heinrich the skeleton who lived behind the kitchen door. Nor was I fazed by the relentless discussion of cancer and Crohn's disease, of dermatitis and diabetes, of Alzheimer's and Aids.

'I've tried it with all three of them,' Anna announced, as she helped me unpack on my second evening in the flat.

I said nothing.

'I met Peter first, in a cinema queue. We chatted and when we got to the ticket counter they had sold out. So we went for a drink and then we found out we lived around the corner from each other and we came back here. Right here to this room,' she said, prodding the carpet with her finger. 'It used to be Peter's and, how do you put it in English? One thing just led to another and we . . . well, you know.' She lowered her voice to a whisper. 'But he's a bit of a brute, a real rational scientist and in the end he didn't seem that interested, but Karl did. He told Peter he was keen on me . . . got his permission, if you like,' she said smiling. 'But that was just a fling you know.'

While she talked she was pulling items of my clothing from a suitcase on the floor and placing them on the wooden shelves next to her. A brown lace-up shoe, white flannel pyjamas, a high-necked, long-sleeved white cotton nightdress. 'You must be joking with these clothes,' she laughed. 'We'll have to sort you out.' She stood up, stretching, as if she were about to leave and wanted to avoid me asking about her encounter with Mischa. She walked over to the window and stood for a moment looking out at the dark grey outline of the *Uetliberg*.

'And Mischa?' I asked. 'What about him?'

'You are talking about me,' said Mischa, peering round the door, a cheeky grin on his impish face.

'Yes,' said Anna, turning round, 'I was just saying how desperately ugly you are.'

Anna was in love with him. That became increasingly obvious to me. But their relationship was anything but conventional. I never saw them touch and Anna insisted it was now no more than a friendship.

Anna and I spent hours together at the interpreters' school learning to become simultaneous translators, indulging in wordplay and simply surviving the rigours of a gruelling programme of practice sessions, of voice train-ing and of memory training to turn women and men in their mid to late twenties into translating machines. A programme where they broke you down to build you up, where the student motto was 'with the hide of a rhino you might get out of here alive.' Mischa and I spent evenings in the apartment philosophizing on the meaning of life. On why we were here, doing what we were doing, choosing above all others the paths we had chosen. And the three of us spent weekends together in cinemas and cafés, strolling by the lake or climbing the *Uetliberg*. Anna, Mischa and I were living proof that three is not a crowd.

One Saturday, we laid out a huge green tartan blanket in long grass in the countryside outside Zurich and picnicked on Brie, French bread and strawberries. Afterwards Anna and I lay back and enjoyed the warmth of the sunshine on our faces. Mischa, in his fourth year of medical studies, was lost in a cardiology textbook. Anna I thought at first had fallen asleep. I was wrong. When I opened my eyes, I saw her, watching him, focused on his hands as he turned the pages. In that split second I knew this 'friendship' was causing her great suffering.

I asked her once why it hadn't worked between them and Anna, usually so direct and forthcoming, was dismissive and reticent. 'It can't work,' she said, pushing her hair behind her ears, 'because it can't.'

'But doesn't it hurt then? Doesn't it hurt spending so much time with him?'

'Perhaps,' she said, 'but I'm a fighter and anyway you know I'm quite batty. Batty, it's such a good word, isn't it, Dominique? I looked it up in the thesaurus the other day. Batty, bonkers, crazy, cuckoo, daft, dumb . . .' And so she went on, lighting another cigarette, having deftly put a stop to my line of questioning.

Anna, the fighter who had made it through a childhood with a mother whose postnatal depression had led her to a mental institution from which she rarely surfaced, and a rich, cold and distant diplomat father, who had palmed her off on nannies. Now, watching her stride ahead of me on the *Uetliberg*, in her black bomber jacket and black leggings, her calves strong and pronounced, I was vaguely conscious of feeling uninitiated and unaware next to her, despite the proximity of our ages. 'Where's Mischa?' I yelled to her. A wind had built up by this time and I couldn't quite make out her words.

'What?' I called.

She put her red-gloved hand to her mouth to propel her words further and yelled back, 'On his way down the other side already.'

That night, after Anna had left, Mischa and I sat together at the long dark wooden table in the dining-room. Often in the evenings we would sit like this and he would talk or read to me while I practised interpreting his words from German into English. During the first months I would stumble, missing out sentences here and there to catch my breath, but as my interpreting skills developed I delighted in my increasing ability to keep up with his words. To practise in Mischa's company made the task at least an aesthetically pleasing one. Though I was in no way sexually drawn to him, to look at his milky-white skin and his piercing blue eyes was a sensory pleasure.

Mostly during these practice sessions he would talk of all things medical and though I struggled with the scientific terminology, the general concepts were in no way alien to me. At times, bored with talk of the medical world, he would relate the general details of his day.

That evening he began with talk of blood pumping through veins and through arteries.

I put my head in my hands to maximize my concentration and focus only on his words, but my eyes were smarting after a day in strong sunlight and I stopped him for a moment.

'Wait,' I said.

I walked to the end of the room and turned down the lights till we were almost in darkness. I went back to my chair and sat down. I resumed my position, closed my eyes and waited for him to begin. There was silence.

'Mischa,' I said, 'Mischa, I'm ready.'

'Oh,' he said, 'sorry, Dom. Sorry. Yes.' And then in Swiss-German dialect, '*Gummir* . . . Off we go.'

Though I could no longer make out his expression, I sensed that suddenly his mood had changed, that there was something he wanted to say, but that he was frightened by it.

'So,' he said, 'Dom, how about interpreting "*A Sunday in Mischa's Life?*" . . . It's the same every Sunday,' he said, as I began to interpret his words. 'Every Sunday I go home and every Sunday my father corners me and he says, "How are the studies son?" and I say "Fine, just fine, Dad," and then he says, "What about women? Anyone special in your life?" and I say, "No Dad, no there's no-one special, not at the moment. Just a bit of this and that." Every Sunday it's the same. He asks the same questions and I give the same answers. But this Sunday it's going to be different. This Sunday, he'll ask me, "How are the studies?" and I'll say, "Fine Dad, fine." And then he'll ask, "What about women, eh?" And I'll take a deep breath and I'll say, "No Dad, no and please don't ask me again. Don't ask me next Sunday, because the answer will always be the same, Dad.

Girls will never be more than friends for me. I'm gay, Dad. Do you hear me? I'm gay. I'm gay." '

I froze in my chair. I had stopped interpreting.

Sobs need no translation.

SIX

Nicholas

My ego is neither exceptionally fragile, nor unusually robust. I do not need constant reassurance of my competence, but like all men I am encouraged by the occasional pat on the back. At Landmark, such positive reinforcement was not forthcoming. I might, I suppose, have taken it as a compliment to know that my occasional telephone conversations from New York to Florence satisfied Grevi that I was pursuing my research as required and he felt no need to make much comment on my progress. I might too have felt encouraged by the confidence displayed in me by Professor Goldmann, my superior at Landmark in New York to whom I reported regularly, giving details of my experiments and the materials I required to execute them. But his belief in my research was revealed more in his readiness to authorize payment for laboratory equipment than in time devoted to talking to me and evaluating my efforts. Though in company his manner was cordial, when he did give me any of his time on a one-to-one basis he was abrasive and to the point. He had never once asked me how I was settling down in New York. He never noticed that I was very much alone. For all the attention he paid me on a human level I might just as well have been a highly programmed robot.

And I was young, still. Thirty-three is very young in the world of scientific discovery, and though I may have the mind of a scientist I am not someone who shuns human contact.

So after a few months in Manhattan, though I was convinced my research into paediatric leukaemia was entirely worthwhile and I had no desire to change my vocational course, I craved the stimulus of teamwork.

Often, alone in the lab, wearing plastic gloves, carrying a bag of blood labelled '*X*'... *Mother, haemophiliac*, to a work surface or another labelled '*Y*'... *Mother Blood group A, Father Blood group B*, I would be startled to find I was talking to myself. No, not to myself, but to the anonymous blood cells trapped in a plastic bag, and belonging to an anonymous child trapped in a body riddled with leukaemia. And on occasions I gave the cells a name. Once, I remember, I called them George and I imagined him, a little bald-headed four-year-old, pale and laughing, running through the corridors of a children's hospital, where I had often walked, with a tube inserted into his skinny arm. And I said, 'OK George, the next few hours are just for you. Entirely devoted to you. *Andiamo*.' I emptied the blood that was George in my mind, into a large fibreglass container and drew my microscope closer.

After a while, as I worked, I took to investing almost all the blood samples with an identity in my mind. I knew only the details of their illnesses and their parents' illnesses and blood groups, but to name them gave me the illusion at least of some sort of human contact and added a sense of urgency to my tasks.

During one such monologue, I felt myself suddenly being watched from behind. When I turned round, I saw Tom, a research colleague, standing just inside the doorway, a broad smile on his all-American face. 'You're losing it there,' he said in his deep voice with the Southern twang. 'Don't sweat. It happens to the best of us after a while in here. I reckon it's time for a break. Are we on for lunch today?'

Embarrassed at having been overheard muttering, I could hardly bring myself to speak. I nodded, removed my goggles and placed them on the workbench, removed my white coat and hung it on the back of the door, removed my plastic gloves, placed them in a black bin marked CONTAMINATED, scrubbed my hands, grabbed my heavy overcoat and followed Tom out of the door.

Ours was a most improbable friendship and though I felt a certain affection for him, we could not have been more unalike. I am loath to stereotype, but he had rarely been outside the US, he adored baseball and was never happier than when he was sinking his flashing white teeth into a hearty burger. Tom worked part of the time in the lab at the other end of the building, researching chronic myeloid leukaemia in adults. The rest of the time he spent on the wards, evaluating the progress of patients in clinical trial. We passed each other often in the corridors over a period of several weeks before we struck up a conversation. Striding past me, he would smile and say in an upbeat tone, 'Hi, how are you today?' and carry on walking. On more than one occasion, I was left with my mouth wide open in mid-syllable ready to answer him, before I realized that in New York 'How are you?' is a rhetorical question.

When, once, I did finally choose to shout after him in a loud voice, 'I'm fine thank you. How are you?' he stopped in his tracks and turned round, surprise registering on his face. Though he walked back to shake hands with me and introduced himself, I often wondered whether we would still have been passing each other in the corridors months later had I not chosen to counter his Americanism with a European response.

From that time on, we would lunch fairly regularly at one of the local delis. Tom would talk of his latest conquest on the woman front and I would sit and listen.

On the day he caught me talking aloud to the cells, we subjected ourselves to the frenzy of the Lunch Club. Fast food, fast service looking out at the furious pace of life on Lexington Avenue.

I sat in front of a plate piled high with rye bread, salt beef and pickles, feeling suddenly a little nostalgic for Florence, and I prepared to listen to Tom.

That day, as usual, I expected him to turn quickly to the numerous sexual encounters in his life. To talk in superlatives as he always did and tell me how his latest liaison had been 'awesome' or 'amazing'.

But there was no mention of nightclubs or women. Instead, the conversation between us took a rather un-expected turn.

'Nicholas,' he said, 'I've got to get the hell out of this place.'

I thought at first he meant the diner and puzzled I said, 'This place. I thought it was your favourite hang-out.'

'No, not the diner, you dope,' he said, a smile briefly crossing his face and disappearing. 'I mean Landmark.'

'What are you talking about?'

'I've had it there. I work my ass off and no-one takes the damnedest bit of notice.'

I nodded in empathy.

'My father has this friend. Walter Zlack. A big shot. Loaded. Absolutely loaded. Supplies the raw materials for pharmaceutical drugs. He's been wanting to set up a small research thing for ages. Keeps on nagging me to go in with him. Says I'll make some real money. Share of the equity and all that,' he said, wiping his mouth with his hand. I handed him a paper serviette.

'And you're really considering leaving Landmark?' I asked through a mouthful of salt beef.

'Nicholas, you're not listening to me! It's not a matter of considering any more. I'm out! And the sooner the better. Give me a few months, till my contract's expired, and I'm gone. This guy's breathing down my neck for a decision.'

I was aware, suddenly, of a tightening knot in the stomach. I pushed my plate away from me.

Tom was the colleague at Landmark to whom I was closest, and though our conversations were light-hearted and rarely touched on the existential elements of life his camaraderie obviously mattered to me more than I had realized. I felt suddenly alone.

'Nick,' he said, 'you look like an earthquake just hit you.'

I snapped myself out of it and cleared my throat.

'No,' I said, 'no, not at all. That's great. Great. It could be a big opportunity for you.'

'And,' he said, pausing for dramatic effect, pushing his chair backwards and standing up, 'who said there might not just be a great opportunity in there for you too? You seem to be doing some pretty hot work. So who knows? You and I could do big things together.' I looked at him, confused for a moment, before I got his drift.

'Me? Oh no. Finding a breakthrough on this leukaemia thing is important to me, Tom,' I said. 'Besides, I've only been here a few months. I could never think of leaving. In any case Landmark would never let me out of my contract.'

Feeling an inexplicable sense of unease, I put a ten-dollar note on the table, gulped back the rest of my glass of water and followed Tom out of the diner. It was time to get back to George.

SEVEN

Dominique

I can lose myself in music, as I once never imagined I would be able to lose myself in love. Words are for analysing, understanding, learning, absorbing, translating. Words have demanded my concentration, my participation. They have exacted emotional response and intellectual involvement and I have given it willingly. As an interpreter I choose words as a sculptor chooses clay. At times, they have sucked me dry and exhausted me. At others, they have excited and exalted me, as I have followed their stream in some foreign tongue without faltering. But always I have paid a price for that exaltation.

Music, on the contrary, has asked nothing of me. As a child, sitting at my walnut baby grand, away from the world in the basement of our house, my teacher wanted me to play only the pieces that brought me joy. On Tuesday afternoons I would sit in school, my gaze fixed so steadily on the big black hand of the clock that I saw even the most imperceptible of its movements. Movements that brought me closer to the music that Livieu and I would enjoy together. He would sit and play me passages by Handel, by Bach or by Beethoven. I can still see his soft brown ageing hands with the ridged nails stroking the ebony and ivory of the keys. When he had finished a piece he would look at me and if I was relaxed and smiling he would lift my right hand to the keyboard and begin to teach it to me. If I frowned or looked disenchanted, he would shake his head and say in his strong Polish accent, 'Dominique, music is for pleasure, not for pain,' and he would move on to something more harmonious still. Sometimes while he played he would talk. '*Allegro, allegro, forte, adagio, adagio. Sotto voce, Dominique. Sotto voce.*'

On occasion he would take me to a concert or to the ballet with other pupils. Invariably late, we would rush through huge high-ceilinged halls to the auditorium and we would flop onto plush red seats, just as the lights went down. Then Livieu would smile, close his eyes and move his head to the strains of the music.

And so these hours in the basement on the piano-stool next to Livieu, or sitting in the plush red seats, were more about the enjoyment of music than the practice of it. Perhaps it was because he preferred to play than to teach. Perhaps because he sensed that I would need music later in life, to give to me and not to take from me. And so music has the power to reach me profoundly, to lead me almost to a trance as no mantra could ever do and as only the most passionate lovemaking has ever done. Music allows me to listen without working. Notes are my antidote to words.

In New York, on Sunday afternoons, after a week of interpreting I would often wander down Madison Avenue into St Andrew's Church just before three o'clock and slip my donation into the green tin on the table inside the heavy doors. Then I would sit down in a pew, with the blues and the greens and the reds of the stained-glass windows to my left and my right, and I would wait for the pianist, the violinist or the orchestra to appear. None of the friends I made in New York expressed an interest in classical music and I was quite happy to go alone. When the musicians were particularly talented I found it to be an almost spiritual experience.

The concerts were advertised on the notice-board in the conference hall building where I worked and looking around the pews, I sometimes vaguely recognized the faces of the doctors, researchers or administrators I had seen during the week. We rarely exchanged words, but there was usually a smile and a nod of acknowledgement.

Three weeks before Christmas, I sat huddled in my sheepskin coat, waiting for the orchestra to appear. It was snowing outside and the church was poorly heated. The programme was Tchaikovsky's Ballet Suites, and next to me were two little girls in navy blue coats with velvet collars. They tapped their feet on the dark wooden floors and moved their heads from side to side, while the orchestra, dressed in black woollen polo-necks and black trousers or skirts, played the opening piece. The children clapped in all the wrong places and laughed. Their mother, a pale thin woman, shook her head and put her finger to her lips. They had obviously come to listen only to the *Nutcracker Suite* because as soon as it was over and they had been allowed to applaud in the correct place, she ushered them out, excusing herself and squeezing past a tall dark man at the end of the row.

The young woman on the stage at the front of the church laid her hands on the strings of the harp. The first violinist rested his violin under his chin and raised his bow. The harpist played her opening notes and then the oboe joined her in the first phrases. Ironically I have always thought Tchaikovsky's *Swan Lake* more beautiful without dancers. As the strains of the music flowed into more lyrical sound, I found myself turning to look at the man at the end of the pew. His high cheekbones. His Roman nose. His long, sculpted fingers. I turned away. The musician at the double bass leant forward ready to play. With the touch of his bow on the string, the music deepened and slowed down. '*Adagio, adagio.*' I remembered Livieu.

I closed my eyes and on the edge of that familiar dream-like state, as a blind man must feel another presence, I sensed someone looking at me. The orchestra quickened their pace again. The double bass joined in. The movement grew dramatic and intense. Drawn into a trance by the music, I willed myself to stay there, as moments before waking you will yourself to stay asleep. But as the sounds sharpened and began to rise and swell, I was jolted abruptly into awareness. The music soared to a crescendo. I looked to my right. He was facing me, as if transfixed, an expression of great intensity on his face. My pulse began to race as the cymbals clashed. The music exploded suddenly then, again and again and again, till, like the aftermath of a firework, it fell in colours to nothingness. Too weak to join in the applause, I turned to lift my scarf from the bench. To my right the pew was empty.

EIGHT

Nicholas

I lay, that afternoon, propped against the wooden head-
board with my leather-bound medical tome from Florence
on my knees. I thumbed the feathery white pages for
hours. I squinted and strained my eyes scanning the tight
black print, but nowhere at all could I find what I was
looking for. I wanted official confirmation of my theories
on the two basic categories of *Homo sapiens*. No, not man
and woman. Not adult and child or black and white. But
listener and talker. Under 'talk' I could find only that, *By
the age of two, the typical child can already utter nearly three hundred
different words. By four it can manage nearly 1,600.* Under 'listen'
I could find only references to the inner, the middle ear
and the outer ear.

I picked up a yellow pencil from my bedside table and,
for once creative, in the empty white margin at the bottom
of the page I added a footnote. 'We are listeners or we are
talkers,' I wrote. 'Listeners can be coaxed to talk and
talkers taught to listen, but much as we may learn from
each other, in our hearts we remain either the talker or the
listener that we became during childhood.'

When, months later, using the book in preparation for
a conference, Dominique stumbled across the footnote,
she underlined the word 'listener' and next to it wrote my
initials and an exclamation mark.

That I am a listener is something I must believe to be true. For I have heard it too often for it to be purely self-analysis. I say that without arrogance, for I place no value judgements on whether it is better in life to listen or to talk.

Once, as a registrar, I was sitting by the bedside of a girl in the final stages of leukaemia. Her mother sat next to me and as dusk fell into night and grew into dawn she told me the story of her daughter's life. How hard it had been to conceive her, how painful to give birth, how exciting to watch her grow and learn to speak her first words. 'She was a talker, doctor,' said her mother. 'Right from the start, I knew my child was a talker. She needed to tell me every thought in her head. She still would if she had the strength, wouldn't you?' she said, gently wiping the sweat from the unconscious child's forehead. Then, with one hand still resting on her daughter's cheek, she turned to me and she said, 'And you, doctor. You are a listener. Thank you.' She got up to go to the bathroom. When she returned, only minutes later, her daughter had died.

After that I heard only wails from her. So the last intelligible words she had said to me during that long night were, 'And you, doctor, you are a listener.' They are words that have stuck with me. Words that for some strange reason came to my mind the night after the concert in the church on Madison Avenue.

The Sunday snow, as it fell, silenced central Manhattan and walking home I could even hear the chirping of the birds above the cars.

'*Nicola, ascolta,*' she had whispered. 'What is it? Can you hear what it is?'

And we would stand together, my mother and I, still as statues in anticipation of the song of some bird or other. I see her still, long shiny black hair pushed behind her ears so she could listen better, her strong hand gripping my wrist while we waited. I remember her in yellow. The yellow of her dress was the colour of the face of the red-necked grebe, that warned us of its coming with squeals and an *aaek, aaeeek.*

In Tuscany in the winter in the lushness of our gardens she taught me to distinguish between the hurried *kier vek, kier vek* of the sandwich tern and the crooning *ah haooo, ah haooo* of the eider calling for a lover. In Sardinia in the summer, on the Costa Smeralda where she learnt her love of birdsong I came to know the pitch and tone of the little bittern with its loud *uh – booh* and the gull with its *gleeeu, gleeeu, gleeeu.*

And I was so proud, always, when my listening techniques became refined and my guess that we had heard the red-necked grebe was rewarded with the sight through the binoculars of a dark rust-brown-necked bird with grey cheeks and a yellow face appearing with a flutter through the foliage, to perch on the branch of a tree at the end of the garden. Or when I had whispered, '*Mamma mamma, e una sterna, e una sterna. Sono sicuro,*' and, minutes later, we might see the slim narrow-winged tern in his white robe and jet-black hat flying above our heads and out of sight.

And so my mother taught me about the birds and the art of listening. She too, with her large grey patient eyes was a listener and I learnt from her example. She wanted always to know everything. Perhaps because she was both mother and father to me. Perhaps because from the time she was in her early thirties, I was all that she had. And she would sit with her square chin in her strong hands and ask and ask about my friends, my fights and my foibles at school. I talked myself out as a child. I talked and talked and if today I am a listener it is because I felt myself to be heard and understood. I am a different type of listener from Dominique. When we first knew each other she was a listener who knew no other way, who had not been heard and knew the value of the words she spoke only in a professional and intellectual sense. I, on the other hand, had been taught at an early age how the weight of my words came from the inner world behind them.

The priest, hidden behind the blue velvet curtain in his little dark brown box, had told me that, when I was first taken as a child to confession. 'The words I hear from you,' he said, 'help me understand the world in your head.'

I remember that first confession, my small hands in his large ones between the curtains and me imagining the world in my head, a globe like the one we had in our classroom, going round and round inside my brain.

Once a week, I told the priest my stories, good and bad. That I helped the boy at school with the broken arm carry his books, but that I had kicked my classmate hard. That I had recognized the voice of the gull, but that I had spent next to no time on my homework. That I had beaten all the other boys in a race by miles and miles, but that I had tipped a whole bottle of black paint over my friend's drawing.

And while he smiled and nodded or shook his head, getting to know the globe in my mind through my words, the lines on his brow deepening or relaxing depending on my story, I wondered if after a few minutes he would stop me and it would be my turn to listen to his stories. He did. And it was. Though not quite in the way I had imagined. My confession slot was early on Sunday morning just before services began, and minutes after the priest had disappeared like Punch and Judy behind the blue curtain, he would reappear in black and white on the pulpit.

My mother would whisper, 'It's your turn to listen.' And so I would concentrate hard on his stories. The stories about shirts made of itchy hair and babies made from thin air. I didn't know if he made them up or if they were all true like mine, but I closed my eyes tightly, focused hard and pictured the pastel colours of the globe with the words on it turning round and round inside his head. When he had finished speaking and the time came to concentrate on the songs of the choir I focused as sharply on the voices and the notes as I did on the cries of the eider or the red-necked grebe.

And though as an adult I rarely attended church, for me it had become a place of listening, of taking in the spirit of the words and the music that wafted towards me. How disturbing then suddenly to feel different sensations that welled up in me in that church on Madison Avenue on Sunday afternoon. Sensations that had nothing to do with the notes of a choir or the words of a priest. Sensations that had little to do with the beauty of Tchaikovsky's *Swan Lake* as it filled the hall, and everything to do with some intense magnetism that drew me time and again to the young woman to my left in the white sheepskin coat.

Yes, there was in that attraction an element of spirituality. Yes, it was elevated by the emotion of the music. But were I not to admit the eroticism of our silent meeting I would be deceiving myself. Were I not to tell you that those dark, often downcast eyes, the thick dark lashes and the way, suddenly and quite unexpectedly, she turned to look at me, were I not to tell you that these things filled me with an almost intoxicating sexual longing, I would be nothing other than a dissembler. And I have no desire to carry with me the burden of falsehood.

I felt guilty enough that in that church, in a place where the body ought to be of the utmost irrelevance, I was closer to my own sexuality than I had been for many months.

And suddenly, while the birds chirped on my way home in that Sunday snow, for once I was overcome by the need to talk. In the space of a week, I had been overwhelmingly drawn to a woman's voice through a set of headphones and, as I then believed, to another woman at the other end of the church pew. I had found myself suddenly under pressure to look my career at Landmark in the face and contemplate the innuendo in Tom's words when he had said, 'Well, who says there isn't an opportunity in there for you too?'

I needed for once to be a talker and not a listener. And I wanted, even if only for a few hours, to be less alone. But Manhattan can be a lonely place. Though I had some interaction with colleagues at work at our weekly meetings and I was slowly getting to know Tom, teamwork seemed to play little part in my professional life and I had not yet developed a network of social contacts, let alone true friends. And so, that afternoon, I felt compelled to put my thoughts on paper, in the form of a letter to my mother who had died some years previously.

NINE

Dominique

E.A.T. The *New York Times on Sunday* spread out on a glass and chrome table at E.A.T. The plate piled high with *pain au chocolat*, next to a cafetière of real coffee, with the gold plunger waiting to be plunged. Manhattanites with scrubbed faces and silky hair brunching in relaxed style. Did these things draw me in from the cold on the corner of Madison and Eighty-First or was it those three huge red letters painted on the glass front of the café?

My table was in the corner right next to the window. The menu said, 'Fresh orange juice'. The juice they brought was blood-red with the pith in it. Freshly squeezed. The menu said, 'Fresh croissants'. They came with the warmth wafting from them.

Two letters in my brown bag. One sent to me by Mischa from Zurich. One that I had begun to write to Paul and come to finish here. Not that we didn't speak on the phone. We did of course, but I came from a family of letter-writers. People say it is easier to speak the truth in a letter. That we have fewer inhibitions. No fear of immediate reaction. It is also, I think, easier to lie in a letter.

There is no trembling to control. No frogs to be cleared from the throat. No quavering to be stilled.

I have only ever seen one letter that I knew in my heart

to be nothing but the truth. I must have been six or seven when I read it. I remember, still, sitting on the floor of my parents' bedroom at the foot of their bed. I untied the green ribbon. I opened the brown folder. I fingered the yellowing envelope on the top of the pile. I asked my mother if I could open it. Letters were sacred in our family. You never, ever read other people's without asking. She said yes. Yes, I could. She said she didn't imagine it was anything very important. It was dated August 6th 1959. It was a letter of one line and though I could read the words, I was too young to make sense of them.

'Until the Rockies crumble.' I read it out loud. 'Until the Rockies crumble,' I said and my mother laughed. I stared at her and listened. My mother laughing. A sound I rarely heard. A sound I struggle now to remember.

'The night before my wedding,' she said.

'What does it mean?' I asked.

'Ask your father.'

'What does it mean?' I asked him.

'It means,' he said, 'forever and ever and ever.'

'Forever what?' I asked, standing next to him at his desk with the yellowing envelope in my hand.

'Forever. Till the mountains crumble into tiny little pieces. It's a line from a song.'

Frustrated, I lost interest in the letter about mountains that would crumble into tiny little pieces. But it was the shortest and I now know the truest letter I have read. For whatever else went on in our household that line of the Fifties song was nothing but the truth. My father often talked to my mother on paper. A poem left on top of the washing-machine in the kitchen. A peace-offering slipped under the bathroom door.

I used to like to sit and watch my mother doing things

. . . peeling potatoes, applying her lipstick, immersing her hands in the soapy suds of the bathroom sink. Only when she was totally absorbed in some physical activity did she forget to be worried or angry. Once, just after one of those fights I was in the bathroom with her, sitting curled up in the dry pink bathtub watching her tidy some drawers, when a folded piece of pink paper slid through the crack under the door onto the vinyl flooring. She opened it sitting there on the edge of the bath and I craned my neck to see the small blue letters. The first word was easy. It just said, 'I' but the second word was too much for me to decipher. Long and written in joined-up writing.

'What does it say?' I asked my mother.

'It doesn't matter.'

'It does. Please tell me what it says.'

'It says, "I understand." '

'What, Mummy? What does he understand?'

'Everything,' she said. 'And nothing.'

'Why don't you write him a letter back?' I asked.

'Because Daddy lives here. I don't need to send him a letter. And anyway I hate to write . . . I used to write though. I used to love it when I was little. When I first came here, I wrote long, long letters back home every day. Letters telling Maman and Papa what I was doing and eating and wearing. Telling them what I was learning and who my new friends were. I wrote even when I couldn't really see their faces in my head any more. I thought my letters would make them remember me.'

I sat still, very very still in the empty pink bathtub, holding my breath while she talked. I can count the number of times my mother forgot herself and began to speak of her separation from her parents in Nazi-occupied France. When she did, she entered an almost trancelike state and I was afraid that if I coughed or sneezed I might break the flow of her thoughts. So I sat there with every muscle in my body tensed as she talked of the 'little holiday' they told her she was going on to the convent in the mountains, of how the 'little holiday' to save her skin had turned into a very very long one, that wasn't of course a holiday at all. Of how they had squashed her against the other children, into boats and trucks and trains till she stood for collection by kind strangers at Paddington station with her name on a piece of cardboard round her neck. She kept on writing the letters, she told me. Letters that were read or not read by some SS officer somewhere and tossed aside with no hope of reaching her parents, for they, by then, had already been burnt. I remember as a child thinking, from the snippets I heard, that we could have done with the Nazis at Brownies and Girl Guides. They were great at making fires and burning things.

'I carried on writing the letters for years,' said my mother, still sitting on the edge of the bathtub. For a moment she was silent. I wanted to touch her back. It looked so soft, so silky and inviting. I stretched out my fingertips towards it. Suddenly she began to talk again. I froze, my hand still in mid-air.

'For years I carried on writing them. Even after I knew what had happened to your grandparents in that place. I would post them in the letter-box with no address on the envelope.'

She always said 'that place'. Never *Bergen Belsen*. Never the hell-hole. Just *that* place. She threw the words away. Mumbled them. Swallowed them almost, as though her lack of emphasis on the words might make them a figment of her imagination and allow her to rewrite her life story. I wanted, when I was small, to ask 'What place?

Where?' but the words stuck in my throat, because once, just once, I had heard my parents' friends talk about camps and I had asked if they were as much fun as the place we went to on a bus for a school trip. But no-one said anything. No-one answered me. And I began to feel this awful shaky panicky feeling. Not unlike the sensation I had years later in the interpreter's booth when suddenly I felt I had lost the speaker's train of thought and it seemed as if the ceiling of the conference hall was about to come crashing down on the makeshift booth. I never mentioned 'the camp' again at home, but I did ask my schoolteacher if we could have those bluey-green numbers stamped on our arms at our summer camp like my mother's Maman and Papa had done at theirs. She said, 'No. Definitely not.'

And my mother, in the bathroom that day coming out of her trancelike state, said that when I grew up I would know why my father understood and yet didn't understand all at the same time, but that it was a very nice letter really that he had slipped under the door.

I, myself, understood next to nothing. And it seems to me still that letters always need translation.

I plunged the gold plunger on my cafetière in E.A.T. I opened Mischa's letter and began to translate.

TEN

Dominique

Dominique . . . mein Schatz,
Ich könnte es gut verstehen wenn Du böse warest. Sicher hast Du
geglaubt auf Godot zu warten.
I'd understand if you were mad at me. I guess you
thought you were
Aber nun setze ich mich hin
waiting for Godot. But finally I have sat myself
down
und schriebe Dir. Ich bin jetzt im halbdunkelen Esszimmer an
dem
to write to you. I am in the dining-room. It's almost
dark in here and I'm sitting at the
langen braunen Tisch wo wir so oft zusammen geubt haben. Du
mit dem Kopf in
long brown table where you sat translating with your
head in your hands and your
den Händen und mit gesclossenen Augen. Ist es möglich dass es
erst sieben oder
eyes shut. Is it possible that that was only seven or
eight months ago?
ach Monate her ist? Es scheint doch wie ein Leben.
It seems like a lifetime.

I turned the page. Mischa had switched from German to

57

English as he so often did. The need to translate his words was no less great.

I have been so caught up with tests at medical school, Dom. It's been a nightmare. I had one test on the immune system. It was crucial. I couldn't sleep the previous night. My head was spinning with all the information I had tried to cram into it. I did the test the next day. I wasn't the only one who was nervous. You should have seen the green and yellow faces in that exam hall.

The results came through the following day and they were as I expected. The exam stress has tired me out though and that I'm afraid must be my excuse for leaving so many of your messages unanswered.

Anna is in good shape. I've been trying to persuade her to come to New York and visit you. She misses you, Dom. We both do. I know I promised I'd come too, but I need to conserve my cash for the moment.

Call me soon. I need to hear your voice.

Mischa

At the bottom of the envelope were four small squares of my favourite Swiss milk chocolate in red paper. He sent them to me with every letter.

But knowing the truth from Anna as I did, I believed little of his letter and as I followed Mischa's words, I read its meaning between the lines.

I've been having medical tests, Dom. It's been a nightmare. They checked my immune system. I couldn't sleep the previous night. My head was spinning with all the information I had crammed into it. I was tested the next day. I wasn't the only one who was nervous. You should have seen the green and yellow faces in that waiting-room.

I tested positive, Dominique. The stress of it all has finished me off and I was afraid to answer your calls in case you heard it in my voice. Anna's taken it pretty badly. I've been trying to persuade her to take a break from me and to come to New York and visit you. She misses you, Dom. We both do. I know I promised I'd come too, but for the moment I need to conserve my strength.

ELEVEN

Nicholas

My microscope is an adult kaleidoscope. As Dominique needs twilight and darkness to work in the booth so I need light and colour. My best working days have always been the bright ones. The days when morning has streamed through the white slatted blinds of the laboratory, scrutinized my activities and inspired me. If I look back, the times when I have felt my work flow, where I have been on the path of progress or the edge of discovery, are times when I have needed only natural light in the laboratory. Light is a person for me. A friend egging me on to greater things.

On that December morning, several weeks before I was first aware of Dominique's voice, several weeks before the Tchaikovsky concert, it was still pitch-black outside save for the street lamps.

The Café Dante, that I could see when I opened the shutters of my apartment on Macdougal Street in downtown Manhattan, and where I drank my espresso every day before work, was owned by Italians and reminded me of home. The green chairs were plastic and the inside of the bar was dark, but Rosa served the coffee in rich chocolate-brown cups, and on the walls the owner had hung old black and white photos of Florence in the 1920s. On the counter next to the silver cappuccino machine were copies of the previous day's Italian newspaper *Corriere della Sera*, that fed my need to be in touch with the Italian world.

Early in the morning and late at night the stress of operating in a language other than my mother tongue was at its greatest. Colleagues considered my English more than good enough for the needs of a scientist, and save for slang and the cinema I had few problems with comprehension. But sometimes during early morning or evening meetings at Landmark, it was as if someone had flicked a switch in my mind and suddenly I understood nothing at all.

It was one of those meetings on one of those mornings. My colleagues and I were gathered together to discuss 'Safety in the Labs'. A researcher working on the brain had picked up a rather nasty case of Hepatitis C from blood samples. When it transpired he had been less than scrupulous in his handling of blood, the pharmaceutical company management was thrown into blind panic. Not one pair of gloves, but two. Not two squirts of disinfectant to scrub your hands when leaving the lab, but four squirts. No examination of material without goggles, ever. No touching of uncovered surfaces. No access to unauthorized persons. Authorization to be given only by senior management.

All this they said in loud twangy voices at 7.30 a.m. and despite the two espressos I had drunk, the words, at first intelligible, began soon to swim past me and swirl round me, amorphous and directionless as the undulating orange gunge in those psychedelic Seventies lamps. They followed me out, as I walked in a haze out of the grey low-ceilinged hall towards the airiness of my laboratory. Towards the haven where at all times I could speak the language of science.

That winter morning approaching daylight had thrown a mauve hue over everything in the lab. As I approached the massive medical freezer where I had frozen the bone marrow of several young leukaemia patients, the adrenalin rushed as it had when as a child I had peered into the initial greyness of my kaleidoscope, knowing all the while that the instant I began to turn the knob at the base of the toy, the greyness would become a crystal rainbow transporting me into another world.

I might occasionally be accused of being less than scrupulous in protecting myself against contamination from specimens, but on that day I feared an inspection and I wrapped myself up like a white mummy. My laboratory was classed as a Level Three, the second most dangerous level in terms of potential contamination, and the penalty for haphazard handling of materials was severe.

Blood, to the layman, pretends to be the purest ruby-red. It is only the laboratory scientist who knows how it is the ultimate joker that cons us every time we bleed. Spun for no more than a few seconds in a centrifuge, a machine whose actions resemble the spinner on a washing-machine, blood divides itself into three different-coloured layers as unwilling to confront one another as oil and water. Shamed into submission the red cells settle at the bottom of the test-tube, topped by a thin yellowy layer of plasma with a layer of translucent white cells sandwiched between them. In my research into leukaemia it was the white cells that demanded most of my time and commitment.

It is they who in a moment of recklessness invite the virus into their midst and leave their hosts to regret their decision, screaming 'impostor' and begging for our help. My ultimate research aim was to find a way to prevent the chaos that stakes its claim in the nucleus of the white cells, as leukaemia takes its hold. When Dominique once asked me to explain the specifics of my leukaemia research, though her understanding of medicine was impressive, I tried hard not to dazzle her with science. Instead I compared the white cell to a runny fried egg with the bright yellow of the yolk as its nucleus. I explained how the yolk contained the genetic material, the DNA, whose chromosomes that should have been in strong intact chains were frayed and torn. And I told her how that fraying and tearing began to take its toll and to beckon the malevolence of the disease. I compared the weakening chains of chromosomes to a string of pearls threatening to shatter and explained to her how I, in this particular area of research, was the medical equivalent of the jeweller, intent on finding a way to restring those pearls.

To that end I had spent day after day, week after week, month after month in cutting-edge leukaemia research, examining the effect of various chemical compounds on affected white cells. I, like all medical researchers, was the weaker party in an unequal battle. As I attempted to keep the sick cells alive to examine their behaviour, so like miniature dodgem cars they avoided me and fooled me, revelling in their agility and dancing their swansong in the little round and transparent Petri dishes.

I arranged six such dishes in a row that morning and squeezed the rubber tip that would suck the thawed white cells into my pipette. I released them then into the first Petri dish. Drop by drop the translucent liquid began to fill the container. I remember thinking that its motion mirrored the work of the research scientist. Slow and laborious. For in our work there can rarely be instant gratification. It is only in the bluest of moons that our observations are anything more than stitches in a massive tapestry that earn us little if any recognition. It is only in the bluest of moons that we are struck suddenly by some great revelation.

And I was wondering that Thursday whether the leukaemia cells might co-operate with me just a little longer. Whether they might be just a little less intent on proliferation. For that day I was trying out a compound that had just been developed in another Landmark laboratory, and hopes were high that this would act on the enzymes within the cell nucleus and begin to repair some of the damage to the chains of chromosomes.

As I unscrewed the top of the purple labelled bottle that contained the compound I found myself speaking to the cells. Not out loud, but in my mind, as I checked each set against the records that told me to whom they belonged. I didn't know the child's name, of course, nor his favourite cartoon character nor the colour of his eyes. Just his code number, age, sex and ethnic origin, his and his parents' blood groups and any relevant diseases they might have had. And in these first five sets of blood cells on that Thursday there was nothing unexpected. Nothing I needed to know, except that all of them were diseased with leukaemia. It was only the sixth set that was different. Only the sixth set that belonged quite by chance to the three-year-old girl from the Bronx who might not have found out for years she was HIV positive had it not been for her leukaemia.

And so I added several drops of the compound from the purple bottle to the first set of cells and I watched as the liquid in the petri dish turned with the effect of the dye from a fluid that was colourless to one that was emerald green. With the second set I did the same. With the third, the fourth and the fifth. And I was lost in my own world watching the colours and shapes through my kaleidoscope, when the ringing began. I ought to have left it. To have let it continue, but the insistence of the sound was such that I stood up, peeled off my thin plastic gloves, scrubbed my hands and walked to the telephone that rang and rang at the other side of the laboratory. Of course when I got there, just as I lowered my hand, just as I touched the yellow receiver, the caller grew tired and the ringing stopped.

I cursed as I walked back to the workbench for allowing myself to be so easily distracted and thought how the isolation of this work was getting to me. How man is not made to spend such protracted periods of time alone. Without feedback. Without teamwork. Without talking. I thought that I ought, at least, to take a day off, to wander round Manhattan and to people-watch.

And now just for one set of cells, just for the sixth set I had to go through the whole procedure all over again. The scrubbing, the gloves, the unscrewing of the bottle, the addition of the translucent liquid that I would leave now to do its work. And as I watched this last set of cells, that belonged to the little girl who not only had leukaemia, but was also HIV positive, I spoke to them and I said, 'I'm sorry, you lot. But you're at a bit of a disadvantage. We're going to have a tough job repairing you.' For I knew from experience that it was only a matter of time till the virus would invade the nucleus of any as yet unaffected cells.

I could have stayed in the lab for the rest of the day, checking my experiments from time to time. Instead I left and decided to leave the cells to their own devices till the following day.

Manhattan is a strange place to be on a weekday if you are not working. You have time to notice the plight of the sallow-skinned sparrow woman holding her child's tiny palm towards you in a gesture of begging. You have time to pity the black woman dressed in a torn grey dustbin-liner, who walks muttering up and down Fifty-Seventh Street with a plaque that says, 'Help me, I have Aids.' And you have time to think that Manhattan is no place to be without a mission.

And so I was grateful the next morning to be walking back into my lab, back over to my workbench, to be peering through my microscope at the chromosomes in the cells in the first Petri dish and saying, 'OK you guys, you're not doing too badly.'

Because in the twenty-four hours that I had roamed Manhattan, been to the movies, slept and come back, the chaos in the nucleus had calmed a little. And the string that held the pearls together looked a fraction less frayed. Quickly I moved the viewfinder to the second to the third to the fourth and the fifth, and saw that in each the picture was much the same. And in the sixth Petri dish, the dish with the cells of the little girl with leukaemia who was also HIV positive, I expected to find pandemonium. I expected to find most of the cells riddled with the virus and I prepared to pour away the waste matter.

But it is nine hundred and ninety-nine times out of a thousand that we are not struck suddenly by some revelation. It is nine hundred and ninety-nine times out of a thousand that we see what we expect to see in the world beneath the glass. And so at first, I was sure that it was entirely my imagination when in the sixth Petri dish I noticed that the virus was not dancing in celebration of its gatecrash into the nucleus of the cells, that despite their crippling disadvantage these cells had kept up with the others that stood in a row in the five little transparent Petri dishes alongside them.

'Manzini,' I said, 'you are seeing things. Manzini, you are losing your mind. You ought to go back to Florence, you know. You're better off as a small-town doctor. Your imagination doesn't play games with you there.'

It's funny how just as one cell divides into two, so you in your mind can become two people engaged in heated debate. The first, the voice of reason that grounds you, that tells you that leukaemia cells infected too with HIV cannot possibly hold their own for as long as those without the virus. And the second, the voice of your gut, that speaks, in spurts of adrenalin, in rapid beats of the heart, and challenges you to believe your eyes.

I hear a thump at the laboratory door. I hear it being pushed open.

'So, do we have a lunch date?'

I turn round. And Tom, as he always does on the days when we have plans, is standing at the entrance to the lab.

'Now?' I ask. 'You want lunch right now?'

'Nick, it's 1.30. I keep telling you. You get too caught up in this stuff. Come, let's go. I'm starving.'

'Can you come here a second, Tom? I need to show you something.'

'Can it wait? I don't have my coat.'

And I was just about to say that yes it could wait. Of course it could wait till after the pastrami sandwiches, when for some reason he thought better of his decision and he said, 'OK, give me a moment.' And in an instant he was back in his white coat saying, 'Give me some gloves.'

He pulled them on. 'What's this about?'

'I don't get it,' I said, pointing to the Petri dish beneath the microscope. 'This lot has leukaemia and they're HIV positive. I put in this new compound and the virus doesn't seem to have taken over. I just don't understand what's going on.'

He grabs the microscope. He yanks it towards him. I notice his fingers. So large they almost strangle its shiny black neck.

'Are you sure,' he says, 'that these guys have got HIV?'

'Yes . . . Let's look at them properly. We'll stain them. I'll show you.'

And with my gloved hands I transfer the cells into a salt-like plasma. I add a solution that swells them, that bursts them like soap bubbles and then I add the emerald dye that will allow us, once we have completed several interim steps, to examine the virus in the cells more closely. And all the time Tom stands behind me. So close that I can feel his breath, so that I have to say, 'Can you move back a little? I have no room.' And I peer then through the lens at the contents of the dish and I see that though the virus has not disappeared from the cells, neither has it penetrated the nucleus.

I move back now to make room for Tom to look.

'There's something spooky going on here,' he says.

I say nothing.

'Nick,' he says, turning round, staring at me. 'How long have you left them?'

'A day and a half.'

'Have you used this before . . . the compound I mean?'

'Never.'

'I don't get it. I don't get it,' he says to me, to himself, to the air. 'Did you use the same stuff in all of them?'

'Yes.'

We look again. We check again. And Tom, wiping his blond hair out of his eyes with his gloved hand, says,

'There's something in this, Nick. There has to be. The virus must have disintegrated. It's not in the nucleus.'

And I'm coming back down to earth now and I say, 'It must just be a one-off. A fluke.'

'So was the discovery of penicillin.'

I lean over one more time to peer again through the microscope that shuns the greys and browns and bursts now with the moving colours of my childhood kaleidoscope.

And I hear Tom saying, 'You have to work on this, boy. You have to. You never know what it might be.'

'It's nothing,' I say. 'It can't be. It makes no sense at all ...You know what, Tom. It's late. And I'm dying for that pastrami sandwich. Let's go.'

TWELVE

Dominique

My neck is the most important part of my body. It is the Eskimo's igloo, the Bushman's straw hut. The shelter to the voice and the throat. We interpreters are as paranoid about our throats as opera singers are about theirs. Pavarotti can feel no greater sense of panic, no deeper sinking feeling than we do, when on the morning of a conference, we wake to find that somewhere between the base of our chins and the nape of our necks, all is not well.

As the pianist must stretch his fingers on waking and the athlete wiggle his toes, even before I open my eyes, I clear my throat. I check that the dust will disperse and the frogs will scurry, leaving me free to practise my trade as best I can.

In a desperate attempt to annihilate intruders, I have squeezed more lemons, spooned more honey, gargled more salt water than I can begin to remember. I have learnt to distinguish between the gravel of the imminent head cold, the grain of the early morning allergy, the pain and swelling of infection as I swallow, and the rare indefinable and inexplicable enemy that attacks my larynx during sleep, sapping me as Delilah sapped Samson and leaving me to wake in a nightmare . . . voiceless.

It was the night before a particularly important conference, where Landmark, as the hosts, had invited eminent professors to present papers on medical treatments for chronic disease the world over. I would, I knew, be under intense pressure that February morning. Two days previously the agency had called me in desperation.

'Dominique, sweetie,' said Deborah. 'I need a huge favour. We're horribly short of interpreters. Could you possibly translate from French, Italian and German on Thursday? I know it's a lot to ask but you're our star translator and I know I can rely on you.'

Her manipulative flattery was successful. I agreed and fell asleep that night with my bedside lamp still on and my crisp white cotton sheets littered with lists of English, French, German and Italian vocabulary. I could do no more than touch the tip of the linguistic iceberg at a conference like this. Only a few of the doctors had provided us with their speeches in advance and the subject of the conference was vast and unspecific. It may sound odd, but in some ways the more specialized the material the easier it is to prepare yourself. I once did a conference on gum disease. Not exactly a subject one discusses at dinner parties. But by the time I walked into the conference hall I could have diagnosed a multitude of periodontic illnesses and recited their names in three languages.

But this was different. This was a conference for which I felt myself to be insufficiently prepared, and my sleep, already disturbed for nights on end by thoughts of Mischa and the burden of the secret I carried, that night was troubled further still.

A sleep where I was knocking on the bathroom door, calling for my mother, begging her to hear me and open up. A sleep where I was standing at the top of the driveway by the back door watching her speed away in her dark grey

Beetle and calling after her to please change her mind and come back. A sleep where I sat with both my parents at the dinner table, my meatballs and carrots untouched, listening to the hostile silence and then saying, quietly at first, that I couldn't eat because I was sure there was a stone in my stomach taking up all the space. I said it softly. Whispered it almost. But no-one heard. I spoke louder, turning first to my father and then to my mother. They carried on cutting, stabbing and munching those meatballs, hearing nothing. And I began to shout then.

'There's a stone in my tummy. I can't eat this. There's no room.' I shouted it over and over again until from yelling I grew hoarse. But my voice wouldn't carry. I was under water, a giant goldfish opening and closing my mouth without the gift of speech. I struggled, swimming upwards and onwards against the current to the surface. I cleared my throat and felt a menacing tightness. I jumped from my bed and ran over to the mirror while the lists of vocabulary fluttered to the floor. I stood in front of my image and opened my mouth to say 'Good morning,' to myself, to check that all was intact.

I watched my lips moving. The sound they emitted which should have been strong, loud and clear was no more than a croak. No point doing voice exercises. There was nothing to work with. I lifted my hand to my forehead. No, I wasn't feverish. I didn't feel ill, just drained and exhausted. I went to the kitchen and reached for the lemons.

As I dressed, in my brown woollen dress, I dared not try my voice again. I promised myself I would not speak till I was in the booth. Not even to call Deborah at the agency to tell her I might be in trouble. I was simply going to seal my lips, cross my fingers and pray on the way to work that when next I opened my mouth behind the microphone, my voice, by then recovered from the exertion of the night, would serve me well.

On the way to work I stopped at a flower stall on the corner of Fifty-Second and Lexington, to buy some yellow freesia. The vendor must have thought me slightly crazy when in answer to his 'good morning' I pointed first to my neck and then to the flowers. He plucked a small bunch from a metal bucket and gave me the freesia and a toothless grin in exchange for my two dollars. As I turned away he hollered to passers-by in a strong Southern drawl, 'Flowers for a good day. Flowers for a great day.'

In the booth I put the freesia in a small carafe at my side of the desk. Anna used to tease me about my habit of placing flowers in front of me while I worked. But I needed in some way to stamp my working environment, to make it my own, if only for a day. When the going got rough, the freesia were a constant reminder of life outside the booth.

In dismay I recognized the grey raincoat on the empty chair next to mine. It belonged to Lisa Marks, a brilliant but frightening and hugely disliked interpreter. She was truly quadrilingual. A French father. A German mother. A childhood in Italy and then England. But she was the most onerous of presences in the booth. She stared at me through her narrow eyes with their colourless lashes while I translated. She took notes and shoved lists of my mistakes under my nose. She huffed and she puffed her disagreement at my choice of words and excelled at making me feel incompetent and inadequate. In her place I would have welcomed the spotty Liverpudlian with open arms. To see her coat on the chair next to mine on a day when I might, I feared, have no voice at all, was almost enough to dispel my belief in the power of freesia.

As host to several medical VIPs, Landmark had added some uncharacteristic touches to this conference. Carafes of orange juice stood on the tables. Cards of welcome for each foreign guest were placed next to them. A massive white screen heralded some visual presentation or other and the sounds of Vivaldi's *Four Seasons* filled the hall from the speakers overhead.

The booths that day were at the front of the hall, beneath the podium facing the delegates. This struck me as a strange and rather ill-considered place for us to work. We would be unable to see the speaker, unable to read his lips as he spoke. And, strange as it may sound, we interpreters rely not only on our ears but on our eyes to confirm what the speaker is saying.

Lisa Marks stomped into the booth, grunted a greeting, and proceeded to complain that we were in direct view of the delegates, available for scrutiny through the glass-fronted booths like monkeys in a cage. I pointed out that I too hated to be exposed to the light and the delegates, but that at least there were curtains we could draw. She scowled in response and said, 'You sound rather croaky. I hope that doesn't mean I will be getting the brunt of the workload.'

I smiled and swallowing hard, assured her in a loud whisper that I would manage just fine. I think as the delegates rolled in it was the *Spring* of the *Four Seasons* we could hear through our headphones. I remember that despite my trepidation at the state of my voice and the unpleasant presence of my colleague I had begun to feel freed and uplifted by the lightness of the music. The orchestral strings heralded crocuses and blue skies. The room filled up, the doctors took their places and Marks abruptly drew the black curtains. The crack between the pieces of material was our window to the outside world and, edging closer to the centre of the booth, I could see the hands of three of the delegates in the front row as they waited for the conference to begin. The first had short plump fingers that he tapped on the black desk. The second, straight ahead of me, doodled with an expensive-looking fountain-pen, held between the large fingers of oversized hands. As the first speaker switched on his microphone and Marks started to follow his words I glanced at the third set of hands. They lay over one another, the skin light brown, the long bony fingers clasped together. Beautiful hands I couldn't help noticing. Eyes and hands are always the first thing that attract me to a man.

The first speaker began and Marks, arrogant but admirable in her fluency, followed his lead.

The price an interpreter pays to attain her level of skill is high. A woman like Marks is rootless. She belongs to every culture and then again to none. All her languages are her own, to play with and dominate as she wishes. And yet at her level no one language is truly her mother tongue. She, like many interpreters, is at home everywhere and nowhere. She is not at peace, never can be, for the words in her head can find no resting-place.

While she translated, I ought to have been concentrating hard, picking up new vocabulary that would repeat itself throughout the speeches of the day. Instead I stared through the crack in the curtain at those three sets of hands. Where was their resting-place? As one wonders fleetingly about the home life of people one sees on the bus or the subway, so I wondered where those hands belonged. The plump hands, the oversized hands, the tanned bony hands. Was the gold band squeezed onto the fourth finger of a chubby hand a symbol of a claustro-phobic marriage? Were the second set of hands those of a lonely bachelor? Were the third set, those that drew me, the hands of . . . ?

Marks glared at me. It was my turn to take over. She pressed the red off button. I pressed the green on button. This speaker would be a tough one. A French professor who had given us no documents to prepare. Would I have a voice or wouldn't I? It was in the lap of the gods. I closed my eyes. My stomach did a summersault.

'*Est-ce que l'on apprend assez l'un de l'autre dans ce domaine?*'

Do we learn enough from one another in this area?

'*Est-ce que nous sommes assez flexibles pour vraiment ouvrir nos esprits aux découvertes . . . ?*'

Are we sufficiently open-minded to discovery . . . ?

What came out was thick and deep and gravelly but intelligible none the less. The freesia had worked. A voice of sorts. Audible, passable, but not my real voice.

I heard Marks get up while I was translating. She pulled open the curtains. Vicious woman. She knew I too hated to work in the light. She knew I wouldn't want to be seen. I was concentrating hard now. No mental space to direct my brain to draw the curtains again. I kept my eyes shut and experienced that childlike hide-and-seek feeling that Mischa must have felt when he closed his eyes to tell me his story. Maybe if I couldn't see the delegates, then they couldn't see me.

Good, the speaker was waxing philosophical. There was much less medical content than I had imagined. '*Ce n'est qu'à travers les études de nos collègues que nous progresserons au niveau mondial . . .*'

'We can only make real progress on an international

level if we take on board the studies of our colleagues . . .'

You rarely have time to think a thought extraneous to your translation when you are working. If ever I envy the factory worker it is at moments like these. He can travel to the Taj Mahal while he sticks the tail on a plastic duck. He can walk by the sea while he glues on its wings. But, rooted to the task, the interpreter's imagination is starved. We cannot create. Only re-create. And eventually if we allow ourselves to be trapped in the world of second-hand words our imaginations shrivel and die.

Only if the speaker pauses for a moment does he allow you a corner of your own mental space. The professor said, '*Nous, à Paris, nous vantons puisque contrairement à ce que l'on prétend de notre culture nous avons la porte ouverte à toute nouvelle idée de nos collègues a l'étranger.*'

He paused for dramatic effect.

Ah, a moment to think. I opened my eyes and saw straight ahead of me a face I had seen before. Black eyes. Black arched eyebrows. High cheekbones. Wide lips that opened suddenly into a half smile of recognition. The face that belonged to the bony hands.

He told me later that I had smiled back fleetingly. I remember only losing my concentration for a moment and casting my eyes downwards. He said he could hear my voice in his ears through his headphones and that from the tips of his toes to the ends of those bony fingers, he was overcome with the conviction that someone, somewhere had just found the last and hitherto hidden piece of a jigsaw puzzle.

And I, at work with my eyes tightly shut, began to feel quite heady, with the scent of the yellow freesia and the sense that the man with the high cheekbones and the black eyes had his gaze fixed intently upon me.

I heard Marks come back into the booth. She had been gone no more than five minutes. Just five minutes. How strange that we can struggle for years to build a career, to learn a language, to know ourselves and others and yet, unsolicited and unexpected, in the space of seconds, in the space of the time it takes to powder one's nose, everything, quite simply everything, can change.

'Do you know that man?' asked Marks, pursing her thin lips as we stood a little later in the lobby during our coffee break.

'Which man?'

'You know exactly the one I mean. The thin dark one you were staring at while you worked. That one there,' she said and pointed to our right.

He was standing there with his back to us, next to a tall strong blond American-looking man who I later discovered to be his colleague Tom.

'No,' I said. 'No I don't know him at all.'

'We will keep the curtains closed at all times this afternoon. It is not advisable to make eye contact with the delegates while you work.'

And so the eye contact we made, Nicholas and I, was not till much later in the day. Much later when Marks had left and most of the delegates had trudged out bored and tired and I was gathering my lists of vocabulary together, still sitting in the booth with my headphones on.

I often sat there alone, in the quiet, to still the buzzing in my head before I tackled the streets of Manhattan. And as the curtains remained closed I had no way of knowing who it was, that I could hear through my headphones, shuffling papers after all the other delegates had left.

Not until I heard a cough and an 'excuse me' right behind me, did I know. I jumped and turned round. He

78

was standing by the door of the makeshift booth. Slightly paler, slightly taller, slightly thinner than from further away. He wore a navy flannel jacket, a white shirt and beige trousers. And I noticed the design on his tie. Tiny little brown sculptures of the Mona Lisa against a blue background.

'May I?' he asked, still at the doorway of my cardboard place of work.

I pointed to the seat Marks had vacated.

'You do a wonderful job,' he said.

'Thank you,' I said. 'Thank you.'

'You've been suffering with your voice today. I heard it.'

I nodded.

'Is it nerves perhaps?'

'I'm not sure,' I said. He's Italian, I thought.

We did invite delegates to come back from time to time to help us with medical terminology. As he was here maybe I ought to ask him for some help. Justify his presence in the booth. Maybe . . .

'Diabetes,' he said, running his finger down one of my lists and sensing my need to find a professional reason for this tête-à-tête. 'Dialysis, dilation . . . It amazes me. You learn foreign languages and then you learn our language.' He paused and then looking up from the piece of paper, turning to me with his jet-black gaze, he said, 'At the concert . . . in the church. I saw you there.'

'Yes,' I said. 'Tchaikovsky.'

'*Swan Lake*,' he said. 'You must be musical.'

'No, no I am not. Not really.'

'I mean to do what you do. To feel and hear languages. You must have a wonderful ear. And to translate as we are speaking. It's such an unusual skill. It astounds me.'

His tone contained no hint of flattery. His admiration was genuine. He simply said what he felt.

'How do you do it?' he asked. 'How do you manage to, what's the expression, *non perdere il filo . . .*'

'Not to lose the thread,' I said.

'Yes. How do you do it?'

'It's like learning to ride a bicycle.'

'Did you?' he asked.

I looked at him. It was warm suddenly in the booth.

'Did you learn as a child to ride a bicycle?' he asked again.

'Yes. Yes I did. A blue one.'

'I bet your father taught you.'

'Yes, he did,' I said, remembering my father's right hand on the front handlebar, his left on the back of the saddle. Remembering how even though I wobbled, even though I had no stabilizers, I felt safe then. If only for a few moments. If only till we got home.

Nicholas smiled and picked up Marks's set of headphones. He bent the wire stand of the microphone closer to his mouth.

'Can I try?' he asked.

For a moment I said nothing. Then I realized what he was getting at and smiled.

I picked up the text of the following morning's opening speech.

'So,' he said, 'what happens here? You read in English and I translate simultaneously into Italian?'

I nodded.

He cleared his throat, then sat up and clasped his hands together as though on the brink of some great discovery.

'I have an idea,' he said. 'Will you go up to the back of the hall and read?'

'What?'

'I mean, why don't you go to the back and see what it feels like to be on the other side. I'll sit here and try and translate for a few minutes.'

I wonder what made me say yes. I wonder how it came to be that I found myself walking the length of the empty hall, unusually aware of how I was moving. I had to go only from one end of a hall to the other, but it felt like a long walk. A very long walk that would lead me who knew where..

At the back of the hall I borrowed someone's microphone, fiddled with some switches and said to the man with the high cheekbones whose name I had forgotten to ask, 'Are you ready?'

'As ready as I'll ever be.'

I held a set of headphones to one ear to be able to hear him speaking. The other ear was free to listen to the sound of my own voice as I read.

He had pulled open the curtains. It had grown darker in the hall. Through the glass of the booth I could see his silhouette, though not his features.

'You promise not to laugh,' he said into his microphone.

'Yes,' I said. 'I promise. But move the microphone a little further away from your mouth.'

'Why don't you forget that medical speech?' I heard him say in my left ear.

'Pardon?'

'I mean, just talk to me. Anything. Just tell me about your day. It will be easier for me to start with.'

'I can't.'

'You can,' he said.

I thought of Mischa. The practice sessions at the dining-room table.

'OK,' I said.

I cleared my throat.

'It's been an odd sort of day really. I mean I woke up with no voice. I was terrified, so on the way to work I bought some yellow freesia to bring me luck . . .'

In my left ear I could hear him, still struggling to translate my first sentence.

'*E stato un giorno. E . . . é . . .*' I suppressed a giggle.

'You promised not to laugh at me.'

'With you,' I said. 'I'm laughing with you.'

And the two of us, at opposite ends of the room, realized suddenly the ridiculousness of the situation and our laughter, his and mine, rang out through the empty conference hall.

'How does it feel?' he asked.

'What?'

'To speak your own words?'

'Sorry?'

'To say what you want to say and not what someone else tells you to say.'

'It feels um . . . um, it feels . . .'

'Yes?'

'It feels . . . sort of like cycling backwards.'

'Unsafe?' he asked.

'Yes,' I said. 'That's the word. It feels unsafe.'

THIRTEEN

Nicholas

In the confines of my lab, over a period of weeks I repeated those experiments time and again. And though the findings the second, the third and the fourth times appeared to concur with the first, on each occasion I convinced myself it was a fluke. Some quirk of nature connected with the cells of the little three-year-old from the Bronx, who had Aids and leukaemia. Some strange twist of fate linked to these cells that I had named Henrietta. But I ran out of Henrietta's blood. The test-tubes that filled the refrigerator, where I froze the samples, and the incubator where I thawed them, all contained the cells of leukaemic patients in no way infected with HIV and I had no way, now, to prove or disprove the possibility that I had stumbled upon a method to arrest the virus. No way, that is, unless I was able to venture into territory that was not my own.

Uncomfortable about discussing such embryonic findings with Tom any further, I felt very much alone.

But water clears my mind. And so down by the South Street Seaport in the cold wind, staring out across the Hudson river at the white fishing trawlers with the sound of the gulls for company, I asked myself why I was loath to go to Goldmann and mention my findings. I wondered why I was so loath to ask for help. And I was able by the water to begin to find the answers. To understand how I feared that I would be inviting Goldmann to join me on some wild-goose chase. That I would appear presumptuous . . . the new boy who had been here all of five minutes and was convinced he'd hit the jackpot.

I was able to understand, too, that this was something that I had no desire yet to share. Because I knew that should my findings ever prove worthy of significant development funding, I would be asked immediately to change my path from leukaemia to HIV research. And though I have said in the past that I was driven by the passion of discovery, I nonetheless had a strong attachment to my field of speciality. And I almost made the decision there and then to leave well alone, to stick to what I knew, to steer clear of dangerous waters.

But as I turned to move away, I was hit by a strong gust of wind that brought with it the sharp smell of fresh fish and the conviction that, despite my reservations, I would not rest till I had taken just one more step.

The next day I crossed Landmark's grey courtyard and made my way along the sterile white corridor to the Virology department. I knocked on a door that bore a huge red circle and the words 'Level Four . . . NO ENTRY WITHOUT AUTHORIZATION'.

For some moments I stood there before the door was opened by a man in a green paper mask that came to just beneath his eyes.

'Can I help?'

'Nicholas Manzini . . . I'm sorry to bother you. I don't think we've met. I work in the . . .'

'The leukaemia department,' he said from behind his mask. 'You're the Italian, aren't you?'

'Yes, that's right. Actually I came to ask you a favour. I won't bore you with the details, but I'm making some comparisons and I could do with some HIV blood. Can you help?'

I have no idea whether or not he raised his eyebrows for they too were covered by a paper cap, but neither his tone nor his demeanour indicated surprise.

'Sure, how much do you need?' he said.

'Two or three test-tubes. I don't know ... whatever you can spare.'

And I stood on the threshold of his laboratory and waited while he filled two test-tubes and handed them to me in two zip-locked plastic bags.

I remember thinking as I walked back that it had been too easy, that his lack of curiosity as to my reasons for wanting the blood was both lucky and unlikely. And I gripped the plastic bags in my hand as I made for my laboratory.

The rules say you must log every ounce of human specimen that you take into the laboratory. The rules say that to begin work with unregistered blood samples or human fluids of any kind is tantamount to smuggling. I leant over and held the bar-code on my badge against the metal strip on the door, I pushed it open and, promising myself I would register the results of my tests when they were done, I ignored the rules.

Unlike other researchers I almost never lock the door, but if I recall correctly I did turn the silver key that afternoon. I turned it both when I came in and when I left. And as so often happened during examinations at medical school, when later that evening I tried to relive in my mind the way I had performed experiments, the images resisted and refused to come to me. It was only during sleep, as though watching my shadow, that I saw myself in white bent over my workbench as I poured the HIV-infected blood into the Petri dish, and I saw how my hand shook as I added the chemical compound from the purple glass bottle and left it then to do its work.

It is strange how sometimes the greatest revelations of your life can be accompanied by an astonishing calm. And so when I saw how the chemical compound in the purple bottle had worked on the HIV, when it was clear to me, beyond all possible doubt, that the liquid had prevented the Aids virus from further hijacking the cells and when it seemed that, quite by chance, I might have stumbled upon a method to further arrest the virus, I did not jump onto my chair or my workbench and shout 'Eureka'. Nor did I run to the door and call out into the corridor, 'Someone come. Please someone come. You'll never believe this.'

I walked instead to the back of my laboratory. I removed a dusky pink file from a pile that stood by the clock and with the fountain-pen that I kept on the inside pocket of my white coat, in black ink and in significant detail I registered my findings.

FOURTEEN

Dominique

Burnt orange. Lighter than Tia Maria. Darker than terra-cotta. I remember the second time I met Nicholas in burnt orange. The syndrome of labelling faces, days and places with a colour, is a recognized one. Krzysztof Kieslowski, the famous Polish scriptwriter and director, named a trilogy of his films in colours. I would find it amusing to hear people say, 'Have you seen *Red* yet? Have you seen *Blue* or *White*?' For some people Tuesday may be brown, Thursday blue, Sunday black. It is a pictorial way of fixing things in their minds. As a linguist I generally remember things in words more than in images, but it is in burnt orange that I recall the second day of the international symposium on chronic disease.

The second day of any conference is always less daunting than the first. You are in the swing of things. The previous day's vocabulary tends to repeat itself. You are familiar with the layout of the room, with the *modus operandi* and the moods of your colleagues. And so, despite unfamiliar sensations that I chose not to question, despite thoughts of Switzerland that never left me, on the night after the first session of the conference I slept better than I had in a long time. I woke early just as night was succumbing to the orangey light of morning. The clothes I had laid out on the rocking-chair were no different from my normal choice of dress. Black velvet trousers. Brown body stocking. Black jacket. I rarely made any attempt to spice up my work clothing but on an impulse I opened the door of my maple wardrobe and reached for the russet velvet scarf that Anna had bought me. I could hear her, as I put it around my neck saying, 'Dominique, you do nothing to attract attention to yourself. Live a little, my friend. Learn to live a little.'

There must have been a spring in my step as I began my day. My aura must have been different because wherever I went, it seemed people were smiling at me. The waiter in the Plaza Diner smiled as he put down my bowl of porridge. The boy at the news-stand smiled as I bought my copy of the *Herald Tribune* and though Marks couldn't quite bring herself to crack her face as I walked into the booth, I was able for once to shrug it off.

I had taken the yellow freesia home with me the night before and placed them on my desk, so I was more than surprised to see that the carafe was filled with flowers. Tulips. Six dark orange tulips.

'Oh Lisa, how nice. You've picked up my habit,' I said pointing to the flowers.

'Not me. They're a total waste of money and they take up all the oxygen in here.'

'So where did they come from?'

'Your time,' she said, 'could be put to better use than asking questions to which you have the answers.'

Today through the crack in the curtains I could see only two sets of hands. The plump hands and the over-sized fingers.

My encounter with Nicholas the previous day had ended abruptly with the arrival of the cleaners into the conference hall and on his way out he had bumped into a colleague, and we had taken leave of one another. I had left the building and jumped in a cab to meet my friend at Sixty-Fifth and Columbus on the West Side.

James was a radio journalist for an East Coast news and current affairs programme and ours was a truly platonic relationship, devoid of any sexual tension or complication. He had never tried. Nor had I. Neither of us had wanted to. But our friendship was an easy one. A bond created mid-air, mid-Atlantic in scratchy blue seats from London to New York.

'It's odd isn't it, how easy and uncomplicated the communication can be when that bubble isn't there?' he had once said.

'What bubble?' I had asked.

'You know, that strange bubble that sometimes, I mean, rarely, once in a blue moon floats in the air when you meet someone. It doesn't happen with a friendship like we have. And it doesn't happen when it's just about lust either. It's just a coloured bubble that dances in front of your eyes and gets in your way. Haven't you ever experienced that?'

I thought of Paul. Friday nights. The Sabbath candles flickering on the table. His family and mine together. Children being sent upstairs to play with Lego and puzzles. Teenagers running upstairs to watch videos. Adolescents sneaking out for a cigarette behind the monkey-puzzle tree in the magic of the garden on a summer's night. And Paul pretending he wanted me to light his cigarette for him and suddenly stubbing it out under his sneaker and kissing me instead. My first kiss at fifteen behind a monkey-puzzle tree. But I couldn't in all honesty tell James I knew anything about that coloured bubble floating in the air, because I hadn't ever noticed it when Paul kissed me. Not then under the monkey-puzzle tree or any time after that.

'Can you describe it to me?' I had asked him and he had said, 'That's like trying to describe a rainbow to a blind man.'

Outside the cinema James, in his black leather jacket, with his pixie face and protruding ears was waiting for me with two tickets for *The Bridges of Madison County* in his hand. He grabbed me by the arm and dragging me inside said, 'We'll miss the beginning, and we're seeing this one for you and not for me. It's a woman's film.'

I was about to protest, as he pushed me laughing through the door of the cinema.

'Dilemma,' he said later over sushi.

'What about it?'

'Her dilemma. Meryl Streep's dilemma . . . to go with the man she loves and pay the price for it. Or to stay. It's an interesting one. What would you have done, Dom?'

'I, I don't know. I don't think anything can tear you apart from someone you love that much, can it? I mean, you know, I'm away from Paul for a while, but I suppose that's only temporary. But a dilemma like that. I don't know. I really don't know. What would you do?'

'I would be true to myself,' he said.

Dilemmas. Had I not buried it so deeply. Had James not been a journalist, ever on the lookout for a story. Had I not been so convinced that an oath to maintain confidentiality was absolute and binding, I might have poured my heart out to him there and then.

I might have said, 'James, do you know that most nights I sleep so badly, because my friend Mischa, the one in Switzerland, the medical student is sick. But I heard something through my headphones, the other day, the other week. I heard these two guys whispering about an idea for a new drug that some whiz-kid has stumbled on and that they want to keep quiet for some reason and I know it's illogical because they can't develop a drug in two minutes, but, well, maybe if I told the Landmark management they might speed things up and help Mischa or use him in clinical trials and, well, I've got a dilemma because I'm bound to confidentiality and so I'm keeping quiet and it killed me when I got Mischa's letter . . .'

I almost did tell James. I sounded even to myself as if I was going to. I said, 'I've got a dilemma,' and he said, 'What, Dom?'

'Sake?' I said. 'Should I have some sake or stick with the mineral water?'

The bottle of Evian in the booth the next day was almost empty.

'He must have used it for the tulips,' Marks growled. 'A disgrace, really, when you come to think of it.'

I said nothing. Just looked at the orange tulips and thought that it had been rather innovative to quench their thirst with mineral water.

'I'll start today,' Marks said and she pulled the medical dictionary over to her side of the booth.

Interpreters at a conference of several days are supposed to take it in turns to open the sessions. It is an unwritten rule. It was fun sometimes to do the 'Good morning, ladies and gentlemen' bit, followed by a few general remarks about the programme for the day or the weather. It eased you in gently to translate these words of welcome. I ought to have said to Marks, 'I'm sorry, but I think you opened the session yesterday morning. Would you mind if I started today?' I thought it. I formulated the words in my head, ready to say them. But they quite simply refused to budge, refused to make the requisite jumps from neuron to neuron, from synapse to synapse, up my vocal cords to my lips.

And so once again it was Marks who got the 'Good morning, ladies and gentlemen' bit, while inside I grew nervous that the next speech was unknown and the speaker as yet unnamed.

'We would welcome more postings to the US branch of Landmark from abroad as we would welcome the opportunity to send some of our people to Europe for specified periods of time. I think to date on the few occasions we have done this, we've found it to be a very enriching experience. It's a case of I'll scratch your back and you scratch mine . . .'

The chairman carried on in this vein and Marks translating from English into French was in her element, unable to mask the delight that glistened in her narrow foxy eyes at her own verbal dexterity, for she had found just the right translation for 'I'll scratch your back and you scratch mine.'

Foxes. We interpreters are foxes and the speaker's words are our prey. We sneak up behind them, snatch them, flip them upside down and play with them as we choose. But sometimes, just sometimes they set us a booby trap. The idiom. Covered over with moss. In no way alarming. Words that are easy to digest and regurgitate. '*Non é l'abito che fa il monaco* . . .' No challenge. 'It's not the habit that makes the monk.' What? We are caught suddenly bloody and exposed in the idiom trap, writhing and realizing too late the meaning of those words. '*Non é l'abito che fa il monaco* . . . you can't judge a book by its cover,' and while we squirm sentence after sentence dashes past us, mocking and untouched.

It was my turn and the speaker was saying exactly that.

'*Non é l'abito che fa il monaco,*' but I'd fallen into that one before and so this time I mastered it without delay.

'You can't judge a book by its cover,' I said, and continued then as following the speaker I translated, 'and though it may seem as if an Italian with a poor command of English like me would find it difficult to fit into Landmark, USA, it has to date proved a most interesting experience. I am researching into paediatric leukaemia and have been posted here for two years with the option to extend my stay. If I were to make comparisons they would be the following . . .'

Your voice. I recognize your voice. I can't see you because the podium is behind me, but I've heard the voice I'm translating before. Just enough time to think those thoughts before he takes off again. Fast. No time to dwell on the words I am playing with. I only know I must be faithful to them. Not lose a moment's concentration. The dash through the undergrowth is exhausting and at the end I switch off my mike and lean back in my swivel chair quite spent and Marks glares at me, baffled by my breathlessness. It's time for a coffee break, but before we get up Nicholas appears at the door of the booth once again and he says, 'Thank you so much. That can't have been easy to translate.' And I say nothing. I just about manage to return his smile. And I can't really see him clearly because the lighting in the booth is so low and because between us at eye-level something obliterates my view. A bubble. A floating burnt-orange bubble.

FIFTEEN

Nicholas

Watches fascinate me. They always have. The Oxford Dictionary describes the watch as 'a small timepiece worked on a coil spring for carrying on the person'. When I was a small boy I would hold the tiny coil springs, the minute cogs, the minuscule corrugated-edged wheels, in the palm of my hand, waiting for the approach of the tweezers to lift them one by one and transform them into a masterpiece that would dictate the movements of its wearers. My grandfather, with his wrinkled olive skin, would pull my little wooden chair closer to his in his workshop on the beach in Sardinia and tell me stories of the princes and politicians whose lives were run by the creation of his intricate artefacts. He would leave the door of the workshop open and craft his timepieces to the sound of the waves. '*Nonno*, you're a genius,' I said to him once, 'You're the man who makes time.'

His creased face had crinkled further still and he had said, '*L'ora la posso creare in un orologio, ma il momento giusto mai.*' I can create time with my watches but I cannot create the right time.

Not till much later did I understand what he meant. He meant that he, that all watchmakers could create the instruments to measure time, but none had the power to influence timing.

I was waiting on a Sunday afternoon for Dominique in the bookstore Barnes & Noble on the Upper West Side. We had arranged to meet at the foreign language section and I, with time on my hands, decided to find myself a decent English dictionary. What made me look up the word 'timing' in the Concise Oxford Dictionary I could not tell you, but I did. The definition of timing read, 'to harmonize with'.

Did my time harmonize with Dominique's? Was the timing of our story fated for good or for ill? There and then at the foreign language section in Barnes & Noble on Sixty-Sixth and Columbus on a Sunday afternoon I asked myself no such probing questions.

I cannot tell you how long I had been poring over the Concise Oxford Dictionary, but suddenly I felt someone touch my arm. At first I hardly recognized her in her weekend clothing. She wore faded jeans and a brown silk shirt. Her hair was tied back with a piece of blue chiffon. Her lipstick was a slightly deeper brown than I had remembered and I noticed a small beauty spot above her lip and a tiny gold Star of David at her throat. Over her arm she was carrying a white sheepskin coat. The coat she wore in the church.

'I'm late,' she said. 'I'm sorry.'

'Don't worry . . . I think I've found it for you.'

I pointed to the medical dictionary section. This was our reason for meeting. I was going to advise Dominique on the best Italian-English medical dictionary to help her in her conference preparation. She walked ahead of me. A little too fast, I thought. She ran almost, as if afraid of something. I imagined the expression on her face. I pictured it as the one she had worn when, at the end of a session a few days previously, I had gone to the booth to thank her for translating. She had appeared both uplifted and slightly alarmed at the same time and I had wondered whether to put it down to the stress of simultaneous translation or to my unsolicited presence.

She was walking on now, past the medical dictionary section.

'Dominique,' I called. It felt new and strange to pronounce her name. 'Dominique, you've gone too far. They're over here.'

She turned back towards me. I was right. She looked slightly, just ever so slightly afraid. 'Oh, here,' she said and walked over to the shelf where I was standing.

'So, which is the best?' she asked, looking at me.

I realized suddenly that I had no clue. How did one compare the virtues of dictionaries?

'I'm not quite sure,' I said, embarrassed.

She smiled then and her face relaxed. I noticed the slight gap between her two front teeth. 'You're the medic,' she said 'You should know.'

'You're the linguist,' I said.

'Well, it's about more than the translation of a condition or an illness. Or a part of the anatomy. I need a dictionary that will explain the meaning of the word to me in layman's terms.'

'So let's pick a word and try out a couple of different dictionaries. What shall we choose?'

'Laryngitis,' she said.

I raised my eyebrows. 'Why?'

She looked away, uncomfortable. 'Oh, just because it's as good as any other.'

And we stood for who knows how long bent over dictionaries. 'Laryngitis . . . a condition that affects the larynx and the vocal cords simultaneously . . . precipitated on occasion by nerves.'

She was standing right next to me. Out of the corner of my eye I could see the contours of her neck. She said, 'I really need my glasses for this,' and leant further forward. Our faces were close together, poring over the dictionary. Almost touching. Almost, but not quite. For a moment I was lost in my thoughts. Thoughts far removed from lexicons and laryngitis.

'This one,' she said in a louder voice than usual, turning suddenly and awkwardly towards me. We bumped noses. We each put a hand up to our faces. 'Gosh, I'm so sorry.'

'It's easy to bang into a nose like mine,' I said and laughed.

'So, um I'll go and pay for this now then,' and she lifted a heavy green dictionary from the shelf.

'And I need to get the *Corriere della Sera* on the fifth floor. It makes me feel at home.'

'Oh of course, you go, I've already taken up too much of your time. I'll be fine . . . Thanks for your help.'

'No, no I'll wait for you.'

'Are you sure?'

'Yes, of course.'

And so we found ourselves on the silver slatted escalators at Barnes & Noble on a Sunday afternoon on the way to the fifth floor. Dominique stood on the step in front of me and I noticed from close up that the blue chiffon scarf had little auburn flecks in it that matched the chestnut streaks in her hair. I noticed too how slight she was and that she stood very straight, almost as if she was carrying the dictionary on her head and not in her hand. When we got to the top she turned round and said, 'The European newspapers are over here, aren't they?'

Le Monde, Le Figaro, Die Frankfurter Allgemeine Zeitung, La

Stampa, Il Corriere della Sera . . . in piles against the back wall
with nostalgic customers huddled round them to breathe
in the scent of home from the black print.

I as usual went for the *Corriere della Sera*. Dominique
reached for the *Guardian*.

'We can buy the papers and sit over there at the café
and read them,' I said, pointing to the tables, piled high
with magazines, newspapers and reference books.

'Um . . . well I . . .'

'I'm sorry, of course, you probably don't have time.'

'Yes, yes, I do. I suppose. Maybe a quick hot chocolate.'

'With cream or without?'

'Without,' she said.

There were no empty tables. I asked if we could sit
down next to a young man in a denim jacket with a poor
complexion and short cropped blond hair. He looked up
from his magazine and nodded. I noticed the title of his
article. 'Support for an HIV Positive Partner'. For a split
second, no more than a split second my thoughts strayed
from Dominique. I looked at her then. She was staring at
the article too. She caught my eye and looked away.

We sat down. She filled her teaspoon with the steaming
chocolate and blew on it before she drank. Between tea-
spoons she asked me questions. Why had I come to New
York? What exactly was I researching? Did I find the work
lonely? Had I made friends here?

And I sensed, while I answered her stream of questions,
that her reasons for asking them were twofold. Yes, she
was interested in what I was saying. She was definitely
interested. She nodded in all the right places and focused
on my words with the eyes of a listener. Eyes that might
have been brown and might have been green. It was
difficult in the artificial light of the bookstore to work it

out exactly. But she had another reason for her questions, I was sure. I don't think she wanted me to ask about her. She wanted to deflect attention from herself. I felt that and I was just about to say, 'That's enough about me. What about you, Dominique? Let's talk about you,' when my instinct and the man with the short blond cropped hair stopped me.

'Do you have the time?' he asked Dominique in a strong foreign accent and she answered with a cheeky grin on her face.

'*Quatre heures vingt.*'

He looked at her surprised.

'How did you know?'

'I'm half French,' she said.

'Which side?'

'*Ma mère* . . . Oh I'm sorry,' she says to me. 'I'm being rude. You don't speak French do you?'

And I say, 'Please don't worry. I wanted a chance to read the newspaper anyway.' And I hide behind the printed sheets and manage with the remnants of my schoolboy French and the strength of the similarities between the two Latin languages to pick up the snippets that float over the top of my newspaper.

She talks to him. She tells him the odd detail about her life because he asks and because it seems the air between them is less charged than the air between us. She tells him words are her passion. She tells him she loves it here in the States, in New York, in Manhattan, in this bookstore. She talks to him and I pretend to read about crime in Milan, but I can't concentrate and I wonder if she's forgotten about me. But then he says he has to leave. He shakes her hand and says '*C'etait un plaisir.*' He stands up, nods at me and goes. And I don't put my paper down straight away, but I look at Dominique and she looks at me and neither of us says anything. A fleeting silence. An eloquent silence, not an awkward one. She looks at her watch then as if she might say she has to go. I look at it too and I think that somehow it doesn't quite suit her wrist. The face is large and oblong and the numbers are silver and I think that a small round watch with Roman numerals in gold would look perfect. She must be reading my thoughts because she says, 'You don't like it do you?' And I say, 'Who bought it for you?'

'Paul,' she says and looks troubled.

I raise my eyebrows.

'Paul . . . my boyfriend in London. He bought it for me before I left, so that I would "feel" every second I was away from him.'

'And do you?'

'I . . . I . . .'

'I'm sorry, I didn't mean to pry.'

'I like *your* watch,' she says.

It is large, old-fashioned and simple, with a black strap, a white face, gold edging and gold numerals. I take it off, lay it on the table and turn it over.

She reads the inscription out loud, '*Ti auguro il momento giusto* . . . I wish you good timing . . . S.M.'

'My grandfather,' I say. 'He was a watchmaker. Try it. See what it looks like on you.'

She holds out her other wrist and I fasten the strap around it and then hold her hand to look at it. I look at it on her wrist for what seems like a long time. It suits her. I thought gold would suit her better than silver. And I notice then in place of my watch, the white band that is a tan mark on my own wrist and her long slim fingers clasped between mine.

SIXTEEN

Dominique

My mother asked, 'Are you happy in New York, Dominique?

We want to know the truth. We worry that it must be lonely for you. I mean don't you miss Paul and your friends from Switzerland? . . . Because you don't have to stay there, you know, just to prove a point. Dominique, you're not answering me. Tell me the truth.'

I was sitting on a low wooden stool in my kitchen by the fridge. I held the phone to my ear with one hand and with the other I searched on the fridge door amongst the jumble of words for the magnetic white strip that bore the word TRUTH.

Ah, yes, the truth. My mother saying, 'Tell us the truth, Dominique.' Still after all these years mispronouncing the 'r' in truth, gargling with it and saying, 'You must always tell us the truth. Only naughty children hide things from their parents.'

'What does the truth mean?' I asked my father.

'It means what is real. It means if you got six out of ten for a maths test, you tell us you got six and not that you got seven out of ten.'

I tried hard, very hard to tell the truth at home and at school. When I was nine we had an assignment. Our teacher handed out blue cardboard folders and two pieces of lined writing-paper and asked us to write about our summer and what it had felt like to be on holiday. I sat at my brown desk, with its woodworm ridges, screwed up my eyes very tightly and tried hard to remember. Then I wrote my story about how the sea and sky in France were very blue all the time and the steak was delicious and the chips were really thin and they called them '*frites*', and how my mother was French so we had our very own translator to explain things to us. And I said that being on holiday wasn't at all like being at home where if my mother and father were shouting at each other I could run upstairs into my bedroom, close my door and cuddle my green stuffed rabbit or my red stuffed bear. Because in the hotel we all had shared one bedroom, my mother, my father, my little sister and me and there was nowhere to go and hide except the toilet. And I would have sat on the toilet for ever but someone else always seemed to want to use it and I wasn't allowed out into the corridor alone, so really I didn't like being on holiday all that much at all.

So I wrote that in my story and I thought I'd get a great mark because I'd told the truth and I'd written even more than the teacher had asked for, but all that Mrs. Graham wrote at the bottom of the page was 'See me, Dominique.' And for some reason that I was incapable of understanding that story seemed to cause lots and lots of tears at home. The ink on the front of the blue folder where I'd written 'My Family Holiday' in joined-up writing got all smudged because my mother's tears dripped all over it and the whole palaver made me wonder whether what they called truth wasn't just one of those things that was harder for grown-ups to cope with than for children. They insisted on it at interpreting school too. Maurice, with his massive moustache, pacing up and down the room saying,

'What do interpreters have in common with the most famous Russian newspaper?' and then answering his own question shouting, '*Pravda Pravda* . . . the truth. A good interpreter will render the speaker's truth in his simultaneous translation. So you must be sharp as a wild beast in danger. Those ears must be pricked up at all times, because in a split second you have to hear his truth in his words and gauge his truth from his tone. I don't care if he's an industrial engineer talking about cranes or a philosopher talking about life, you only deserve to call yourself an interpreter if you tell his truth.'

That worked most of the time. You got as close to the speaker's truth as you could. On a good day after a few sentences you took the whole of your being and in your mind you sat right inside his head. You lost yourself entirely, so that the whole of you was no more than a piece of sophisticated software programmed to convert his words into some other language. Once, though, Deborah from the agency had asked me to work at something they called 'An International Forum for Ideas'.

The room was full of writers and philosophers in ghastly patterned shirts, ill-fitting trousers and open-toed sandals and I was concentrating hard, translating the philosophical ideas of an elderly Brazilian man. He spoke in French, but with a heavy Portuguese accent, and translating his words was the mental equivalent of doing press-ups with the flu. I was focusing so hard that it was only after I had finished translating, only after I had interpreted his ideas that I realized that I had said, 'One might perhaps suggest that the severity of the conditions in one or two of the concentration camps was marginally exaggerated by those who worked there.'

Oh I had been truthful of course. Entirely. I had

rendered the speaker's words and his tone exactly and precisely. He even came and thanked me for all my hard work. But I wondered for a long time after that whether there might not just be the odd occasion in my professional life when I would be better off to lie than to tell the truth.

And now sitting on the kitchen stool, with my mother in my ear saying, 'Tell me the truth, Dominique. Tell me the truth,' I told her what I could of it.

'Yes, Mum, I'm fine here. But yes, I do miss Anna and Mischa and if I sound stressed it's just because there are things on my mind. Work-related stuff, you know. Don't worry Mum, don't worry.'

'And Paul?' she asked. 'What will happen?'

The words echoed from her kitchen in London through the airways, rebounded and got caught in the cracked paint on my ceiling. 'And Paul, what will happen? Are you excited about seeing him?'

Almost exactly what he was to ask me on the phone the next day. 'Dominique, I can't wait to see you.'

'Yes, me too.'

'You don't sound convincing.'

'What do you mean?'

'I mean that you seem to have got used to being without me.'

'Don't be ridiculous.'

'I booked my ticket yesterday.'

'You'll love it here. You'll love New York.'

'Dominique.'

'Yes.'

'I'm not coming for New York. I'm coming to see you.'

'I know that.' I took a deep breath. 'I can't wait.'

The truth. What happened to the truth? I think then,

during that conversation it was the hard gristly ball that lodged itself somewhere in the region of my belly button and refused to budge. I recognized the feeling of that gristly ball stuck there. Like some chronic condition it had ensconced itself there so many times over so many years. Yet now instinctively I felt that were I not to squeeze my stomach muscles tight and encourage it to bury itself between fold after fold after fold of intestine, the truth might rush upwards unchecked through my oesophagus and my throat and burn the inside of my mouth with its unfamiliar acidity.

But the gristly ball of truth, unaware that its days in hiding were numbered, succumbed to the tightening of my stomach muscles yet again and I said, 'Paul, Paul. I really am looking forward to seeing you.'

I hung up, leant against the pull-out table in the kitchen, opened the refrigerator door, took out a paper carton and drank a glass of milk, that would, I knew, calm my discomfort within minutes. Too tired to talk any more that evening I walked into my bedroom to switch the phone to the answering machine and came back to the kitchen.

I sat there for a long time sipping my glass of milk and writing down in black ink a list of my favourite places, so that Paul's days in New York the following week would be filled with interest and activity. I wrote down at first the Metropolitan Museum, the Museum of Modern Art and the Guggenheim. I looked at the words on the paper, thought about them and slowly drew a line through each. And instead by their side I wrote the Empire State Building, the World Trade Center and the New York Stock Exchange. He would prefer these places, of course. How silly of me not to realize that straight away.

The phone rang three times while I was writing my list and leafing through my New York guidebook. I heard the machine click, but I had turned down the volume of the answer phone and couldn't tell who had left the messages.

I might easily have fallen asleep the moment my head hit the pillow, but I am someone who can sleep only in pitch-darkness. A chink of light through the curtains or from under the crack in the door has always disturbed me. My curtains were lined, my door firmly shut but even through closed eyelids I sensed the insistent flashing of the tiny light on my answerphone. I dragged myself out of bed, walked towards the light, pressed the button to the right of it and in the blackness now that I needed for sleep I listened to my messages.

The deep voice of a young woman with no more than a hint of an accent.

'Dom, it's Anna. You never seem to be home. I think you're getting quite out of control there. I need to speak to you. By the way did you get Mischa's letter? He told me he wrote to you. He really doesn't know I've told you anything yet. I want to talk. About him. About everything. Call me. *Un baccione.*'

A click. And then a fast voice. A good solid radio voice.

'Hi, it's James. Just checking in to make sure you're not drowning under a pile of vocabulary somewhere. Dom? Dom? Are you screening your calls? I have a feeling you're there. . . . Oh well ignore me if you must. Speak soon.'

Click.

A man's voice again. A deeper voice this time. An accent not dissimilar to Anna's.

For some reason I open my eyes, and in the dark in my mind I see him as he begins to talk. He says something about Sundays in New York and something about Barnes

& Noble. He says he went to another concert in the church on Madison Avenue . . . Mozart's Clarinet Concerto in A and it was beautiful, really beautiful. He asks, 'Do you know it Dominique? Have you heard it? . . .'

He says goodnight and that he'll speak to me tomorrow, and I fall asleep. The next morning when I wake up my throat is dry and I stumble into the kitchen. I must have slammed the fridge door hard the night before because under my left foot I feel something. I bend down and pick up one small white magnetic strip that has fallen off the fridge and I turn it over in my hand. Ah yes, the strip I had been looking for. The strip that in tiny shiny black letters bears the word TRUTH.

SEVENTEEN

Nicholas

Tom is faster than I am. His trainers are Nikes. New well-padded Nikes. He finds it easier than I do to talk and run at the same time. His breathing is less erratic than mine. He's been doing this for years. I've only been at it for a few weeks. I haven't got round to buying a decent pair of running shoes. I'm still wearing my old tennis shoes. The rubber's worn down and the laces look grey. I feel the soles of my feet each time they thud against the gravel. It's the first time we've run together. He sprints ahead for a bit, then slows down to fall into pace with me.

'You don't have to, Tom,' I pant. 'Go ahead.'

'No big deal Nick,' he says. 'Just keep at it.'

I nod. No point wasting my aerobic capacity on superfluous words. The sweat is pouring off me. I feel my grey T-shirt sticking to my chest. My white shorts are nylon. They cling to me and feel uncomfortable against my skin. Must buy some cotton ones.

'So, where are you up to?' Tom asks, running to my right. I hear the regularity of his breathing with each stride. 'Never get time to talk these days,' he says.

'What?'

'Your research?'

'Freezing . . . Bone marrow . . . it's a great thing.'

Up the slope, past the patchy grass on either side, towards the start of the exercise path they call the loop.

'I don't mean that,' he says. 'I mean the other stuff. The stuff you showed me.'

'I've done a bit more,' I say. He hasn't asked me about it for weeks. I thought he'd lost interest. I was dealing with it in my own head. I didn't want to make a big thing of it.

'What d'you mean "a bit"?' he says over his shoulder.

He's slightly ahead of me again. I notice, as I run, the strength and solidity of his shoulders. His running gear's professional. Red shorts and sleeveless vest. They look good with blond hair.

'What did you say?' I called ahead of me. I'd heard him the first time. I needed a few strides to contemplate my answer.

He turned his head for a moment.

'I mean, any more exciting news?' he called and brushed his hair from his face as he carried on running.

I thought I'd be grateful for Tom's company. I'd been pleased when he asked me to run with him. I thought it would motivate me. But it struck me suddenly, as I propelled myself forward, that I preferred to run alone. I felt the weight of my Walkman clipped to my shorts. I longed to switch it on, to pull the headphones out of my pocket and over my ears. I longed to run to Cat Stevens. I couldn't do it though. Far too anti-social. Far too ungrateful. Tom was doing me a favour here by training with me. A favour as a friend.

'Nick,' he called. 'You in a dream world there? Is there anything exciting or isn't there?'

'Not sure yet,' I puffed. 'Really not sure.'

Yes, I thought. I was better doing this alone. Less pressure running alone.

'You haven't discussed it with Landmark have you?'

I shake my head. I feel the beads of perspiration on my face.

'Don't,' he says. 'For God's sake, Nick. Don't.'

I say nothing.

I feel the beginnings of a stitch in my right side. I will myself on. My calf muscles are pulling. I'm sure he can't feel his. His movements are so fluid.

'You ready to talk about it?'

I hadn't realized I was so unfit. I'm concentrating on my running, concentrating on how to answer, but Tom shows less patience here than he does with my lack of stamina.

'Someone wants to talk to you about it. Now,' he says. 'Can't wait much longer. You know, the guy I'm going to work with. My father's friend. I've told him about you. He needs us to talk.'

I keep going, though the stitch is getting worse. I keep running. Alongside Tom now. Alongside the cyclists. Haven't done too badly. Thirty minutes isn't so bad for a start. The light is brighter now. Tens of helmeted cyclists bent over their bars whizzing past us. I notice the splashes of colour as we run. The yellow of spring's first daffodils sprouting through patchy grass. A red helmet. A purple helmet. A green one.

'So Nick, how about it? Uptown sometime next week.'

I'm coughing a bit now. That's enough for an early morning run. Tom shows no sign of stopping. I begin to feel winded. I stop and bend over. I rest my hands on thighs, breathing heavily now.

'OK Nick?'

'Fine,' I pant.

'Great, I'll set it up. I'll let you know when.'

He's jogging on the spot. Not ready to stop. And I'm

still standing there bent over, staring down at the gravel waiting for my heart rate to slow down.

'I'm going to keep on going for a bit,' he says. 'I guess I'll see you later.'

I hold up my hand. 'Thanks. That was good.'

He sprints off and I turn towards the exit at Seventy-second Street. I'm walking. Slowly at first. And I'm thinking about Tom as I walk a little faster and approach Fifth Avenue. Then I press the button on my Walkman and I turn the volume up loud. In my ears Cat Stevens is singing at the top of his voice, '*Oh, I can't keep it in. I can't keep it in. I've got to let it out. I can't hide it and I can't lock it away, I've got to show the world. The world's gotta see . . .*' And I'm running again now, my feet pounding against the gravel and Cat Stevens is singing '*I can't keep it in. I gotta let it out.*' The beat is fast and the music is loud and I feel suddenly strong and powerful.

Just before I pass the high dark green hedge that separates the rest of the world from Central Park a vision of a mouth moving behind glass flashes through my mind. Cupid's-bow-shaped lips painted russet-brown moving fast and furiously. Lips that, as they open and close, reveal a tiny gap between the two front teeth. And I think that I must ask her to come here with me. Not to run, but to talk. To walk and to find out who she is.

EIGHTEEN

Dominique

Nicholas laid his hand on the sleeve of my black jacket and he said, 'Look, look over there. You see that runner. The one in the green shorts. See how fast and confident he is. He runs like you work. I wanted to tell you that the other day . . . when I was here with my colleague Tom. I saw a runner like that man over there and I thought of you. That's what you sound like in the booth.'

'Do I? Do I really?'

We walked from the entrance of the park in the direction of a shadowy area of bottle-green foliage that I knew by now would give way to a clearing and the blue of the lake that is Central Park's *pièce de résistance*. As we approached the water an orange plastic ball rolled towards Nicholas's feet. He bent down to pick it up and a small blond boy came running towards him. The child came up very close and Nicholas dropped the ball into the podgy hands that were cupped and waiting.

In jest the child tugged at Nicholas's denim shirt and where it rode up the darkness of the markings on his belt contrasted with the skin on his lower back. A young woman came and dragged the toddler away and as he stood up Nicholas said to me,

'I need to be near the water, you know. This is the first time I've ever been so far from Sardinia. I spent all summer every summer there as a child. The water is turquoise there. Turquoise or navy depending on the time of day . . . I suppose this is better than nothing though,' he added, pointing at the man-made lake. 'This little pond in the middle of the city.'

He tilted his face upwards and said, 'Look. Look where we are,' and he gestured towards the zigzag outline of the high-rise buildings.

The weak late afternoon sunshine fell on his cheek for a moment, till turning his face, he banished it.

'I have this crazy dream you know, that I walk out of my apartment in the middle of Manhattan barefoot, over the road and straight into the Mediterranean. Sometimes I can almost feel the salt water on my skin. It's odd isn't it?'

I laughed and that spring afternoon walking by the lake in Central Park I saw myself instead walking with him by the sea. A sullen stormy dark grey sea. A dramatic sea. A sea with waves that thrashed and threatened and threw their spray about without regard. The line of poetry that imposed itself suddenly and from nowhere on my mind was a disturbing one: 'Wild waters whose foamy waves deny yesterday's frivolity to all who pass by . . .'

I racked my brain to try and find the author as we followed the contours of the lake. I could see the black print of the poem on the page. The way the first word of each verse began with a curly italic capital letter, but no name came to me.

Nicholas interrupted my thoughts.

'Where did you go to be near the water when you were small, Dominique? And now where do you go when you are back in London? Or maybe you are not someone who needs water in that way. Do you, Dominique? Do you?'

He always seemed to ask one question after the next. He wanted an answer to the whole, not just to the parts. So he lumped them together. Like a cut-out paper chain he sewed the question marks together, because he knew full well that one lone question would never have made its mark with me. He knew that I would almost certainly have mistaken his question for a rhetorical one. I was familiar with those . . . the rhetorical questions. As familiar as I was with French or Italian or German. I recognized the curve peculiar to the body of those question marks. But the real ones, the ones that scratched beneath the surface, they were new territory for me. And so to make sure, he joined them up and gradually as I came to know him, so I came to understand this new language.

He asked me that string of questions in Central Park with the same jet-black intensity in his eyes as when he had asked me in the booth, 'Did you ride a bicycle as a child, Dominique? Did you?' He asked as if he had to know, as if it was of the utmost importance to him to understand whether or not water was a crucial part of my life.

'Yes,' I said, 'I do need to spend time near the water. That's why I rented an apartment right opposite the Hudson. I love water. It calms me.'

'So where did you go then? As a child.'

It was not the lake itself, that day, that jogged my memory. It was not the way the sun bounced back off the water, nor the coloured sails of children's boats that commanded by a string meandered in and out of lines of ducks and swans. No, it was Nicholas's question and the ducks and swans themselves that were my *madeleine*. And in their wake the ducklings and the cygnets whose fluffy backs I longed now to touch as I had then.

'You can't Dom. You can't touch them.'

My father held me back as I leant over the side of the rowing-boat on the lake in Hyde Park.

'You can't, because the older ducks wouldn't allow it. They'd bite you. Look at their beaks. Look how sharp they are.'

So I contented myself with throwing the rough, dried-out pieces of bread into the water and watching the splashes and the ripples as the duck families and on the rare occasion the swan families came to fight for them.

They were precious, those pieces of bread. Precious crumbs won from my mother earlier in the day with anger and with tears.

'Wasting bread on ducks. It's a scandal . . . *Un scandale*, Dominique. Do you hear me?'

And she would glare at my father as he took the oldest and most dried-out bread from the earthenware bread bin, broke it into pieces, shoved them into a plastic bag and handed them to me. I felt, as I stole out of the room with that plastic bag in my hand, as if the bread bin were her jewellery box and the crusts of bread were her gold watch or her diamond ring.

Once, when I had tiptoed downstairs in the middle of the night for a glass of water, I had seen my mother in her yellow sleeveless nightgown sitting in the corner of the kitchen by the bread bin, stuffing pieces of hard dry bread into her mouth.

'Mummy, what are you doing? That must taste horrid. Why don't you eat the soft bread Mummy? Look there's some here,' I said and rushed to hand her a slice of soft white bread. She pushed my hand away and cried then. Uncontrollable sobs that she fought hard to stop as she struggled to swallow the last mouthful of hard dry bread. She didn't begin to explain to me. She didn't even try.

What could she have said? 'When I was your age just one corner of hard, dried-out bread found in the transit camp was manna from heaven. When I was your age the sight of sprouting green mould meant hidden treasure beneath. When I was your age, my parents were in a place where those foul and rotten crumbs of bread made the difference between life and death.'

And the ducks in the lake at Hyde Park were so close to the edge of the boat. Four furry brown ducklings huddled together while suddenly and unexpectedly their father in his shiny green waistcoat and their mother in her brown fur coat went for each other, ostensibly over the end piece of a processed white loaf.

'Why are they fighting?' I asked my father.

'Probably over the children,' he said.

'You have an unbelievable memory,' said Nicholas.

I'm not sure quite how many times we'd walked round that lake in Central Park when he made that remark. But as we had strolled he had said almost nothing. He must have prompted me of course, though of that I have no recollection. He must have encouraged me, because all the way round the lake I talked. I talked as if I were talking to myself. As if I were telling someone else's story, translating someone else's words.

It had been different last week. Quite different here with Paul. After the New York Stock Exchange, where I had stood and waited for him, watching from behind the glass as white-shirted arms with tensed fingers gripping receivers waved and gesticulated to each other. I had watched him through the window as he moved from hand-shake to handshake, from one useful contact to the next in this world of finance, that was his world. I looked at him through that floor-to-ceiling pane of glass as though for the first time. I stood there thinking, 'I have known him for ever. He has been part of me for years, but today, here, now, seeing him in New York for some reason I don't know who he is.'

And I was overcome by a feeling of panic. I felt the sweat under my hair at the back of my neck, the tingling in the right-hand corner of my mouth and the tightening in my chest. I felt the sensation of panic of the child separated from her mother in a shopping centre, her throat tightening, her eyes darting around her. All of the adult women she sees towering above her look a little like her mother though none of them is her. And all of those brokers and traders looked like Paul, clean-shaven, freshly laundered and assertive, but it seemed for a few moments that none of them was him. I stared through the glass at one of them. Medium height, medium build, regular features. I knew him and I didn't. That is what filled me with panic. That is what caused the sweat to pour. His movements behind the glass were familiar but strange.

He must have crossed the trading floor and come round to my side of the glass because I heard his voice. Unusual for me to be behind glass and to hear a voice next to me, speaking at me directly and not through headphones. 'Dom, Dom are you OK? You're in another world.' The voice was as familiar and as unfamiliar as the physique, the features and the face, but I was unable to place it.

'Dom what is the matter with you?' he asked, irritated.

I caught sight suddenly of the brown birthmark by his right ear. The birthmark that I had always thought was shaped a bit like France. My breathing began to slow down again. Paul, yes Paul. Of course. It's funny how difficult it can be sometimes to recognize someone you know even from so close up, even when you have known them for ever. I've often thought that.

'You had this blank expression on your face, Dominique,' he said in the elevator going down. 'As if I was a stranger. It was really scary for a minute. You do still love me, don't you? You do still feel the same?'

The elevator kept on going down and down. One of those elevators that lurches and makes you feel sick to the stomach when it gets to the bottom. One of those elevators that threatens to crash right through the floor. I answered his question of course, but somehow it was lost in the crush of people pushing their way in as we pushed our way out.

And Central Park after the Stock Exchange was meant to be calming and soothing. It was meant to be the antidote to the tension of the trading floor. The park, I have always thought, is where couples go to discover intimacy that might be, to build on intimacy that is and to dig for intimacy that was. To agree to ride or run or roller-blade is one thing, but to say yes to an unstructured stroll is quite another. You know, from the moment you agree to that walk, that you will be exposed solely to one another for that period of time. That there will be no dinner menus to distract you, no waiters to offer interruption, no agonizing decisions between *tarte aux pommes* and *tiramisu* to take up your time.

'How was it?' Nicholas asked.

'How was what?'

'Your time here with Paul last week. Didn't you say you came here?'

'Yes, yes we did.'

'And how was it?'

'Different.'

'Different from what?'

'From this.'

'How? How was it different?'

The shape of the question marks looked somehow different. But I couldn't explain that to Nicholas. Because I didn't understand it myself. And Paul and I of course had touched as we walked round the lake. We must have done because he had come all the way from London to see me. But for some reason I cannot remember the feeling of his hand in mine. And Nicholas and I, together in Central Park for the first time, can't possibly have touched there and then because we wouldn't have done. When he had laid his hand on top of mine in Barnes & Noble it had been quite by chance. It had been only because he was trying to fasten the strap of his watch around my wrist. But in Central Park, I don't remember any physical contact with Nicholas though I do remember the feel of his words.

But with Paul, the week before, I remember distinctly that he had turned me to face him, held on tightly to my shoulders and he had said, 'Dominique, when are you coming home? I need you home now.'

'It's good practice for me here. I'd never get this type of interpreting experience in London.'

'Sometimes,' he said, with his face close to mine and pointing his forefinger, almost poking it into the side of my head. 'Sometimes, I think you have no more than a language laboratory up there . . . I mean I know you're brilliant at what you do. But you can be a parrot at home, as much as you can here. Can't you?'

It had been early evening already and it was getting chilly. The hairs on my arms were standing on end and on the way home in the taxi I must have been very quiet, because I remember repeating a line of a poem over and over again to myself in my head. A line of a poem by Jacques Prévert, about a little boy at school who says one thing and means another. The line goes, '*Il dit oui avec la tête. Il dit non avec le coeur . . .*' He says yes with his head and no with his heart.

And all the way home in the taxi that line did multi-coloured acrobatics in my head. I saw the little boy in his maroon shorts that stopped just above the knees. I saw him standing by the white board with the royal blue felt-tip in his hand doing some complicated calculation or other, pretending all the while that he was happy to be here, to be doing what he was doing, confined to this classroom with the teacher breathing down his neck while instead of running wild and free outside he was forced to do these mental gymnastics in the confines of his head.

And that line of the Prévert poem stayed with me as I climbed out of the cab and walked up the two flights of stairs to my apartment with Paul behind me. It stayed with me as I struggled to fit the key into the rusting lock of my front door and to pull off my jeans. And later in my bedroom, when the lights were out I was that little boy.

The child who said yes but meant no. Except unlike the teacher, standing by the blackboard, who had no idea that the boy was bursting to run to the classroom door, to yank the handle and to escape, Paul must have known. He must have felt the jagged bits of the N's of the word '*Non*' as they stuck into his ribs. He must have felt them because I did. I felt how they lodged themselves between us and stayed there with their sharp intrusive edges. And in the morning as the first light came through the window I could have sworn I saw the shadow of the 'O' from the word '*Non*' on the white sheets.

What did Nicholas learn of that from me a week later

in Central Park and what did he glean? Did he take my monosyllables and string them together to make sentences? Was it on that day that I told him about the 'N' and the 'O'? Or was it the following evening? Was it in the park or in his yellow kitchen as he was putting the basil on the plate next to the fresh tomatoes or as he was pouring the olive oil onto the blue saucer or at the round table as he was filling the long-stemmed glasses with the red wine?

He must have known some of it at least by the time I felt myself moved by the depths of Mozart's clarinet concerto with the scent of orange incense around us or by the time the clock in its wooden case on top of the black piano said one a.m. He must have known most of it by the time we sat close to the tall brass candle-holder with the three flames that lit the titanium sculpture of the man and woman lying interlocked, her back to his chest. Curved around her like a question mark that wanted to know. A question mark next to her. So she could feel his warmth. His mouth on the curve at the back of her neck where she could feel his breath. Her head arched backwards. His legs and his ankles straight pressed against hers, the stem at the base of that question mark. Against her but not crushing her. So she could feel the asking, the wanting to know. Gently. Hardly at all. Brushing her back. And then again with more urgency as the candle flickered and threw light and shadows over the two of them.

NINETEEN

Nicholas

'Nicholas . . .'

'Who is this?'

'It's me.'

'Who? I'm sorry?'

'It's Tom . . . Only a foreigner could miss my Texan twang.'

'Tom. Hi. Sorry. I didn't recognize your voice . . . You're not phoning to ask me for another run are you?' I say laughing, holding the phone between my ear and my shoulder, turning up the gas flame under the heavy silver pan on the stove. 'You almost finished me off last time. I need to do some serious training before you and I run together again.'

'No, I'm not calling to get you pounding round Central Park again. Don't worry . . . How're you doing anyway?'

'Good. Good. And you?' I ask lifting the lid now from the pan, the steam rising towards me, lifting a fork, prodding the pasta in the boiling water, wondering why he has called me at home. He never calls me at home.

'Fine, just fine thanks Nick.'

'I didn't even realize you had my number here,' I say, bringing a steaming green pasta shell to my mouth to check it. To see whether it is cooked *al dente*.

'I got it from the lab.'

The pasta is boiling. Boiling enough to burn my tongue. For a moment I can't speak and then I say, 'From the lab?'

'Yes . . . from one of your files in the lab. You didn't lock the door. You ought to, you know.'

'I turn on the tap, reach for a glass, fill it with water.

'Nicholas? You still there?'

'Sure. Sure.'

'Looks like you've been working pretty hard.'

'Yes.'

'Listen, how's it going? I could hardly discuss it with you on the run. You were too busy trying to breathe.'

'Fine. Fine. It's going fine,' I say, my tongue still smarting from the heat of the pasta.

'Talk to me boy,' he says.

'Sorry?'

'I've come to the conclusion you're a genius.'

'Tom, I'm sorry. I'm not with you.'

'You think you've cracked it don't you Nick?'

'What do you mean?'

'I said you think you've cracked it don't you?'

Gulping down the rest of the glass of water before responding, putting it on the ridged stainless-steel counter next to the sink. Walking over to the window, the telephone in my hand now. No longer between my ear and my shoulder. I see that picture so clearly. Me looking out and the light from a window above the Café Dante in an apartment opposite shining in on me.

And if in years to come someone sits me down on a sofa and puts a remote-control changer in my hand, if they bring me face to face with a video of my life, if they turn to me and say, 'You can edit out any two moments. You can obliterate them, change them, do as you will with them and in their place you can insert a new scenario,' then this precise moment, the one after I have gulped back the water and walked over to the window, is the first one I will obliterate. I will annihilate my vanity. I will annihilate the sudden and unusual need I feel to share with Tom more than I already have done. I will press the pause button at that question, 'You think you've cracked it don't you?' I will turn up the volume full blast and listen again and again to that question till each of the words reverberating round my kitchen is so loud that it causes my ears to throb. Till for the fifth or the sixth time I hear *'cracked it, cracked it, cracked it'* and the drilling *'crrrrr'* of 'cracked it' sends a sharp and shooting pain through the side of my head. The conversation in that best of all possible worlds will go like this.

'You think you've cracked it don't you?'

'I wish. I don't know if you saw the stuff in that file, but it's just the stuff of my dreams.'

And he will say, 'Oh how disappointing. I thought it was for real. I thought you'd got farther than last time we talked. Listen boy, we really must do that run again. Get yourself in shape. Anyway. Maybe I'll see you for lunch this week.'

But it is that conversation that is the stuff of my dreams. It is that conversation which will never happen, because it is of course only in our fantasies that we can be the editors of our lives.

In reality the words of my conversation with Tom were quite different.

He said, 'You're a genius. You think you've cracked it don't you?'

'Oh Tom. What do you want me to say?'

'I want you to talk to me boy.'

'OK. Listen, in a nutshell I could, I might, be on my

way to something. Not a cure, but something that will complement the triple therapies. But I have a long, long way to go. It might be nothing anyway. And if I do pursue it I have to decide how and when to approach Landmark. I'd need so much funding. I don't want to appear pre-sumptuous. You know what I mean . . . the new boy who thinks he's a hotshot. Goldmann's miserable enough to deal with as it is. And anyway, I'm serious about the leukaemia business. I don't intend to abandon it just like that. I'm going to take some time to think about things. It might be nothing much after all.'

'Nicholas.'

'Yes.'

'They didn't ask you to research anything other than paediatric leukaemia did they?'

'No.'

'You stumbled on this by chance, right?'

'Right.'

'So, I guess you know who owns the patent don't you?'

'Who?'

'Well it isn't Landmark.'

I was quiet on the end of the phone. I could hear my own breathing.

'I've looked into it,' he said. 'I spent a whole day looking into it for you. In the Medical Law section at the library. It doesn't belong to Landmark at all, because it wasn't in your mandate to research it. And it won't ever belong to them unless you're crazy enough to hand it over.'

'I'm not sure you're right and even if you were . . .'

'Look, you remember that meeting I told you I was going to set up with my father's friend . . .'

'Which friend?'

'On the run. I told you about him on the run.'

'Yes, I remember.'

'Well, I've done it. I've organized it. He might make you an offer. But you'd have to be prepared to move fast. He has the whole of the rest of the team in place. He needs one more researcher. You have to come, Nicholas. Just to hear what he has to say. A week from today 6.30 p.m. at the Four Seasons. Ask for Walter Zlack. I'll be out of town for the whole of next week, so I won't see you till then. But I'll call to confirm.'

'I can't next weekend, Tom. I have plans.'

'Nicholas.'

'Yes.'

'Cancel them. This thing wasn't easy to set up. He's only in from DC for a day. He's an important man. A heavyweight. You gotta be there.'

'Tom. I really do have plans.'

'Yes, you do. With me. You know where the Four Seasons is don't you? It's on Fifty-Seventh between Park and Madison on the south side of the street. They do the best cocktails in the city. I'll see you there if not before.'

'But Tom, could we perhaps make it some other time? If you want me to be honest with you I've met this woman. An amazing woman. I don't know what's going on with me. I haven't felt like this for a while. For a long time. Ever really. And that's really the main thing on my mind. So perhaps we can, what's that expression you use, put a rain check on it?'

No answer.

'Tom?'

No answer except for the loud hum of the dialling tone. I put down the phone and ten seconds later it rang.

'Nicholas.'

'Dominique.'

I exhaled.

'Is it a bad time?'

'Not at all. Why?'

'You sighed.'

'I did? Oh I just had a heavy work call.'

'On a Saturday? What about?'

'Oh just boring stuff.'

'Nicholas, where are you?'

'In the kitchen. Why?'

'Just wondered if you were in the lounge. Anywhere near that sculpture. You know the one of the man and the woman together.'

'Hang on,' I said, walking with the phone still to my ear, out of the kitchen, past my bedroom and into the lounge. 'Now I am. I'm right next to it . . . Why did you ask?'

'No. No reason. I just like it.'

I wonder sometimes if Dominique hadn't called at that very moment, if she hadn't distracted my attention over the phone with her voice, if I would have called Landmark there and then and left a message on Tom's voicemail telling him that the following Saturday was out of the question. I wonder whether it was the timing of her phone call that led me to believe it was meant to be that I should go to that meeting with Tom and his future employer at the Four Seasons. I wonder if I had gone not on that day, but on some other day whether events would have panned out in a very different way.

TWENTY

Dominique

Torrential rain and brilliant sunshine at one and the same time. Coincidence in the truest and most dramatic sense of the word. Coincidence fêted by the purples, the oranges and the ochres of the rainbow. An upside-down capital C, the master of all coincidences, that offers you proof of its existence, but no explanation.

Deborah called from the agency. She said they needed me for *chuchotage* on Friday. She said there was a small meeting on leukaemia, an Israeli professor coming whose English wasn't great and I might have to whisper things in his ear from time to time. I didn't want to do it. I had a heavy week ahead of me. I said, 'No Deborah, I'd rather not. If you don't mind. I've got a tough few days ahead of me.'

There was a silence and then she laughed. 'Dominique, my goodness. I've never ever heard you say no before. Life in New York must be teaching you things. And normally I'd leave it at that, because you're so obliging and you must have your reasons for not wanting to do it. But you have to sweetie. You have to. Because I don't have any other interpreters on my books right now who do Hebrew and know the medical stuff as well as you do. So you have to do it and . . .'

The dictionary really offers no insight into coincidence.

It feels so heavy and authoritative when you hold it in your hand, as if it is bound to shed more light on the nature of coincidence than the rainbow. You turn to the *co's*, you run your finger down them in expectation till you reach the feeble and disappointing offering next to coincidence . . . 'Unexpected incidents that occur at the same time'.

I remember when I looked that up, I had this image in my mind of the compiler of that dictionary. An un-imaginative grey-faced man in a moth-eaten grey sweater and grey trousers thinking to himself, 'Co incidence. It comes from the Latin. *Co* . . . together. *Incidentia* . . . happening.' Two events happening at the same time without prior planning, and he must have tapped the words out distractedly with his unkempt nails on the black keys of his typewriter without considering the events of his own life, without considering the converging paths that had led him to cheap grey sweaters and trousers and stifled imagination.

And when I walked into the meeting-room that Friday morning, through black wrought-iron gates, through a courtyard planted with spring flowers, with my brown leather folder stuffed full of documents under my arm, I was introduced to Professor Weiss the Israeli, to Professor Sand and Professor Goldmann both of whom I vaguely recognized from Landmark, and to Dr Manzini.

'This is Ms Green, our interpreter.'

Nicholas smiled when Goldmann began to introduce us. He said, 'Dominique and I know each other from Landmark. She interpreted some of my papers and I've given her some help with technical vocabulary,' and we all took our seats at a round black table, next to a window that overlooked the courtyard. The owners of the building obviously took great pride in those few metres of garden.

As I worked I could see the anemones, the tulips, the daffodils and the freesia beneath us.

The French and the Italians, usually freer and more imaginative with their language than the British, don't do a much better job with coincidence than we do. '*Coincidenza*' in Italian pronounced '*coincheedenza*', and '*coincidence*' in French pronounced as coincidence except with a French accent, but however many dictionaries I have pored over in each of those languages none of them has come up with explanations that have excited me. Astonishing really, when you think of all the momentous Latin love stories initiated by chance meetings and doomed or blessed by external events. But no, they can't do it either, the French or the Italians. And I don't really have any clues from my childhood, because the first time I heard my parents talking about coincidence they didn't agree on the meaning of the word. They were in the bathroom. The door was locked and I was outside, sitting on the scratchy carpet listening, holding my little sister still and very close to me with my hand over her mouth so they wouldn't know we were there and I heard my father say, 'Her headaches always come the day after these fights, Sonya. I'm telling you it's no coincidence.'

And my mother said, 'Nonsense. Don't talk such nonsense. One thing has nothing to do with the other. Of course it's coincidence.'

So my first exposure to the concept of coincidence left me none the wiser. How could it, when even at home my parents who were both great with words didn't seem to know what it meant?

And at one side of the black table, Professor Goldmann was speaking and I was sitting very close to Professor Weiss, ready to whisper in his ear whenever he nodded.

That was our code. He would look puzzled and nod and I would lean forward and whisper in Hebrew in his large ear. I was glad, very glad that there wasn't too much he didn't understand, because his right ear with which I was forced to make almost physical contact had grey hairs sprouting from it, that on one occasion tickled my lips and disrupted my concentration. And behind it, tucked away at the back was a tiny white hearing-aid that I was terrified I might dislodge with some impromptu movement.

Nicholas was sitting to my left. I had my back to him with my chair turned towards Professor Weiss, but I could feel him behind me. I heard him as he moved his chair backwards so that we weren't very far apart at all. Goldmann said, 'The teenager I'm referring to found a donor almost by coincidence.'

Weiss, sleepy by now, was finding it hard to concentrate. He nodded at me and touched my arm. '*Ha gever matza be mikre . . .*' I translated. '*Be mikre*' . . . by chance . . . the Israelis put a different slant on this coincidence thing. They call it simply chance. Chance at least is slightly less practical. Chance gives us a little peephole to the spiritual or the mystical. As if there is at least an element of coincidence that transcends the purely random occurrence of events.

Professor Goldmann closed his white folder. I moved back from Weiss's ear. He sat up with a jolt and poured himself a cup of cold coffee from the Pyrex carafe. And I noticed suddenly how close to his temple on the right side of his face he had a brown birthmark, not quite the shape of France like Paul's, but not dissimilar. France, distorted just a little. Its terrain a touch darker. And though I had no time now to think in words, there was time enough to feel a pang. To feel it and in a split second, before it was gone again, to interpret it as guilt.

Weiss was about to speak of his recent findings and I could see from the way the heavy wrinkled folds of skin on his eyelids were drooping that he was having problems keeping awake.

'What language do you want to talk in?' Goldmann asked him. Weiss, bilingual in Hebrew and German, chose to speak the latter. He was born in Poland, but someone told me later he'd spent the war in Auschwitz and the Nazis had taught him fluent German.

It was coincidence, pure coincidence that both Goldmann and Sand understood German too. So neither of them would need my services. In fact Professor Goldmann had just turned to me and said from under his gold-rimmed half spectacles that rested on the bridge of his nose, 'Ms Green, I think we can cope without you now,' when he remembered something and said, 'Oh wait a minute, of course you don't speak German do you Nicholas? How silly of me.'

Nicholas shook his head and I could see a wry little smile forming in the right hand corner of his mouth.

'Sorry, Ms Green,' said Goldmann. 'Sorry, we're not going to let you out for another twenty minutes after all. Dr Manzini needs you.'

And Nicholas said, 'Yes Ms Green, I do need you . . .' and then, 'why don't I bring your chair round to my other side, so you can see Professor Weiss speaking while you translate for me. It will be less of a strain for you.'

And I remember as Nicholas lifted the chair with the black leather seat and the chrome arms round to his left side, I felt a mixture of embarrassment and amusement and I tried hard not to make eye contact with him in case I should start to laugh. The amusement though outweighed the embarrassment. And I enjoyed the secret. This kind of secret was nothing like the other kind. Nothing like the onerous sort that consumed you, that hung like a dead weight round your neck day in and day out. No, there was an excitement in this secret, looking at Nicholas with his light blue shirtsleeves rolled up to the elbows, looking at him lifting my chair and knowing.

I sat close to him, poised to pour a stream of *chuchotage* into his left ear. In a brief moment of panic I wondered if I was professional enough not to be distracted by his scent that was both new and familiar at one and the same time, by the five o'clock shadow that was beginning to show on his face and by his hands that if I closed my eyes for just a second I could . . . I had to be professional enough. Weiss's words were crucial.

'*Wir brauchen unbedingt eine Zunahme der Prüfungsmoglichkeiten fur Minoritätsgruppen . . .*'

'We need much more bone-marrow testing for minority groups . . .'

'*Die Juden, die Schwarzen, die Italiener, haben grössere Möglichkeiten unter ihren eigenen Minöritaten eine passende Gruppe zu finden . . .*'

'As you know the Jews, the blacks, the Italians are far more likely to find a matching donor from their own minority group . . .'

For a split second I felt the swell of pride. Nicholas was any other client in need of translation and I was a professional. The scent and the five o'clock shadow registered dimly through my words, but in quite another part of my mind to which I had no access till Weiss had stopped speaking and the others had left the room ahead of us. Because Nicholas and I were both slow in gathering our papers together. And the *chuchotage* carried on beyond the end of that afternoon's interpreting session, though it was not me now, who whispered words, but Nicholas. Words that bore no resemblance to medical terminology. No resemblance at all.

'We couldn't . . . expect you . . . to work . . . this hard . . . any longer,' he said, his words missing my ear and brushing its lobe and the side of my neck instead.

The Germans seem to come closest in their choice of word for coincidence. They call it *Zufall* which means, literally, falling together. At the same time. Falling deeply and having no say in the matter. No control over depth of the fall. But even the German word, even the word *Zufall*, gives no indication of whether that falling is for good or for bad. Of whether coincidence is good or bad. No language gives us a clue to that.

TWENTY-ONE

Nicholas

Dominique was in white. A white nightdress against white sheets. The expanse and the dazzle was broken only by her chestnut hair and the blue cornflowers on the bedside table. She looked different that morning. Perhaps it was the way the light fell so that for the first time I noticed that she had a small beauty spot below her right eye just like the one above her lip, and that though her bone structure was delicate, the set of her chin was almost determined. I remember standing in the doorway, looking at her and thinking that the discovery, the unveiling of another person was as exciting, and as unpredictable as scientific discovery.

But Dominique was no experiment for me. I would describe her more as a slow explosion in my life. A slow explosion that like the roll of amber lava picked its moment and with a gesture almost cruel in its flippancy exposed me to emotions both new and overwhelming.

We, all of us, are easily fooled by our own perceptions. We think, sometimes, that we are so clever, that our insight is such, that very quickly we have seen and understood another person. We think that if only we behave in a certain way then things will follow a certain path.

And we are so sure, when we have known someone

intimately, that we can predict exactly how she will move when we call her name or when we touch her. We imagine we can predict the tone of her voice when we ask her a certain type of question. Or that we know almost exactly how she will react when we make a certain type of comment.

You think you know all that, and because of it you are in control of yourself and of what goes on between you. You think it and most of the time you are right. Most, but not all the time. I had not imagined that Dominique would want to know any more of my professional world than I told her. Not that I didn't want to share my work with her. Nor that I didn't want to let her into my world. But to me she was an artist. Her voice the brush. Her words the paints. And though her father was a medic, I had no reason to believe that her interest in science went beyond the words that described it.

As time moved me further away from my experiments with the HIV-contaminated blood, though the results of my experiments remained irrefutable, I questioned more and more the possibility that I, Nicholas Manzini, newly arrived from Florence, could have made so potentially huge a breakthrough. Time and again I heard Grevi's words in my head, 'Don't get big ideas about yourself,' and I felt that to talk of my findings to Dominique would have appeared ludicrous. Adolescent almost. As if I were trying somehow to inflate my importance in her eyes, trying to sell myself with my achievements.

On the morning of the white sheets and blue cornflowers, she sat suddenly bolt upright in bed and she said, 'I want to see your lab.'

'My lab. Why?'

'Because it's part of you.'

I moved from the doorway to sit close to her on the bed.

'When can I come?' she asked.

'Dom, it'll be so boring for you. What are you going to do? Watch me fill up test-tubes with blood?'

'You've been in the booth. You've sat and watched me work for hours. You weren't bored were you?'

'No. But that's like watching the eighth wonder of the world.'

I felt from under the duvet a playful kick against my thigh.

'Flattery,' she said, with her head cocked to one side, 'is a useless diversionary tactic . . . So when am I coming?'

She was still in white. Though this time a white coat, a white cap and a white mask. I'm not quite sure why I asked her to wear the mask for there was little chance of her coming into contact with noxious substances. She saw that I myself was barefaced, she looked at me and raised her eyebrows.

'Why do I have to wear this thing? You're not wearing one.'

I smiled and said, 'It's to keep you quiet. It's so that you don't give away any of my secrets. But I'll put mine on if it makes you feel better.' I reached for a paper mask in a drawer under one of the benches.

'Do you have any?' she asked distractedly, taking in the unfamiliar surroundings.

'What?'

'Secrets? Do you have any secrets from me?'

'Do you?' I asked. 'Do you have any secrets from me?'

She looked at first as if she might say something. Not of course that I could see the movement of her lips for

137

they were hidden behind the mask. But she stood very still for a moment and I thought I saw, in her eyes, a need to talk.

Instead she laughed. A muffled laugh through the mask and she asked me muffled questions as she moved around the lab, touching the Formica work surfaces with her gloved hands.

'What's this?'

'It's a centrifuge. It's where we spin the blood to separate the layers so we can analyse them.'

'And this?' she asked, leaning against the cold white freezer. 'No, wait,' she said and held up her hand. 'It's where you freeze blood samples isn't it?'

'Dr Green,' I said laughing. 'Where did you get that one from?'

'It doesn't all go in one headphone and out of the other, you know. Some of it does, but not all of it.'

She moved away from the freezer over to one of the workbenches and turned to face me. 'Nicholas . . . Nicholas. It's so silent in here. Don't you get lonely?'

'Here, sit here,' I said, pulling out a high stool for her. 'Sit here and close your eyes for a minute.'

I took a key from the pocket of my worn brown leather briefcase. I walked to the far end of the laboratory, leant down and opened a small cupboard. Out of the corner of my eye, on the shelf above the cupboard I caught sight of the dusky pink file that contained my research notes. Again, the thought of mentioning it to Dominique crossed my mind and I laughed at myself. It really would look as though I were boasting, as though I were flaunting my credentials. I knelt down further. Amongst the square plastic cases I found what I was looking for.

'Nicholas, can I look now?' she said. 'What's going on here?'

'Two minutes.'

I locked the door of the cupboard, stood up, reached around inside my briefcase and from behind I placed the headphones of my Walkman over Dominique's ears. In contrast with the stillness of the laboratory, the music must have made its impact. She turned to look at me. Above the mask her eyes lit up and she smiled a knowing smile. '*Swan Lake*,' she said.

For a few moments she sat on the high stool and listened. Then she removed the headphones and she said, 'So that's what keeps you company. But what about people? Does anyone ever come in here and talk to you?'

'Goldmann comes in from time to time. But you couldn't exactly call him company. And my colleague Tom comes in. But I talk to myself sometimes and to the blood samples and the cells. I . . . I pretend they're people.'

Embarrassed suddenly by my admission, I turned my back on Dominique and walked towards the cupboard as if to replace the CD.

But suddenly from behind she stopped me in my tracks and put her arms around me. I had never felt a woman's arms around my neck in the lab before. And never, since my arrival in New York, had anyone spoken to me in Italian in the laboratory. Of course I might well have misunderstood her words through the mask but I thought I heard her say, '*Ti voglio bene*.' I was sure, in fact, that I had heard her say it, but I am not as quick with words as Dominique and before I'd had time to digest them, she had turned away, and it might just have been my imagination that right here, right in the middle of the laboratory, in one of my white cotton coats and quite out of the blue she had told me how she felt.

The white coats, the gloves and the mask must have come between us, for within seconds she was at the other side of the laboratory, standing by my workbench.

'Ah, your microscope,' she said and touched its black shiny neck.

'I call it my kaleidoscope.'

'Can I look through it?'

I turned the knob at the base for her and remembered how she had adjusted the microphone in the booth for me.

She leant forward and put her eyes to the lenses.

'What am I looking at?' she asked.

'Cells.'

'What sort of cells?'

'Leukaemia cells.'

'Is this microscope powerful enough to see everything?' she asked.

'Not everything. Sometimes we need a more powerful one.'

Her head down, still looking through the microscope, she said, 'What about an Aids-infected cell? Could you see Aids cells through this?'

'You could,' I said. 'But you'd have to prepare them first. An electron microscope would make it easier.'

'Oh,' she said. 'I see,' and she lifted her head to look at me, while the white paper cap slipped down half covering her eyes.

TWENTY-TWO

Dominique

I have my own oasis in Manhattan. Tucked away behind high hedges, set in gardens with huge heart-shaped lily leaves in its pond, barely mentioned in guidebooks, the off-white house-cum-museum on the Upper East Side is the place where, during my first months in New York, after a heavy interpreting session, I would come to hide from the dust and the discord of the city.

Though the Frick Collection stuns you with its Titians, its Turners, its Manets and its Renoirs hung nonchalantly behind doors and casually under stairwells, I went there as much to think, as I wandered through the thickly carpeted rooms, as I did to admire the art. The Frick was my oasis. Not one that I had stumbled on, but one that I had sought. For everyone, I think, in every city, needs to find their own oasis. Mischa taught me that.

In Zurich, I came home stressed and in tears one day after a rigorous session at interpreting school. It was Mischa with a box of pink and blue tissues in his hand at the foot of my bed who said, 'Dominique. You go to interpreting school and you come back home. Every day the same places and the same faces. We need to find you an oasis in this city. We need to find you a place where you can go to be peaceful and escape.'

It was Mischa who had come to the side of the bed, sat

next to me and then late on that early autumn afternoon had dragged me out of the flat, down the leafy streets alongside the tramlines and up the steep cobbled slopes of Zurich's Altstadt.

We walked upwards, past the tiny galleries, the arty cinemas and past the teashops. Mischa, strong and fit and healthy, then, always ahead of me. We walked and walked till all at once there was just us. Just Mischa and me in a cobbled square. Just Mischa and me standing above the city on a plateau they called the Lindenhof. And all around us and beneath us, like a three-dimensional painting in browns and blues, in greens and greys, the steeples of the churches, the slated roofs of the medieval buildings, the sinewing of Zurich's river, the Limmatquai. Awe-inspiring, I thought. Awe-inspiring and hypnotic. And at first I wondered whether I might one day come here to share the romance of this oasis with someone. But, then I thought no. No, this would be my oasis, this plateau on top of the world, and whenever I escaped to it, after that, I was grateful to Mischa for letting me into his secret. For knowing what I needed. For knowing it better than I knew it myself.

Each time standing there, on the plateau above Zurich, looking over the edge of the world a line of poetry came into my mind. A one-line poem. The shortest poem in the whole world.

'M'illumino d'immenso,' which you can't really translate but if you could you would say, 'I am dazzled by the vastness.' And in Zurich I went there often to escape when the going got rough.

For a long time in New York, after I had found my oasis, I shared the secret only with Mischa. On a postcard of my favourite painting. Renoir's children at the piano in faded pinks and blues. I remember standing there in that tiny museum shop, buying the card and writing on it simply, 'Mischa . . . I've found my oasis! Thinking of you . . . Dominique.' And ten days later in my mailbox, lying there without an envelope I found an addressed photograph of our plateau above the world that had inspired him too to think of poetry, because on the back in black italics he had written four lines by Goethe. '*Uber allen Gipfeln ist Ruhe, In allen Wipfeln spurest Du kaum einen Hauch, Die Voglein singen im Walde, Warte nur, Balde ruhest Du Auch . . .*' A poem about peace above the treetops, quiet between the pine needles, birdsong in the forest and the certainty that each of us too would someday find that sense of peace.

For a long time I never actually said the word 'Frick' to anyone. It was as if the instant I mentioned it, my secret would be out and the place would cease to be my refuge. In the same way as I was happy to be alone at the classical concerts in the church on Madison Avenue, I had no need for company as I moved from room to room, and stood in contemplation before the masterpieces in their gold-leaf frames.

When my parents came to New York I made no mention of the Frick. When Paul came I left the museum off my list of places to visit. I couldn't imagine spending time there and being obliged to talk. For me it was a place of serenity. A place where I could put words to rest and where I would be able to go only in the company of someone with whom quasi-silence was in no way awkward.

Nicholas and I were walking down the sweeping stairway of the Frick the day after I visited his lab. The permanent exhibition was in storage and in its place the museum was showing the work of a young gay artist by the name of Ted Swain. As we reached the foot of the staircase Nicholas said to me, 'This place sort of belongs to you doesn't it? You're at home here.'

'Yes. I suppose I am.' I smiled at him. At a slow pace, a very, very slow pace I had begun to feel less afraid of his powers of perception, less astonished that he would take the trouble.

'Who taught you to be alone? To go places and do things alone?' he asked me.

Two massive canvases hung on the yellow wall in front of us. The first against a blue background was of a strong healthy man in blue jeans and a bare torso standing in front of his reflection.

I looked at the painting and I thought. Mischa taught me to do things and to go places on my own. Mischa on Saturday afternoons in Zurich would bound into the flat, sit down at the brown dining-room table, his face flushed. His piercing blue eyes shiny with excitement at the latest exhibition he had just seen, he would talk to me of the golds of Klimt, the pastels of Cassal, or the pointillism of Pissarro. He sat there once for hours with the poster of Klimt's *Kiss* he had bought and talked to me about the clinch and the colours and the way he could lose himself standing in front of a painting. I remember once asking him, 'Why do you go alone?' and he said, 'Because you were asleep and I called Anna but she was out and why would I want to give up on anything in life just because I'm alone? And anyway I would only want to go with someone who wanted to see it as much as I do.'

And so I learnt from Mischa. I learnt both how to be alone and how to derive pleasure from painting and from sculpture without the need to intellectualize and to analyse it.

And at the bottom of the stairs in the Frick, I turned to

Nicholas and said, 'Mischa. He taught me to go places and to do things alone.'

Nicholas knew of Anna and Mischa's existence in my life, though not yet of their importance. I am sure I must have talked more of Anna than of Mischa at that point in time. For to speak in detail of Mischa would surely have opened sluice-gates. Had I begun to talk of him, I would have been threatened by my own growing need to divulge. Threatened by my knowledge. No, not knowledge perhaps, but strong suspicions that I had fought hard to suppress since that day at the conference, that someone, somewhere was withholding valuable information.

Nicholas pointed to a water-colour in twilight. A fading blue sky streaked with red, in a rough wooden frame. Beneath it, on a bench by a lake, two men sat, their bodies towards the water, their faces turned to one another, their foreheads touching. Perfectly still in their closeness to one another. Still, not because this was a painting, but because whatever had been before or would be afterwards, this moment together, touching foreheads, towards nightfall was an epiphany for both of them. Mischa had told me that. Not that I had asked of course. But I was on my way home from tea with Anna when I saw him on the bench, by the water, with a man.

Minutes earlier Anna and I had parted ways outside Sprungli, Zurich's olde worlde teashop, and as I walked up the Bahnhofstrasse towards the lake, past windows of clothes and of watches on both sides of me, I held in my mind the image of her, across the table from me at Sprungli. Not as the other customers must have seen her, bold, blonde and brash with a butterfly tattoo on her arm, incongruous in the gentility of the setting. No not like that. But, Anna, framed by the walls of the tearoom, lifting a teacup to her lips, letting the warmth of the liquid touch her mouth, as though to give her courage, deciding suddenly then that she would talk instead of drinking, looking at me with her green eyes, a streak of blonde hair falling over her left eye, and saying. 'We've never really spoken about it, have we?'

'No.'

'I couldn't. I mean I still can't really. But, I will. I must.'

She lifted her hand to the corner of her mouth to wipe away a crumb that wasn't there. I noticed how her fingers trembled slightly.

'I have to accept it,' she said. 'You probably think it's pathological, don't you? That I only ... that I only ... only love ... that I only feel like this because he is and always will be unavailable to me. But it's not true. That's not the way it is.'

I realized suddenly that I was holding my breath. Anna had never really opened up to me about Mischa before and just as I had felt sitting in the empty pink bathtub, afraid to interrupt my mother's stream of consciousness lest she should clam up, so I was afraid now to react to Anna.

'You know,' she said, 'you can try to sleep with other men to banish it. You can try to throw yourself into work, but if it's there ... I mean really there ... I don't suppose it ever goes away.'

'*Kann ich Ihnen noch etwas bringen* . . . Can I bring you something?'

In his white shirt and his black bow-tie, it was the waiter who broke the flow of Anna's thoughts and instigated the return of her composure, so that seconds later she was flirting with him and I was left sipping my tea and thinking how it changed things when the words were out. How Anna might have hoped that if she found the courage to speak the words, if she actually said, 'That I only ... I only ... only love ...' then no sooner out of her mouth, the words, like ladybirds, might settle for a few moments at most on the white tablecloth, but that they would raise their fine black spotted wings then and fly away. She might have thought that as a reward for her courage in speaking them, the words and their meaning would leave her purged. I sensed that she felt that. I sensed it by her swift move to the superficiality of her flirting with the waiter. I didn't want to disillusion her, to tell her she was entirely wrong. That speaking the words, far from strangling them, would give them a truth. Speaking them would lend them a life of their own, allow them to dance free, released from the confines of her mind to decide on their own direction. They didn't need to be carved into the wall of a cave, engraved on the bark of a tree, or penned on a piece of parchment to continue to exist. She was fooled by the words she spoke in the booth ... words that did float out of your mouth, out of the door, out of the room to dissolve outside into nothingness. By speaking other people's thoughts she was fooled into thinking that her own, when she spoke them, would be as easily soluble.

The timing was strange that day. For it can't have been more than twenty minutes later, in the twilight with the red streaks in the sky, that I had caught sight of the two young men on the bench, facing each other in profile, their heads close together. Though it registered only after I had passed them. And when from a distance I turned round to check, Mischa had lifted his head and was looking at me. It was several days later that he told me how that moment, that moment of touching foreheads had been a revelation for him.

When I turned away from the painting in the Frick and

looked to my left Nicholas was no longer standing there. I walked into the next room. The walls were slightly darker. A mushroom colour. I didn't see him, but from behind I felt him put his arms around my waist and clasp my hands in his. Over my head I heard him say, 'You were so deep in thought, I didn't want to disturb you.'

I stretched my arms up behind me and felt his face with my fingers. The curve of his forehead. Of his nose. Of his lips that moved as I touched them and he said, 'Who did that painting remind you of? The one in the other room?'

'Mischa.'

'Why doesn't he come out here with Anna to visit you?'

'Because . . .' I said, my fingers still on his lips, 'because, he's busy.'

'If he's so into art, he'd love it here. You should persuade him to come. It would be fun for the three of you to be together again.'

I am glad, when I think back and I relive that picture of me in front of Nicholas, leaning against him slightly, of the two of us in front of an almost black canvas in a darkening room with my arms stretched up behind me, that it was my fingers that were on his lips and not his on mine. For he would have felt my mouth open as he said, 'It would be fun for the three of you to be together again.' He would have felt it open wide as if to release words in thick black capital letters. And he would have felt it close again then, before I had spoken, or shouted or screamed,

'Mischa's sick. Don't you understand?'

Because that pose of the woman in black, surrounded by darkness with her mouth open was a painting.

I had stood in front of it with Mischa in the Kunsthaus, Zurich's main art gallery, in the late autumn of the previous year, just before I had left for New York. As we had walked through the door of the modern building with its white-painted walls he had said to me, 'So who's going to drag you to these places in New York?'

'I'll go alone, if I have to.'

'You're learning, Dom. You're learning.'

But in the exhibition hall the smile was wiped off his face and off mine. We were surrounded in that room by greyness and blackness. Not the greyness and blackness of a deepening night sky. But the greyness and blackness of sadness and sickness. Munch's sisters, sad and sick. Munch's mother sadder and sicker.

'I hate this,' I said to Mischa. 'I hate it. I hate it.'

He had beckoned me into the next room and as if as a balm, it was filled with fjords and fabulous colours, with late sunsets and with light.

And standing there in front of Nicholas in the Frick, his arms around my waist, instead of staying there still, my mouth wide open as if in Munch's *Scream*, I closed it and began again. I turned around to him and told him of the fjords and the light that went on for ever.

'You know, Dominique,' he said, looking at me with a very serious expression on his face. 'You reminded me of a piece of art the first time I saw you in the booth.'

'Which one?' I asked, smiling now.

'You won't take this the wrong way, will you?'

I laughed. 'Are you about to insult me? Are you going to tell me I remind you of one of Toulouse-Lautrec's fat, ungainly prostitutes?'

'Now that I think of it . . .' he said.

'Nowa data I tiiiink of iiiit,' I said, exaggeratedly imitating his accent.

In mock anger he grabbed me. He laughed for a few moments, then fell silent, took a few steps backwards and stood and looked at me, his head to one side as if contemplating a canvas.

'No, it's a sculpture,' he said. 'Just a head.'

'Just a head?'

'Yes. A head cast in bronze. She has eyes everywhere like the *Mona Lisa* and . . .'

'And I have ears everywhere,' I said laughing. 'Anyway where is this masterpiece?'

'Paris,' he said and his face lit up. 'Come with me to Paris. We'll go to the Rodin museum. We'll stand in front of *Mignon* and we'll see if you feel even a tiny little bit as if you're looking in the mirror.'

'I can think of plenty of reasons to go to Paris, but I am *not* going there with my . . . with my . . . lover, to see if I look like a bronze head.'

We were both laughing now. Still in the room with Ted Swain's paintings around us, laughing at our ludicrous conversation, and at ourselves, as weeks before we had laughed with each other from opposite ends of the huge conference hall.

'OK I'll make a deal with you.' I don't know what made me say that and when I said it I'm not sure I knew how I would finish my sentence. But quite suddenly, quite out of nowhere, in the way that clairvoyants must do, I had a picture in my head.

'A deal?' he said.

'Yes, I'll . . . um . . . I'll meet you in front of the bronze head when we're old and doddery.'

He raised his eyebrows. It looked more than quizzical, almost funny in fact when Nicholas raised his eyebrows. They were so dark and black and bushy.

'When we're old and doddery?'

'Yes I mean, if we're not together. Maybe not when

we're old. We might not get up the stairs. But if we ever split up. I'll meet you a year from the day we separate, at midday under the sculpture.'

'Dominique.' He leant forward and cupped my face in his hands.

'Dominique,' he said. *'Sei proprio impazzita?* Have you lost it? There are some very peculiar thoughts in that head of yours . . . Come, let's go,' and he took my hand as we turned to leave.

Out of the front door of the off-white house, out of the high iron gates onto Fifth Avenue, I turned back to look at the Frick and thought of Mischa's words. 'We need to find you an oasis. We need to find you a place where you can be peaceful and escape,' and I wondered if it was only a place that could be an oasis. Or if a person could be your oasis too.

Nicholas and I crossed Fifth Avenue and began to walk slowly downtown alongside the park. Alongside the trees whose leaves rustled as night began to fall.

An oasis. Water in the desert. Passion in blandness. Lushness in an arid wasteland. As we walked I looked up at Nicholas from the side. He was lost in thought, a slight frown on his brow. So lost in thought as he walked next to me, his hand under my hair at the back of my neck as I sang the notes but not the words of a song that I had memorized.

'You are my oasis. You are my oasis until tomorrow comes again.'

TWENTY-THREE

Anna

My name was written in huge black letters on a large white board held up in the baggage hall of JFK airport on my arrival in New York. I had not wanted to leave Zurich, but for weeks on end Mischa badgered me and finally when he told me I was beginning to look almost as bad as he did, I agreed to go. Dominique had told me she would send a car to collect me and as I walked down the steps towards the carousel I was looking out for the driver. I smiled when I saw the sign that was held up, for it said simply, 'ANNA'. As I approached a face peeked out from behind it and beamed. It was Dominique. We laughed out loud, hugged and then stood back, our arms on each other's shoulders. Ask me to pinpoint the physical changes I saw in Dominique in those moments in the baggage hall, while over the loudspeaker a voice boomed, 'Stand back from the carousel,' and I would say that they were minimal. I noticed she wore the orange velvet scarf I had bought her. Her hair might have been slightly shorter and the shade of her lipstick might have been a little darker than when I had last seen her in Zurich. It might have been, but I cannot be sure. But while I stood with my hands on her shoulders, I felt something about her to be unquestionably different.

'What?' she asked me later that night, while we lay feet touching at opposite ends of her brown suede sofa.

'What's different about me?'

'Your aura,' I said. 'It's your aura. It's . . . it's a different colour.'

And what changes must she have seen in me that day? Black rings under my eyes that I pretended at first were the result of a long-haul flight. A tired and dull complexion that I put down to the jet lag. We both knew of course that the bags under my eyes went deep, very deep, far deeper than shadows go when you have missed just one night's sleep. That the greyness of my skin that she saw from the other end of the sofa went far below the surface. We both knew the reason for my insomnia, yet on that first evening of my visit to New York neither Dominique nor I could bring ourselves to talk of Mischa.

'Dominique.'

'Yes.'

'Are you going to tell me about it?'

'What?'

'Your aura.'

I knew nothing. At least I knew nothing for a fact. She had made no mention of Nicholas in her letters or during our phone calls. She had made mention only of an impending visit from Paul. But I had seen Dominique and Paul together in Zurich on many occasions. I had seen her after his weekend visits, and the aura I saw here in Manhattan, on her brown suede couch, bore no resemblance to the one I recognized from those times.

'I'm waiting,' I said to her.

She gave me a playful kick with her bare foot.

'What do you want to know?'

'Do I need to spell it out?'

'Yes.'

'Dominique,' I said, emphasizing each word, 'who is

he?'

'Who is who?'

'The man responsible for stripping you of your virginal air.'

'Paul doesn't know yet.' she said.

'Neither do I. Dominique, I'm going to scream in a minute. Who is he? *Chi è? Chi è?* Do I have to beg you?'

My talented friend, my brilliant, linguistically gifted friend was quite unable to find the words to tell me who he was.

'Fine,' I said. 'Let's play twenty questions . . . Is he an interpreter?'

'No.'

'A doctor?'

'Sort of.'

And so by the time the brown suede sofa had been converted into a bed and I fell asleep I had joined up at least some of the dots. But had she told me everything, had she been unencumbered by guilt towards Paul and told me all the facts, I still don't think I could quite have understood. It wasn't till the next night that I got the picture.

'I've booked a table to take you for a welcome dinner,' she said, standing at the kitchen sink with her back to me.

'Great.'

'Anna.'

'Yes.'

'Would you mind if I brought a friend?'

'No,' I said, 'I wouldn't mind at all.'

The walls in Café des Artistes are decorated with Renaissance frescoes in pastel colours. The lighting is low and the atmosphere is one of subdued elegance. It is the sort of restaurant you might expect to see in a black and white Forties movie. The sort of restaurant they might choose as the setting for a love scene.

The three of us that evening spoke in Italian. Nicholas and I joked about the rivalry between true Italians and Swiss Italians from the Tessin. We compared notes on Sardinia and on Tuscany. We lauded Italian cuisine and teased Dominique about the ignorance of the British palate.

The art of interpreting had taught me to talk and to think at the same time. To look into the eyes of the person next to me as if the whole of me were there, involved and immersed in that conversation. To give no inkling of the thought processes on an entirely separate subject in an entirely separate compartment of my brain.

What I thought, while the three of us ate lobster from white plates on a white tablecloth and talked of eating pasta from earthenware crockery on a wooden table, was that Nicholas and Dominique bore some physical resemblance to one another. It was something in their colouring, their bone structure and the slant of their eyes. What I thought as the evening progressed from lobster to *crème brûlée* and coffee was that if I had been watching that black and white movie, the directors would have found it hard to create the sense of something as vast or as deep as that which I saw between the two of them that evening in Café des Artistes. It wasn't what they said to each other. Nor the way they looked at one another. It was something intangible, a feeling that washed over me as the Chianti began to do its work, that whatever it was I was privileged to witness between them could not be searched for or rationalized or even put into words. I was watching a scene in a film and my curiosity to know what would become of the characters was overridden by the desire to freeze that picture so that nothing ever would change for them. I wanted the mood that evening to stay exactly as it was, but it was Dominique who poured the glass of wine with a glug glug that threatened to loosen my tongue. And I am almost sure that it was me and not Dominique who brought up the subject of Mischa. I remember thinking that Nicholas was a doctor and it wouldn't matter if I told him about Mischa's illness and his prognosis in all its graphic detail.

I told him how, as a medical student, Mischa had wanted to experiment with the drugs. How he had waited till the illness had progressed significantly before he agreed to swallow handfuls of green and yellow and pink pills a day, how though they had temporarily improved his condition, his immune system had already been impaired to such an extent that the future looked bleak. If one could talk of a future at all. And I think it was when I said that word *'future'* . . . *'futuro, futuro,'* that I felt myself begin to crack, which in front of a complete stranger would have been highly embarrassing had it not been for the Chianti. I don't recall leaving the restaurant or walking back to Dominique's flat, but I do remember the immediate and almost physical tension in the air whilst I sat and spoke of Mischa. Even through the haze of alcohol, I saw the tightening of the muscles in their faces. Of course I would have expected Dominique to be distressed by the conversation, but there was something strange and at the time inexplicable in her expression. Both she and Nicholas were upset by what they had heard, though during that part of the conversation there was no direct communication between them. They were entirely separate in their reaction to my story. And so when I relive that evening, when I put myself back there in the Café des Artistes with the lobster, the *crème brûlée* and the Chianti, I remember witnessing both a great togetherness and a great separateness that I was unable at the time to explain.

TWENTY-FOUR

Nicholas

Manhattan was muggy and oppressive. The sky felt like
the low and suffocating ceilings of a cramped and airless
apartment. Spring pretending to be the height of a
sweltering summer. Spring warning Manhattanites in a
freak forty-eight-hour heat wave of what was to come.
The city was crowded, Fifty-Seventh Street crowded
further still. A large pothole in the road was separated
from the relentless passing of frenzied feet only by the thin
rope that encircled it. A black sign with white letters read
'CAREFUL. YOU MAY FALL.'

I attempted a detour, but the crowds were so thick that
I was forced to retrace my steps along a narrow makeshift
cardboard pavement under several feet of scaffolding, to
cross over Fifty-Seventh Street and back again. As I stood
in the heat by the pedlars flogging 'leather' handbags that
were plastic and 'Cartier' watches that were fakes, I looked
over at the gold and chrome façade of the Four Seasons,
the black-and-gold capped doormen who spent their lives
opening and closing the car doors of the opulent. Next to
me, a young boy with a teddy-bear rucksack stepped off
the pavement into the street. I watched a dark hand reach
forward and yank his arm back. His mother yelled at him
over the honking of the horns as she pulled him back.
'You'll kill yourself,' she said.

I turned to my right and saw her bend down to him, ruffle his hair and say, 'Don't do things without thinking. Do you understand?'

The flashing sign in white capital letters changed from 'DON'T WALK' to 'WALK'.

I crossed the street and walked through the sliding doorways into the entrance of the hotel. They had overdone it on the air-conditioning. My body temperature dropped instantly and radically. Ahead of me a flight of marble steps led up towards the reception desk. I felt the damp patch at the back of my navy linen shirt. Behind the desk the young woman with white-blonde hair scraped back off her face reminded me of Carla, my friend in Florence. I felt a moment of guilt. I had not responded to her last letter. She had written that the pressure of the operating theatre was overwhelming and she had decided to 'change her ideas' as they say in Italian, and to come and spend a few weeks in New York. 'I don't know where your life is right now,' she wrote, 'but perhaps we could spend some time together, unless of course you are seeing someone. I would appreciate your honesty.'

Seeing someone? Should I write back and say that I was seeing someone? Spending time with someone? Museums, movies, Central Park on Sundays. Should I write back and say that? Or should I write and say, 'I thought up till this point in my life that nothing was more important than my work. I thought that nothing was more important to me than saving a child with leukaemia. I thought that, when I was in Florence, when you and I were "seeing" each other. And it's not that it isn't still hugely important to me. It's not that I care any less about the pale little faces I imagine behind the blood cells that I scrutinize. It's not that I care any less about discovery . . . about what I have . . . I mean what I might have stumbled upon quite by accident. No, I don't care any less about these things at all. And you can't compare passions, of course. I know that. It's a ludicrous concept . . . the idea of measuring a professional and a private passion. The idea that passion can be measured. That it can be lifted in cupped hands, placed gently on a scale and weighed. Because what would be the point anyway? If it weighed too much, if it was taking up too much of your headspace could you tame it, trim it, prune it, cut it down to size? Could you . . . ?

'Good afternoon, sir. How can I help you?'

'I have an appointment with a Mr Walter Zlack.'

'Mr Zlack, of course. The presidential suite, sir. Take the elevator behind you to the fifty-second floor.'

The notice on the inside of the elevator said, 'Capacity 24 persons'. I was alone. The carpets were new and soft. The lighting was low. I remembered my childhood fear of elevators, of being stuck for ever between where you had come from and where you wanted to go.

I turned to look in the mirror that covered the back wall and for the first time that morning I dared to broach the subject with myself. No-one could see me. Who cared if for a moment I engaged in conversation with my reflection.

'Nicholas,' I said, 'what the hell are you doing here? What the hell . . . ?' And it was in the ping that announced my arrival that I knew I had come not just as a favour to Tom but out of my own sense of curiosity.

In the mirror, I saw the doors begin to open. Tom came towards me beaming, teeth whiter than ever against a turquoise shirt. The elevator opened right into the presidential suite. It opened in effect right onto Manhattan, for only the glass of the floor-to-ceiling windows separated us at eye-level from the silver spikes of the city. The tips of the World Trade Center, the Chrysler building, the Empire State Building were close enough to touch. To the left and beneath us a plane, tiny as a toy from where I stood, was taking off from La Guardia. To my right another was coming in to land at JFK.

'Awesome isn't it Nick?' he says, beside me now, looking out at the view that surrounds us.

'It is. It's amazing . . . but Tom. I'm not totally sure what this is all about . . . I wish you'd prepared me better.'

His call the previous evening had been from a mobile phone, the reception had been terrible and he had simply shouted over and in between the crackles, 'It's all arranged Nick. 6.30 in the presidential suite at the Four Seasons. Ask for Walter Zlack.'

And now standing here in this huge room with brown and yellow prints of presidents on the walls, with green and gold lawyers' lamps on the sideboards, with a long shiny chocolate-coloured boardroom table and Tom hopping from one foot to the other as though waiting for the start gun of a race, I wish for a moment that I was on my own territory. In a restaurant downtown or in the Café Dante, because you always feel more in control in familiar surroundings.

'Just you wait,' Tom said, 'to hear what he's going to say to you . . . I've told him you're the hottest thing to hit pharmaceuticals for years. You'll thank me for getting you in here, boy. Believe me,' and then looking down at my feet, at my brown suede lace-ups he says, 'nice shoes, Manzini . . . well done,' as if he's giving me his approval, telling me I look the part.

He walks over to the antique drinks cabinet, unlocks it, takes out a whisky bottle and crystal tumblers and begins to pour himself a drink, showing me he's at home here, as comfortable in the presidential suite of a five-star hotel as in his own living-room.

'What can I get you Nick?'

'Just a mineral water thanks.'

He laughs. 'You're going to have to learn to live the high life . . .' and then in a half-whisper, 'for God's sake Nick, when Zlack comes in show your enthusiasm.'

And it is as he says 'enthusiasm', just as the word has come out of his mouth, that at the other side of the chocolate-coloured table a man stoops to avoid the door-frame and walks through from the adjoining room. He moves towards me, thin, upright. In his late fifties perhaps. His greying hair cropped short. His grey suit well cut. A starched shirt. A slither of a tie. A firm handshake.

'Walter Zlack . . . You must be Nicholas.'

He gesticulates towards the table. Tom pulls out his chair for him. We sit on either side of him. In front of each of us is a document in a transparent blue folder. Through the plastic I can make out the heading, 'ZLACK ENTERPRISES . . . THE DEWAR/MANZINI PROJECT.' The words feed my curiosity and ignite my discomfort.

'So, Nicholas, I've obviously heard many good things about you. You're from Florence I believe.'

'That's right.'

'A wonderful city. I've been there on business once or twice. You must miss home.'

'Yes, I suppose I do. Manhattan is not the easiest place to get to know people.'

'No, I don't imagine it is,' he says, and covers his mouth as he coughs a smoker's cough. 'I hear you were hand-picked to come over here.'

'I wouldn't put it quite like that. I was fortunate to be given the opportunity and I took it.'

And Tom says, 'Cut out the modesty, Nick. You were hand-picked and you know it. You were their star performer.'

This small talk won't last long. I feel it. Such niceties pain Zlack. There is a stiffness in his manner. He wants to get straight to the point.

'Let's get down to business,' he says, laying a dry grey-skinned hand on the document in front of him. The expression on Tom's face is one of nervous anticipation. I notice he has coloured slightly. I've never seen him ill at ease. Zlack says, 'I'm very pleased to hear that you wish to join our new venture, Nicholas.'

A moment's silence. An awkward silence and then I say, 'I'm sorry Mr Zlack, I . . .'

'Call me Walter.'

'I'm sorry Walter, I'm not sure that I quite understand. Tom's told me about you of course, but we never got this far. I came today, because I was interested to hear what you're planning.'

In the sharp features, the thin lips, the small eyes, I see a mixture of irritation and surprise as he says, 'Tom, there seems to be some confusion here. I hope I'm not wasting my time. I was under the impression that Nicholas knew all about our project. Have I mis-understood?'

'Of course he knows about it. That's why he's here. But perhaps he needs to know more. Let me fill you in, Nick. Basically Zlack Enterprises . . .'

Zlack stops him. Snaps at him, 'Tom, I'm sure Nicholas doesn't need you to write my CV. *I'll* tell him about us,' and he turns to me then, and in the lighting of a long thin dark brown cigarette he resigns himself to a lengthy explanation.

And I remember at that moment realizing that Tom must have led Zlack to believe that he and I had discussed their new venture over countless beers. That he must have told him I was bursting to leave Landmark, that he must have assured him I was all but in the bag.

It was the only way Zlack would have agreed to this meeting, for I saw within minutes that he was not a man to bother himself with preliminary discussion. Though then, of course, at the beginning of that meeting in the Four Seasons, I had little idea why it was me that they wanted. Why my skills were not interchangeable with those of any other research scientist.

He offers me a cigarette. I decline. Tom takes one from the packet, accepts the flame from Zlack's thin silver lighter.

'I started in the late Sixties importing raw materials for pharmaceutical companies from all over the world . . . from Italy, Israel, India and China. My imports have contributed to the make-up of diabetic drugs, chemo-therapy medication, the contraceptive pill . . . the list is endless.' He looks at me, inhaling, reading the interest on my face and carries on, less irritated now. Because every-one, even the least talkative of men, can be encouraged to speak of himself and his achievements. Even the least communicative of men, once he is in the groove and faced with a listener, will talk of himself.

'Though I say so myself we have an exceptional track record and we've played a part in improving the lives of millions of people I haven't even met. I'm not a business mogul in the conventional sense, Nicholas. Money is not my primary motivation. Though of course financial success is a welcome by-product. But America has been good to me and I like to think I give something back through my company.'

All the time Zlack is speaking Tom is nodding. In agreement. Out of deference. I've never known him to be this quiet.

'Tom will have told you I've been contemplating the establishment of a new research division for some time. A pharmaceutical company with a young dynamic team. A company at the cutting edge.' As he is talking, he walks over to the sideboard, picks up the whisky bottle from where Tom has left it, brings the crystal tumblers to the table. He doesn't ask. He doesn't want to interrupt his flow. He just pours the drinks and hands one to each of us. Still standing, glass in hand he moves towards the window and turns to face us from there. 'It's all about people and I am certain that with your support I have the right team to make this thing work . . . We have a top Harvard biologist, a wonderful French chemist, a lawyer on hand to patent any discoveries and two sharp medical researchers . . . you and Tom.'

Zlack was the one who had talked and talked, but it was I who felt breathless. As though I had just run round the loop in Central Park, as though I were on the beach in Sardinia, tugging at the reins of the big grey horse as he canters ahead disobeying me, moving too fast despite my resistance, threatening to throw me and I say, 'Your achievements sound incredibly impressive. And this is all fascinating and exciting, but why me? I'm not even sure I'm experienced enough to join you. I've only been in research for just over two years.'

'Oh come on Nick,' Tom says, 'you know you've got what it takes.'

And Zlack, clearing his throat, coughing again as if to call order, says, 'Nicholas, maybe there are crosswires here, but this is the bottom line. Tom led me to believe that you were most unhappy at Landmark, that he had discussed my proposition with you and you were ready to join Zlack Enterprises. The draft we have prepared gives the two of you the opportunity to develop your careers in an exciting environment financed by a major organization and working with a committed team. The only reason for my visit today was to meet you in person and to sort out any problems that might arise from the contract, and I'm planning to put the wheels in motion for the establishment of the new division as soon as I get back to DC. But Nicholas,' he says, turning to the side, blowing out smoke, 'maybe I have misunderstood the situation. If you're happy at Landmark, if you feel it's the right environment to develop your ideas, if they can provide you with the same incentives as I can then that's fine by me. If this is not for you, it's not for you. If you feel you're involved in teamwork at Landmark the way you want to be and getting the feedback you need to get, then you can walk away from this with no hard feelings . . . But if I were you, Nicholas, I would probably let Tom take me through the proposal to pick out some key points. If by any chance it does appeal to you and you do decide to go ahead then all I need is your signature on the document.'

'But Mr Zlack.'

'Walter.'

'Walter . . . I'm flattered of course. And it's true, there isn't much feedback at Landmark. None really. Although I do enjoy my leukaemia research. I feel committed to it . . .'

And Zlack, standing behind his chair now at the end of

the table says, 'Nicholas, you can always go back to leukaemia at my company in a couple of years, but that other research work of yours that I've read, it's so impressive. It has such potential, that it must surely take priority . . . Now if you'll excuse me, I have some calls to make.' He stubs out his cigarette, turns to leave, stooping again through the door-frame as he goes.

'What other research work, Tom? What's impressive? What's he seen of mine?'

And Tom, wound up now, too involved to contemplate his words, says, 'The HIV stuff. The stuff in the pink file.'

I remember once at medical school learning the physiological reasons why shock can render you momentarily speechless. The vocal folds rely on the requisite amount of air for free movement. In the complex interplay between breath and movement of the vocal cords it takes no more than a fraction of a second for something to go wrong, for your voice to rebel and refuse you freedom of speech, till your pulse has stopped racing and your breathing has resumed its natural rhythm.

I find myself over by the window, staring out. The sky, darkened by now, is studded with the lights of the skyscrapers.

'I did it for your sake, Nick. I knew you'd never let me show it to him. You're too damned modest for your own good.'

Not turning round, not looking at him, I say, 'You can't just go round stealing people's files.'

'Stealing? Don't be ludicrous, Nick. I was trying to do you a favour as a friend. I was trying to get you out of there. I saw your face that day in the diner when I said I was leaving. I'm trying to help you, damn it. Don't you see that?'

'It's an odd way to go about it . . . And anyway, it's ludicrous to offer me a position on the basis of those findings. They may amount to nothing at all.'

'That's not true for a start, and you know it. But, I just don't get it, Nick. I don't get it at all. You're acting like I'm trying to harm you in some way. I mean for God's sake. D'you think I'm doing this for me or for you?'

His question was a clever one. A gamble, but a clever gamble. Because if someone puts it to you like that, in your mind you have to go one way or the other. You have to make a choice. To decide on the spot whether this person is a friend, whether or not he has your interests at heart.

'Show me the contract,' I say.

And as I follow him back to the chocolate-coloured table a wave of unreality washes over me, up there above Manhattan, in the presidential suite of the Four Seasons at night.

He takes the document out of the transparent blue folder, hands me mine and not waiting for me to open it begins to read extracts out loud. His voice is high. Excited. Like a child almost.

'Get this, Nick, get this . . . "A remuneration package of $250,000 in the first year of employment . . .

' "A five per cent share in the equity . . .

' "Use of state-of-the-art equipment . . ." '

While he is talking I have begun to read the document for myself.

' "Any certified drugs resulting from research carried out during employment at Zlack Enterprises to be the sole property of the company which will have exclusive development and marketing rights.

' "All findings to be jointly attributed to Tom Davies and Nicholas Manzini acting as a team.

' "The signatories will join Zlack Enterprises within one month of the date of this Agreement." '

I have little idea why I picked up on this last phrase as opposed to the others. I have little idea why this was the one objection I raised.

'Tom. I can't leave now. I'm morally and legally bound to Landmark for another five months and even after that, I can't work with any other pharmaceutical company for another six months.'

'We can sort out the time issue, Nick. That's easy.'

He knows now he has aroused my interest. He senses it. He snatches it and he goes to the bedroom door, knocks, disappears for a moment, for long enough to whisper information and comes back with Zlack.

He walks back to the table and says, 'So, have you worked things out?'

'The offer is interesting,' I say, 'but there's no way I could leave Landmark for another five months. And even after that I'm contractually bound to a restrictive covenant. Even if I did decide to go for it, I couldn't join your company for a year. Why would you wait that long for me?'

Zlack looks concerned. He is silent for a moment and then he says, 'Nicholas, I believe you are worth waiting for. As long as we can get something signed tonight, I'll make that concession.'

'I'm sorry. I appreciate your offer, but I need some time to think about what it would involve.'

'Time?' Tom says, 'what do you need time for?'

'In business, Nicholas,' says Zlack, inhaling the smoke from his long thin cigarette, 'one has to be decisive. But I'll give you your time. You can even take this document home with you. I don't leave till 9.30 tomorrow morning.

If you decide this offer's not for you then so be it. But in case you do decide to join us, Tom and I have already signed all three copies. You can keep one and return the other two signed in the morning prior to my departure.'

He extends his hand, grips mine again in his firm handshake.

'I hope you make the right decision Nicholas,' he says and is gone.

I stand up to leave. I need to go outside. To breathe some fresh air. Tom follows me to the elevator and he says, 'You know what this is about, Nick, quite apart from the money. It's about teamwork. You and I working together with guys on the same wavelength as us. And Zlack's no Goldmann. There'll be dynamism, camaraderie. You won't have to stand there and talk to yourself any more. I'm no idiot, Nick, and I've signed this contract haven't I? D'you honestly think I would go with something that wasn't a great deal?'

The elevator arrives with a ping. And even as the mirrored doors are about to close in his face, Tom is standing there, talking to me, convincing me. 'You'll never get another offer like this, Nick. This is a once in a lifetime thing. Don't throw it away.'

When an army of arguments, their sleeves rolled up, their muscles flexed, their best foot forward have positioned themselves in your mind each ready to fight his corner, each ready to annihilate the others, there is no way to be but alone. There is no place to be but in your own four walls, ready to referee their combat. I stilled them at first in my apartment with the warm jets of water that ran over my face and my body, skimming the surface of the tension, and then in my towelling robe in the kitchen, with a glass of red wine, with some Brie and some olives I sat myself down to listen to all sides.

To the side that said, 'OK Manzini, this has taken you by surprise, but maybe that's the way things are with you. Didn't Grevi force you to make an overnight decision about moving to New York? And you managed to make up your mind in a night on that one, so what's the problem here? Let's say you don't take them up on their offer. Let's say you stay with Landmark, then what? You would go to Goldmann now and tell him about your findings and he might well not believe in you. You're a leukaemia researcher after all. He might ridicule what you've done, tell you like Grevi did not to get any big ideas, to stick to your own territory. But Zlack and Tom clearly do believe in you. More than you believe in yourself. So what about this Zlack thing, Manzini? What do you think? The way Tom went about it was odd to say the least . . . or maybe it was just immature. Maybe he just didn't think it through properly.

'Let's say they are using you. Does it really matter? It's not like they're trying to take your ideas without involving you. So let's say I go. Let's say I do decide to take them up on it. Then what? It's a risk . . . a new venture always is. It could fold. But so what? When am I ever going to take risks in my life if I don't do it now? And the money's unbelievable. Don't pretend that doesn't seduce you just a little, Manzini. Who wouldn't be seduced by it, for God's sake? If they're crazy enough to offer you that kind of money are you really going to say no? And the delay? You're going to be sitting on that research for months. But what's a few months in this game? It's nothing really, is it?

'Now hang on a minute. Take a few deep breaths. Consider a different scenario. Say Goldmann does think you're onto something, say he asks to see the results of your experiments and moves you straight to HIV research. You'd work in the Virology department, maybe even with a team, but by the very nature of the set-up your project would be led by other scientists, because otherwise it would put too many people out, you moving to a new department and immediately running your own thing. And you've forgotten something, Manzini. Goldmann is going to ask you where you got the HIV blood from and you're going to have to admit that you smuggled it into the lab without registering it. That's a great start isn't it? And the truth is you're not that enamoured with life at Landmark are you? Sure they brought you over here, but your obligations don't run to self-sacrifice do they? Be honest with yourself. How many people get an offer like you just got?'

And so through the night the arguments sprang back and they sprang forth. The pro-Zlack arguments bolstered by the contract in the transparent blue file that I took with me to bed. The pro-Landmark arguments weakened by its pages and by the isolation of the past few months. So that by 7.30 I was up and dressed and shaved and ready to make my way to the Four Seasons to hand in the two copies of the contract to Zlack. So that once again I had made a major career decision in one night. Though this time I had allowed myself to be convinced by a vociferous team of arguments in my mind, and not by the voice of my gut that had brought me to New York in the first place.

TWENTY-FIVE

Dominique

Balance can be so temperamental. So capricious and underhand in its ways. Like a hedgehog, unthreatened, as long as all is well, balance is a nonentity. But threatened, it stiffens its bristles and pricks us hard into awareness of its existence. Balance has no colour in the patchwork. It is the invisible thread that holds together the quilt of our lives.

During those first few months, both Nicholas and I were oblivious to balance within our relationship. Between us, there was no feeling of competition or insecurity. No sense of the abyss on either side of the tightrope.

On Memorial Day Landmark threw a party in a garden that rolled down to the water's edge in Amagansett, a small town at the eastern tip of the Hamptons, where New Yorkers escape from the city at weekends. The mansion belonged to one of the pharmaceutical company's founders and though Landmark could not always be lauded for the way they treated their staff, on that day no expense had been spared. Plates of shellfish and smoked salmon, bowls of peaches and strawberries, carafes of red wine and bottles of champagne on white-clothed tables adorned the lawns. A disc jockey had been hired and from the terrace, decorated with fuchsia and yellow flowers in massive terracotta plant pots, the music wove its way to the buffet table, in and out of our conversations. The day was perfect. The weather wrapped us in its warmth.

I stood, with a plate of oysters in one hand, half a glass of champagne in the other, talking to a young German interpreter in a red dress. And normally we might have spoken of the ardours of our profession, of how we were no more than tools, of how we were undervalued and underpaid. But on that day there was none of that. She was laughing and joking about some translating anecdote or other and when for a moment I looked away from her, towards the far end of the buffet with the rest of the guests mingling between us, Nicholas and I caught each other's eye and standing quite still, we held one another's gaze.

Towards evening we moved in the direction of the house and began to dance on the patio. Fast breathless tunes at first. Music that, after all the food and wine, left us panting and laughing. And then without comment the disc jockey decided in the semi-darkness to change the mood and to play some corny oldies. Except by that time the line between corny and romantic had blurred. Next to us, on the ground as we danced I could see a saffron shadow and I wondered whether it was his or mine. And I remember him asking me very quietly if I had danced as a girl. He didn't mean this sort of dancing of course. In fact I'm not sure by the time he asked if he knew what he meant at all. And I don't even know if I answered him. But in some very fluid and late-night way I thought about it. I danced as a girl. Of course I did. Ballet all the way into my early teens, and I remember it was all about balance. All about standing on my points in my yellow tutu and keeping my balance. I had wanted a pink tutu like the other girls, but my mother had some old taffeta at home and she wasn't going to waste it. 'Dominique,' called the teacher above the music, 'up on those points and balance. You know where it comes from don't you? From the base. From your tummy muscles and the arches of your feet. Balance from the base, Dominique. From a position of strength. Don't forget that. It can only work if there is a solid base.'

And I thought as I danced amongst the wood and the mirrors of that practice hall that my balance was solid. I felt strong on my points. I felt strong as I rehearsed the part of Tarantella, the peasant woman who stood for a second quite motionless and then scurried on tiptoes from one stall to the next at some street market or other. But balance had fooled me. It had given me a false sense of security. Because the night before the dress rehearsal was one of those nights when I lay on the scratchy landing carpet with my ear to the floor, and the next morning one of those mornings when I forgot all about my ballet. It was far less important than making sure my mother would allow my father to kiss her before I left for school. I worked hard. He kissed her and I was happy as I ran down the front path with my brown satchel slung over my shoulder, because if things went according to plan it would be at least a few days now till the next fight. And there were no headaches that day. No coloured dots in front of my eyes. But my balance was a little off. My dancing was not what it had been the day before and hard as I tried I couldn't seem to stay up on my points and my ballet teacher didn't want to take a risk. After all, the performance was the next day, so the understudy took my place. My teacher said she didn't have my flair, but she was good on the balance side of things and sometimes I couldn't get that quite right. It took me a long time to understand why, though I think that now I do. I remember

175

my surprise the night before when I had heard from the upstairs landing, not my mother's shrill tones, but my father raising his voice at her. One of the rare occasions when I ever heard him shout. Something about him loving her more than she loved him and that it was all lopsided. And I wondered if what went on between two people was sort of like dancing. If it was the same as the way you needed to put your weight on the tips of the toes of both feet at the same time. And how could I possibly get that right at ballet if my mother and father didn't have a clue about it even though they were supposed to be grown-ups?

Nicholas said as we danced on the terrace that night that my cheek was wet against his. It must have been the alcohol. It had been a long time since I'd last drunk champagne. The heady effect of it sent me quite off balance and I struggled, as I spoke, to form my words clearly.

Just like in the booth, when you were interpreting and at first you had got it just right. You wanted to stay up there, triumphant on the bright blue surfboard, riding the crest of the wave behind the speaker's words, but sometimes the spray was too strong, some outside noise distracted you, or your headphones dug into your ear and you began to wobble. You missed a word, a sentence, an idea and right there in the booth you lost your footing and you toppled.

One night, at the end of a session that had gone on till dark, Nicholas had come from the lab to find me. I had been sitting at the back of the hall in the booth, memorizing the last of the next day's lists of words. And when I think about it now, I'm not sure whose hand it was that reached out to dim my tiny blue reading-lamp to nothingness. But I remember that I for once said nothing in the booth.

Effortless balance for as long as it lasts is harmony. Harmony can be about wanting the same things at the same time. About sensing the shape and the flow in the silence. About the ballerina on her tiptoes engulfed by the music. The surfer, euphoric on the crest of his wave.

TWENTY-SIX

Nicholas

From time to time a blackness crossed Dominique's face. Its rarity rendered it all the more noticeable. When I look back, though, over that spring and summer in Manhattan, most of the images of her that I have in my mind bear no similarity to that darker picture. Instead I see Dominique behind smoky glass, her eyes cast downwards and a half smile on her lips. Dominique against the counter in my kitchen watching me as I crush garlic or grate Parmesan. Dominique nibbling her lower lip as she did when in serious contemplation of an answer to one of my more probing questions.

As spring heated into summer I began to see slight changes in her. I noticed that when we lay in June on the green checked rug in Central Park, our bare feet touching and I asked about her mother's past she needed only a little prompting to talk. That when in mid-July we sat one night in the garden of Barolo, an Italian restaurant in downtown Manhattan, and I asked about her relationship with her father, she needed no prompting at all. She tilted her chair towards me and, animated, spoke of the understanding between them. An understanding built on a passion for words, yet one which needed few words to express itself.

'So why did he choose medicine, Dom? If he was so talented with words.'

'Why did you?' she asked me, leaning back in her black sleeveless dress with a neckline that looked to me ever so slightly lower than any I had seen on her before.

She saw me looking and she laughed.

'Dominique.'

'Yes.'

By the tone of her voice I could tell that she had heard the change of tone in mine. I waited before speaking. She made no attempt to rush me. I filled our glasses with white wine. I put the cork back in the bottle and the bottle back in the ice bucket.

'Dominique . . . I . . . I don't need to say it, do I?'

She looked at me, she shook her head and for a moment at the table, in that garden, at Barolo opposite each other we were silent. I have talked of a moment that I wished with a passion I could have erased from my life. But this moment, this one here, was one that I would be happy to repeat again and again just as it was. One, in fact, that I did repeat often in my mind just as I recalled it, though expressions of course fade very fast as does the sound of a voice. I remember once looking back and laughing at a fantasy I had about that moment. I thought I should have turned to the waiter and said, 'Thank you. Thank you, yes, I'll have that one to take away. It was delicious. Too delicious to enjoy just once. Perhaps you could wrap it for me.'

Dominique twisted her spaghetti round her fork, said, 'Now answer my question,' and lifted the fork to her mouth. But I was too caught up in my thoughts, I was too busy thinking that it was a shame really that spaghetti took so long to eat because I wanted to get up there and then, to leave some money on the table, to take her by the hand, to run home with her and . . .

'Nicholas. My question.'

'Which question?'

'Why did you choose science over words?'

'That's an odd thing to ask, Dom. You know why.'

'Tell me.'

'Because words are not my talent. They're yours.'

'You're wrong,' she said.

'What do you mean?'

'I mean . . .' and she dropped her napkin on the ground, perhaps to give her time to disappear for a few seconds from my scrutiny and contemplate what she was going to say. I smiled and wondered whether she herself knew why it was that she had disappeared under the table.

She surfaced and she said, 'I mean . . . that you know how to make people talk.'

She didn't mean people, of course. She didn't mean the man in the grocery store or the woman at the dry-cleaners. She didn't mean the receptionist at the restaurant or the waiter. But she used the third person. She said, 'You know how to make *people* talk,' to distance the comment from herself. To save her from having to say, 'You know how to make me talk.'

And now when I think about it, I know that though she had begun to flirt with the edges of the chrysalis, it was not till a little later, not till events shook her that Dominique was totally comfortable in the first person where it mattered.

Was I wrong to believe that the blackness of which I have spoken appeared only on the rarest occasion? Was I wrong to imagine that everything then in our lives was secondary to our mutual, as yet unspoken conviction that we had 'come home'?

During those weeks of June and July I worked long

hours. The free time I did have was spent with Dominique and I saw little of Tom in that time. We arranged lunch at the deli on one occasion but I found a reason to cancel. For the time being I felt I needed some distance to digest my decision. I wanted to put the thought of leaving leukaemia research to the back of my mind for I knew very well that when the moment came it was likely to be a wrench, and I was relieved that it would be some months before I reached the break clause in my contract and needed to hand in my notice.

The hours for reflection at that time were in any case very much limited. In late June my boss Professor Goldmann, who had strong links with the paediatric leukaemia department at the Sloane Kettering Hospital, told me there was a short-term opening for a specialist in the field to combine laboratory work with some clinical research. He told me, not, I am sure, because he was interested in the development of my career on a personal level, but because the liaison would carry with it significant prestige for Landmark. I hesitated when he asked me. I had moved away from the clinical side. I had moved away from the trauma of the day-to-day contact with sick children. Why would I go back to it now, a short time before I was due to leave Landmark? Even if only two days a week? Even if only for a period of a few months? But I reasoned with myself. In the short time since I had moved into research our collective efforts meant that huge advances had been made. The anti-rejection drugs meant that bone-marrow transplants had higher chances of success. A greater sense of optimism pervaded the hospitals. And how after all could I call myself an authentic researcher if the closest contact I had with the illness was with a bag of blood?

So I agreed that for four months I would go twice weekly to the Sloane Kettering, to the children's oncology ward and I would contribute to the analysis of certain patients under the care of the department. My contact with the sick children drained me emotionally then as it had done in the past, but now when I peered over blood cells in the laboratory a new set of children's faces spurred me on to more intensive research. Maggie, in pink pyjamas with a furry giraffe by her bedside who said she absolutely had to be better for the school sports day. Daimon, who wore his blue baseball cap even at night to hide the ravages of chemotherapy, and Sophie, a little olive-skinned girl with huge dark eyes who said little but looked at you as if she knew it all. I thought every time I saw her that Dominique must have been just like her as a child.

I suppose it may appear strange that having stumbled on a potential breakthrough in Aids research, I was able to put it to the back of my mind, albeit for a limited period of time, and to continue my work in another area. But you cannot run two races simultaneously. You cannot, as we say in Italian, '*mettere il piede in due scarpe*', put one foot in two shoes. I told myself there was nothing wrong with putting my HIV research on hold till I moved to Zlack Enterprises. I told myself there was little I could do now, here, in this interim period, where no-one at work except Tom knew of my findings and it would have been foolish, while I was still employed by Landmark, to spend time on research in an area that I now needed to divorce from them entirely. Of all these things I convinced myself, and then as much as was possible I banished the subject to the back burner to be retrieved, or so I thought, shortly before I reached the break clause in my contract with Landmark. In truth, I don't think my bosses concerned themselves with my contract for even a moment. I am sure that in Florence, Grevi assumed I would feel so privileged to be here in Manhattan, rubbing shoulders with the *Who's Who* of the scientific world, that I would never, not even for a moment consider leaving before I was asked to. And Goldmann still had shown no interest in my well-being or lack of it.

With sessions at the hospital, long hours in the lab and the occasional conference to fill my mind, perhaps I over-looked some of Dominique's moments of sadness. Perhaps it suited me to let them wash over me. But there are two such moments, two moments of blackness that come to me.

The first is Dominique standing waiting for me one evening outside Landmark, her chin in her hands, her bare elbows on the rough stone of a brick wall. I saw her from afar as I crossed the front courtyard of the premises and normally I would have called out to her, '*Ciao bella,*' but something in her stance suggested she was deep in thought, and so I walked up very close to her before I spoke. I stayed on the other side of the brick wall. I leant against it, so that it stood in between us and I could see her only from the neck up, and facing her I said, 'You look really sad.'

'I was thinking.'

'What about?'

'About Paul. How am I going to tell him, face to face, that I mean it? That we're like brother and sister, but it's not enough. That . . .' and she leant her head forward so that her face was hidden from me and her forehead was against the top of the wall and she started to cry. The first time, I think, that I had seen Dominique cry and she said in a whisper, so that I didn't know if I had imagined it, 'It's easier to stay asleep.'

'What?'

'Nothing . . . nothing. It doesn't matter,' and she wiped her eyes with the back of her hand and walked around to my side of the wall. And though it pained me to see her unhappy, for me the salt water that ran down her cheeks dragging with it a black streak of mascara was a sign. A symbol of the fact that she had let me in. Because seeing Dominique cry for the first time was as private as making love with her, as intimate as finding her voice in my ears.

It can have been no more than two weeks later that we sat one scorching Sunday afternoon drinking iced coffee from tall glasses in silver holders, on the front terrace of the Stanhope Hotel, opposite the Metropolitan Museum and the park, with piles of newspapers in front of us. Dominique was too immersed in her novel to touch the papers.

'I'm sorry,' she said, and touched my cheek, 'I'm not much company. I just can't put this thing down.'

I looked at the cover. *Washington Square.*

She was three-quarters of the way through the novel. The pages looked crinkled, as if she'd been reading it in the bath.

'What's it about?'

'Tragic love,' she said.

'Explain.'

She looked at me with mock exasperation on her face. The expression one wears when immersed in a gripping novel one is wrenched from the urgency of the story by some insignificance in the outside world.

'It's about this young American woman, Catherine Sloper. Her mother dies in childbirth. Her father never forgives her and then she falls passionately in love with this man. It's the first time she's ever experienced true happiness and that's as far as I've got.'

'So why did you say it was about tragic love?'

'I just have a feeling. Maybe I'm wrong. But I also think she's going to triumph in some way . . .' She turned her eyes to the vanilla ice-cream on the top of my iced coffee.

'See, I told you you should have ordered some too,' I said, filling a long-handled silver teaspoon from the scoop and moving it towards her mouth. She smiled at me and she parted her lips. Centimetres from her mouth I stopped. I held the spoon there and I said, 'This doesn't come free, you know.'

She frowned.

'The price for sharing my ice-cream is that you have to read to me a little from your book.'

And so Dominique is there, next to me in her jeans and white T-shirt with her sunglasses pushing her mahogany-coloured hair back off her face, and we are not separated by different reading material. Not transported into different worlds with me grappling with a political analysis and her lost in Catherine Sloper's mind. No, we are both in the same world and I listen uninterrupted for some time to the movements of Dominique's voice. I listen and I focus not on the story, not on Catherine's distress, but on the movements of Dominique's voice. Dominique speaking words that enthral her. Not words imposed on her as they were in the booth. Not yet words of her own making either. But words that fulfil and stimulate her and when I look up at the entrance to the restaurant I see a street artist. Thin with a shock of silver hair and a long beard, with his portable easel in front of him and I know, as if by instinct, that he is going to move in our direction. He catches my eye and holds my gaze till he has manoeuvred his way through the tables and is standing next to ours. He startles

Dominique and he says in a heavy French accent, 'Excuse me, but I would like to draw the lady.'

And Dominique would normally have shrunk from such exhibitionism, from making herself the focal point, but she is charmed by his manner and by the fact that he is French. We ask the head waiter's permission and he agrees and the artist unfolds the legs of his easel and unrolls his canvas close to our table. He lays his pencils and his pieces of charcoal out on the little ridge at the side of the canvas and he asks Dominique to lower her book a little but to carry on reading. She does and I am half listening to Catherine's story and half watching Dominique as she reads. And I sense suddenly that she is not quite as engrossed in the story as she was before and I see a darkness cross her face. I take her hand and I ask her what she is thinking about and in a very quiet voice she says, 'Mischa. And Anna. They're on my mind all the time.'

I feel half sad and half relieved when she says that. Sad because of the effect Mischa's illness has on Dominique. But relieved that the sombre expression I see on her face has nothing to do with me. Relieved because I don't imagine then that it is something that will come between us. And it crosses my mind that to speak to her of my findings, of the hypothesis that they might at some point, when it was far too late to help her friend, be developed further, would be almost cruel. Like showing newly planted crops to the starving.

As he begins to dismantle his easel the artist says, 'Would you like to see the drawing?'

Dominique, suddenly embarrassed, says, 'You look, Nicholas.' I go round to the other side of the easel. And the pencil lines on the paper do create a true likeness of her. The curve of her jaw and the slant of her eyes are the same. The shape of her lips is the same. The beauty spot above her mouth is in the same place. But what shocks me, what takes me quite off guard is the harsh charcoal shading. What shock me are the layers of pencil. The layers of darkness, that whichever way I look throw an unmistakable blackness over her face. And it is with a distinct sense of unease that I watch as the artist rolls the canvas and hands it to me.

TWENTY-SEVEN

Dominique

'I'm dreading it,' I said, sitting cross-legged on my bottle-green rug on my wooden floor, twisting the white plastic cord of the telephone round and round my wrist.

'I'm terrified.'

'Of?'

'Of Paul's reaction.'

At the other end of the phone line James, my journalist friend said, 'Go . . . just go.'

'What do you mean "Just go?" ' I asked, irritated that he should make it sound so easy.

'What do you mean what do I mean? I mean just get on that plane back to London and go and tell him. I can write the script for you if you want. Just say, "I loved you once, and now I don't." '

'You're wasted, James. You should be writing screen-plays not radio scripts.'

'Oooh aren't we getting feisty? Reserved and reticent Ms Green seems to be finding that voice of hers.'

'It's a big deal you know. Finding the right words for this one. I can't just say "I don't love you," because it's not true. It's just not *that* kind of love any more.'

'Dominique. D'you think some pop psychology might help?'

'Like what?'

'Like, "Feel the fear and do it anyway."'

'Unlikely.'

'You don't have any doubts about it though? About what you're doing?'

'No,' I said. 'No, I don't think I do.'

'Anyway what does what's-his-name, your doctor friend say about it?'

'Nicholas?'

'Yes. Nicholas.'

Strange, so strange that in the throes of an *angst*-ridden conversation, that quite suddenly and from nowhere one can feel soothed and lightened. Strange that you can feel, for a moment at least, as you do when shivering with cold you take that first step into the hot bubbly water.

'What does he say? . . . I suppose he just listens to me really. He says that I'll confront it in my own time, when I'm ready.'

'So have you seen that coloured bubble yet?'

'What?'

'Remember that coloured bubble we talked about that time on the plane? The one you see when it's the real thing.'

'James, leave me alone,' I said, laughing.

'I want to know if you've seen it.'

'I might have done . . . And I'd love you to meet him.'

'I'll make a deal with you, dinner on me for the three of us at the venue of your choice when you get back from Europe.'

'It's a deal.'

'Listen to me, Dominique. Get it over with. You know I'm right.'

I listen to him, but mostly I listen to myself and I am standing there in a silk sundress outside the doors of the

British Airways offices in Manhattan. I am standing there on Fifth Avenue between Forty-Fourth and Forty-Fifth Street and normally I would be bursting to rush in and to buy my ticket. Because the feel of a passport in my hand would send a surge of adrenalin through me. Because if I close my eyes and breathe in deeply I can conjure up the smell of an airport or a station. I can re-create the feel of the stainless-steel stairs up to the plane beneath my feet, of the quasi-jump between the platform and the train as you board. The sensation of creeping to the door of my mother's bedroom the night before we were supposed to travel. Of peering through the crack between the hinges of the door to watch her hands with the long tapered fingers as she folds and packs. Of listening for the rustle of the tissue paper as she covers her clothes and knowing that at any moment she could stop and call out to my father, 'Phone the airline. See if you can get your money back. I'm not going.'

And he would come bounding up the stairs as I scurried back into my room and I would hear him say, 'Sonya, you can't do this again. You can't do this to the girls. Dominique's so excited. She's packed all her own things.'

He was right. I was excited, because just as my mother was folding and packing her clothes between tissue paper I had managed somehow to pack away the memory of the layers of tension we brought home with us from the last holiday and the one before that. I had managed to push them down, one on top of the other so that there would be room, in my shiny green suitcase, for my swimming-costume and my story-books. And what propelled me now to sit by my bedroom door with my hands clasped together, saying, 'Please, please, don't let her say we can't go,' were the exotic sounds I knew I would hear in Italy or

Spain and the memory of the sand between my toes.

'I'm not doing it. I don't feel like it. I can't bear it,' she would say. 'You take the girls. Go without me.'

'I'm not going without you.'

'I don't want to pack. I can't pack any more.'

'Come,' he would say, 'I'll do it for you.'

And sometimes, the better times, she would acquiesce and I would lie awake watching the fluorescent hands of my alarm clock till it was morning and we were on the move.

But there were other times. Times when I knew that his comforting, his coaxing and his cajoling were destined to fail. I knew it as soon as I heard her shout, 'You don't know what it feels like. What it felt like then to pack and unpack and pack and unpack and pack . . . What do I want it for any more? Why would I want to run any more? Who am I running from now?'

And my father would say, 'But the girls, they will be so disappointed.'

And I would hear her then through the walls half crying and half shouting, 'Disappointed? Disappointed? They should be happy they have no-one to run from.'

And so now when I travel, it is not just where I am going that matters. It is the fact that I am going at all. The fact that from the moment I feel the laminated plastic of that passport in my hand, from the moment I slip the maroon-bound pages into my bag I am free to reinvent myself. And it is not the exotic that enthrals me. Not so much the ancient pink of Petra nor the deep dramatic reds of Arizona. No, it is not that which excites me so much as the prospect of slipping in Rome into the language of the Romans. The prospect of trying for as long as I am there to immerse myself in them as I walk their streets, of testing myself to see how well I can melt into the sounds and colours of their world.

But this journey, this one ahead of me, filled me with none of the multicoloured butterflies that in the past had marked the build-up to my departure. No, standing here in front of the British Airways sales office in Manhattan, I felt none of that thrilling tingle of anticipation as I crossed the blue carpeted floors with the red specks that matched the British Airways insignia, as I approached the sales assistant in her short-sleeved dress that matched the carpet.

But though I bought the ticket for my trip to Europe without excitement, though I signed the credit-card slip with a feeling of foreboding, I bought it, too, with a great sense of compulsion.

I had discussed my journey with Nicholas. I had told him I was going to London to visit my parents and Paul, to Lugano to work at a conference with Anna, and to Zurich to visit Mischa. I expected him to ask me questions, to need to know and understand the thinking behind my trip. But I was wrong. This time he asked me nothing. He just smiled and said, 'You'll bring me back something fabulous, won't you?'

And I knew in the way that I had known when I sat by the sculpture in his apartment, when I listened with him to the movements of Mozart's Clarinet Concerto in A, in the way I had known when I left the booth, crossed the conference hall and spoke into the microphone for Nicholas to translate my words, that this journey was one which would in some way make its mark.

TWENTY-EIGHT

Nicholas

She flew to Europe for two weeks and for the first time I was alone with space to think of her. She left me with her aftertaste. For everything, I think, has its aftertaste. The weight and the aroma of wine is at its most delicious once your glass is emptied. The colours of a painting more vivid once you have averted your gaze. A piano concerto more profound once the last note has been played. The impact of a conversation more far-reaching in the silence it precedes. Aftertaste speaks of pleasure or of pain. It is the reverberating voice that cements the memory and draws you back to savour the experience again and again.

Once, Dominique and I talked of the idea of aftertaste. It was the night of the party on the lawn in Amagansett. We had stayed in Bluff Cottage, a little inn right on the water, and all night long through the open windows we could feel the sea, we could smell the breeze and the salt. The air was warm and as we lay half covered by a thin white sheet, in a room that would have been pitch-black had it not been for the reflection from a lighthouse, Dominique turned her face to me. She moved as if to look at me, though even in the semi-darkness I could see that she kept her eyes closed, and she said to me that it was now, in the moments that followed euphoria, that she knew, that she felt quite sure, and half asleep she

193

murmured something about the aftertaste and of it being like the feel of a foreign language on your tongue. I laughed at the comparison and I asked her what she meant. On the edge of sleep she struggled to be lucid in her reply. She said that seconds after you had spoken just a few words in a foreign language you knew whether or not it could belong to you. You knew by the taste that it left on your palate.

She called when she left for Europe from a payphone at Kennedy airport to say goodbye and as always when I spoke to her on the telephone I imagined myself to be hearing her voice through headphones. 'Interpreter context,' I said down the phone.

'What?'

'I need to know precisely where you are standing and what you are wearing.'

I could hear her smiling. 'Departure lounge. Next to one of those silver AT&T phones. Uncovered. On the wall. A grimy receiver in my hand. A little girl with chocolate all over her face crawling round and round my feet.'

'And?'

'And what?'

'Clothing.'

'My auburn scarf.'

'Just that?'

'Nicholas!'

'Disappointing . . . What else?'

'Short black skirt?'

'How short?'

'Nicholas, I've been gone for five minutes. Can you possibly have lost it in that time? You're not going to use some of your hocus-pocus potions in the lab and conjure yourself into a different person while I'm gone, are you?'

'I'll try not to . . . Dominique, is there anyone behind you in the line for the phone?'

'No.'

'How do you feel about being the last person to get on the plane?'

'Any particular reason?'

'Yes. Then we can talk till you board.'

It didn't happen like that though. It rarely happens the way you plan it. She had just started to respond to me. She had just said, 'I wish you . . .' when the operator cut in and said, 'Please deposit twenty-five cents to continue this call. Please deposit twenty five cents to continue this call,' and the line went beep, beep, beep, beep. She would call back, of course. I knew that. If she didn't have a quarter she would walk over to the mother of the child with chocolate all over her face and ask for change for a dollar and she would rush back to the phone on the wall and press the little silver squares with the numbers on them and we would talk till she heard the last boarding-call.

And I sat for a while by the sculpture in my living-room and waited. Certain for the first few minutes that she was having problems finding change, I waited till the chiming of the clock chose to taunt me. Till it chose to tell me that her plane must certainly have taken off. I even called the airline to check that it had departed on time, so that I could get up from my sofa. So that I could give up waiting for Dominique's phone call and imagine her instead in her black skirt and her auburn scarf sitting in her seat in mid-air, her hair falling over her face, her head bent over her novel.

It may still seem unnatural that I had told Dominique nothing of my findings over those months. As if I felt I had something to hide or hold back from her. It may seem peculiar that I should fail to discuss an element so central to my life in a relationship where layer after layer of withholding and inhibition fell away as if in a slow-motion film clip of the shedding of leaves. But whatever seeds of discovery I may have made were no more than a tenuous beginning, that day in the lab, when, though it was still winter, the sun shone through the slatted blinds so strongly that it blocked the view in my left eye almost entirely. A beginning before her time. A beginning that could never have helped Mischa and therefore seemed irrelevant to my relationship with Dominique.

If I made an active decision not to talk to her of my HIV findings, it was out of a wish not to tantalize her.

In the time that she was in Europe I began again to wonder about my agreement with Zlack and Tom. One evening in the Café Dante I found myself sitting with the *Corriere della Sera* in my hand. I found myself clutching it so hard that the black print came off on my fingers and though my gaze rested on an article at the top of the page, I could have told you nothing of what I was reading. The newspaper was an excuse for thought. An excuse to sit and think alone in a public place. Briefly it crossed my mind that to arrest investigation of my findings, while I waited for my contract with Landmark to expire, was perhaps the wrong path.

Briefly I considered that it might be better to go to Goldmann there and then, to march into his office, to stand in front of his massive desk and to say to him, 'Look, I think I may be onto something. I want the funds for development, but I want to do it in my time and my way and I want for once to be given some feedback and to work with a team.'

I entertained that scenario for a few moments and then dismissed it. And I thought, when the article in the newspaper in my hands came back into focus, that the slightly sour aftertaste on the roof of my mouth was due to the bitterness of the espresso and I beckoned to the barman to bring me the sugar bowl.

With Dominique out of town, there was time to sit here in the evenings on the green plastic chairs at Café Dante to read the papers, to drink my coffee and to listen to the words of the Italian songs that overwhelmed the café. I knew of course that Dominique would see Paul on her trip, but that meeting I can honestly say caused me no restlessness. I knew without question that she would not move backwards, that in that encounter between the two of them I had little to fear. And yet, when I thought of her in Europe, when I thought of her in Switzerland with Anna and Mischa, I could not help but acknowledge the fingers of inexplicable anxiety that brushed in warning against my upper arm. She had not said she would call during the time she was away and I had not pushed. Between us there was an unspoken understanding that she would deal with whatever she had to deal with alone and then would return to New York.

Aftertaste is short-lived. Quickly it glides into memory and from there, if the memory is a pleasurable one, it melts into anticipation.

TWENTY-NINE

Dominique

London, July 28th

We are sitting, my father and I, on white wrought-iron garden chairs on my parents' back lawn. My mother has taken to gardening and the flower-beds are still ablaze with colour. Drowsy with jet lag I watch her in her light blue sundress as she reaches upwards to sprinkle the white rose bushes. As she stretches her arms towards the highest bush. I watch and I don't want her to stop. I am hypnotized by the sight of her watering those roses, detached by this practical task from worry. And I think, as I sit there in the sunshine on this first morning of my trip back home, that however much you have moved forward in the outside world, however much you believe yourself to have over-come feelings that went hand in hand with the tensions and traumas of childhood, the minute they open that front door to you, the minute you breathe in the unchanged scent of your mother's skin, it is so easy for all the learning to fall instantly away. It is so easy to be pulled back again into those same patterns. And when my mother turns towards me and smiles, the open end of the green hose-pipe in her hand threatens to suck me back into the way that it was.

But the suction this time is not strong enough. I am no longer sitting curled up in the dry pink bathtub, waiting to hear her voice. Instead she and my father in his straw sun-hat are waiting here in the garden to hear mine. They ask about my career. About the conferences and my colleagues. They ask about my apartment and the neighbourhood in which I live. They ask about these things and concentrate on my answers. I observe my mother listening to me. She wears an expression on her face that is foreign. One that didn't belong to the repertoire I knew growing up. She wears her new listening expression. But the questions they ask are just a prelude to the main one. I know it. I can feel it looming. My father goes inside and comes back with a wooden tray with a jug of lemonade and three glasses. And it is just after I have taken my first sips that I hear him say, 'You haven't mentioned Paul.'

I cannot speak at first, with a mouth full of lemonade, so they assume I don't want to answer and my father says, 'Come on, Dominique. We want to know.'

And it crosses my mind that breaking it to them is the dress rehearsal for breaking it to him.

I swallow my lemonade and I say, 'I came home to tell him that it's over.' And neither of them says anything and then both of them start talking at the same time. A jumble of counsel, concern and consternation.

'But he'll make you happy.'

'But he knows you so well.'

'But you have the same background.'

'But he understands you.'

'He doesn't.'

'What?'

'He doesn't. He doesn't understand me at all.'

The garden has become suddenly small. My mother standing there with the green ribbed hose-pipe and my father with his hand on the brim of his straw hat, could quite easily have been mistaken in that instant for wax models.

'She has someone else,' says my mother to my father, as though I were out of earshot. '*Elle nous a quittés* . . . She's not with us any more.'

I say nothing, but I nod in the silence in the garden and my father hears me. My mother says, 'I've folded back the bedspread in your room.'

'I think I'll have a rest,' I say and I stand up. I take the empty glass from my father's hand. I take the half-full one from my mother's hand, because I know that now she will not drink it. I put them on the tray and I turn round to walk inside aware that all the time, all the way to the French windows at the other end of the long garden, their eyes are on my back.

I take off my suede sandals to walk upstairs. At the top on the landing the carpet is scratchy beneath my feet. I push open the yellow painted door to my bedroom. To the room that was my bedroom with the single bed and the purple flowers on the wall. With the picture of my little sister and me on the dresser. My little sister who had grown up with my hands over her ears, so that she could choose a different path. So that she could become a writer without detour. Straight from university.

Suddenly exhausted, I flop down on the yellow nylon bedspread that has been folded back. I close my eyes and turn to face the wall. The mattress feels lumpy and uncomfortable and sleep evades me. Perhaps because I am overtired. Perhaps because the acoustics in the room are as sensitive as they always were, and through the walls as I lie in this single bed I hear the sharpness and shrillness of raised voices. Even though, when I go to check, there is no-one in the bedroom next door. Even though it is the middle of the day and my parents are still outside on the back lawn.

And when I climb back into bed I stare at the walls and I see where they bulge under the paper, where the paint is cracked close to the skirting-board. And I realize that the angry words and the raised voices must just have stayed there all these years, throwing themselves against the layers of plaster of the walls, fighting to rip the paper and to crack the paint, desperate to get out and evaporate into thin air.

'I don't think I'll be able to come back for a while after this,' I say the next morning, spreading marmalade. 'The autumn is a crazy season for conferences in New York. It would be nice if the two of you came to visit me again in Manhattan.'

'Now that's an idea,' says my father in his navy pyjamas, pulling the butter dish towards him.

'Perhaps,' says my mother, pulling it back and looking suddenly old, 'but I suppose you won't really have time now that you have someone else.'

She says that 'someone else', even though I have told her nothing of Nicholas. But she is my mother and she has sensed it. She says it as though she and Paul were one. As though in leaving him I have betrayed her, because he, this 'someone else', this as yet unnamed unconfirmed figure, was not in her master plan for me. He is an unnecessary outsider, an unknown entity and even after all these years, for my mother, strangers are a threat. Sinister until proven otherwise.

July 29th

'Paul Ellis,' he says. 'Hello. Who is this please?'

'It's me.'

I can hear the background noise of the trading floor. Even over the phone I can hear the figures frisbeed through the air from desk to desk. I can feel the urgency in the air that is pregnant with profit and loss.

'Dom?'

'Yes.'

'What on earth are you doing up? It's the middle of the night for you.'

'No it's not. I'm here.'

'What do you mean?'

'Here in London. At my parents. I'm . . .'

He lets out a shriek. A sound not dissimilar to those I have heard when he checks his computer screen and sees that his shares have hit the roof.

'Why didn't you tell me you were coming? When did you land? You wanted to surprise me didn't you?'

'Paul, I . . .'

'D'you hear that guys? Dominique's in town . . . Hey wait a minute. I'm not going to be able to get out of tonight. My parents are taking me out for an early birthday celebration, because they're away next week. You'll have to come with us. They'll be so excited that you're home. I can't believe this. Hang on.' His voice is slightly fainter. He moves away from the mouthpiece for a moment and then comes back.

'What? How much? . . . Sorry Dom I've got to go. The Footsie's going mad here. I'll pick you up at 8. 30.'

I sat by the phone at my father's mahogany desk that was piled high with medical books. I stayed there staring at the dark grey cover of a book entitled *The Psyche*, until I found the strength to pick up the black receiver from the old-fashioned telephone, to call again so I could tell him that dinner with his parents was quite out of the question. That I absolutely needed to speak to him alone. That his interpretation of my unexpected visit was all wrong.

'Sorry, Ellis is out of the office.'

'When will he be back?'

'Not for the rest of the day. He's out with the partners.'

I call him on his mobile. It rings and rings. I envisage him in some boardroom somewhere, pressing his phone to his ear, hearing me say, 'I need to see you alone,' and guessing what is coming. In my mind I see the colour draining from his ruddy cheeks. I see his colleagues turning to stare at him. His mobile phone goes on ringing and ringing till a recorded message says, 'The number you have called has not responded. Please try later.' I hang up.

Later from the upstairs window I watch him draw up in his low silver sports car. I feel a strain as I stare out of the window. The strain of the child craning her neck to look for a car that is similar in colour. Standing there after almost all the other children have been collected outside the school gates, making bets with myself. Betting that if I can balance on one leg for more than thirty seconds, then this time I will be the second last and not the last child to be picked up. But invariably my leg begins to wobble. I lose my bet. The other straggler's mother arrives and I am still there in my green jacket and beret waiting for that overwhelming rush of relief as I hear my mother hoot her horn.

Paul hoots too. He hoots three or four times, but the effect of the sounds is quite different now as I stand there resting my head against the cool pane of glass of my parents' bedroom window. I walk out of their room. I look into the yellow and purple bedroom where I spent the night and shut the door firmly behind me. I walk down the stairs, across the hallway. I unlock the front door from the inside and pull it firmly closed from the outside. I turn my back on the house and I walk down the front path towards his car. He leans over to open the passenger door. He pulls me in and he stretches to put his arms round me. But he can't quite reach. It is awkward to hug in such a sports car. The seats are low and far apart.

'I can't believe you're here,' he says. 'Let me look at you.'

'It's only been a few weeks,' I say.

He revs the engine.

'We're so late. They'll be waiting for us. I haven't told them you're here. I wanted to surprise them.'

I talk all the way. I babble from Ladbroke Grove to Little Venice to avoid conversation. We drive up alongside the canal towards the restaurant and park the car. As we get out, through the window of one of the barges at the edge of the canal, I see a couple standing holding each other. The reflection of the light from the window makes a diamond shape on the black water. The music that wafts from the barge is classical. A Mozart concerto.

I turn away and begin to run up the hill towards the restaurant. Paul has to lock his car and remove his radio. He calls out, 'Dom, hang on. Wait for me. Why are you running?'

I am breathless, almost at the door of the restaurant, drawn by the promise of momentary refuge like a blue-bottle to a light-bulb. Paul catches up with me inside. He grabs my arm. 'Dominique what is . . . ?'

But the waiter is already pointing to our table in the far right-hand corner. As though she has heard him point, Paul's mother, sitting with her back to me, turns round. She opens her bright pink mouth wide. She stands up with her arms open to envelop me. And I feel as she crushes me against the diamanté buttons of her pink suit that I am accepting this embrace under false pretences.

'We didn't know,' she says, shaking her head. 'How exciting.' 'Yes, exciting,' says Paul's father from behind his ginger beard. 'We didn't know. Why didn't you tell us, Paul?'

Behind me now, he says, 'I didn't tell you Dad, because I didn't know either. She surprised me.'

We sit down and I am in the corner squashed by the table with my back to the wall. I am hemmed in, but facing outwards and I am grateful for the clatter of knives and forks, for the loudness of the conversations on either side of us, for the fact that Italian restaurants do not dictate decorum. All three of them have their bodies turned towards me. But Paul's mother at first chooses to chatter and not to ask questions. Sitting there in her pink suit she talks in a loud voice between slurps of minestrone about the failing health of her Highland terrier, and every time she parts her lips I see where the pink lipstick has rubbed off on her teeth. And I am just beginning to feel a little safer, to consider that I might get through this evening without incident and be able afterwards to sit alone with Paul and break it to him in the way that the textbooks say one should, when the main course arrives. Paul's mother struggles to pierce the stem of a button mushroom with her fork. She misses once, twice but on the third go the prong shoots straight through the stem and as it hits the mushroom's centre she looks at me and says, 'So you came specially for Paul's birthday?'

'Well, actually I um . . . I um came for . . .'

'Can I pour you some more wine?' says the waiter, appearing again between me and Paul. He leans over me to fill my glass. The smell from under his spotless white jacket hits me hard.

'Dominique, you look a little pale,' says Paul's father. 'It must be the jet lag.'

Paul puts his hand on my left shoulder. The jet lag grips tighter. The restaurant begins to swim. I feel myself turn green. I get up. I push my way past him. His father has to stand up to let me through. I say, 'Sorry I must get some air.' As I make for the door of the restaurant the lights go down. Ahead of me, to my right from the direction of the kitchen, I see flickering candles. The waiter moves past me towards our table with Paul's birthday cake as I move towards the door. Paul has followed me out. As I am standing with my head over the edge of the pavement, I hear the restaurant break into song. I hear the chorus of 'Happy Birthday Dear Paul', as he stands there next to me by the gutter while his cake with the thirty candles approaches the table. I take a few deep breaths. I open my mouth, not at first to vomit as Paul thought I would, but to say 'Happy birthday'. But I am shocked by the words that I hear. Words that without preamble push their way up and out of me on the edge of this pavement. They come straight from the gut and I am powerless to stop them. They spill onto the pavement, as ugly to Paul as the sound of my retching.

'I have someone else. I'm so sorry, Paul. I have someone else.'

Lugano, July 30th

I flew over mountain peaks on my way to Lugano. The plane with its ten passengers felt light. A hang-glider in comparison to the jumbo in which I had flown from New York to London. There was a slight wind but the sky was clear. Fifteen minutes away from Lugano, the captain said, 'Ladies and gentlemen, on your right as we approach you will see the bay of Lake Lugano beneath us and the mountains San Salvatore on your left side and Monte Bre on your right.' As he spoke in my head I could not help but translate his words simultaneously into French.

The seat next to me was empty and I moved across to look out of the window. The pilot flew low over the lakes and the mountains. Even now, even in the height of summer, the peaks were coated in white.

I felt the plane's contact with the wind. I saw by the movement of the wings how we tilted to the left and the right. How we were jostled a little in one direction and then in another. I caught sight of the white line traced by a plane that had passed close by and I thought then how ingenious it was that despite a plethora of uncertainties in the sky, despite the fact that the control was in our hands only in as much as we had chosen to take this flight, we would still land at the port for which we were destined.

I was afraid, normally, in the air. Excited and afraid. But something in the captain's voice had calmed me. A confident reassuring voice. Intonation that was familiar. English spoken with a slightly Italian accent. I smiled to myself. In a few days I would be back in Manhattan.

Lugano airport is tiny and pristine. Between the small silver baggage belt and the arrival hall there is a huge window. Her nose squashed against the glass, her red lips pressed against it in a kiss that she leaves behind when she sees me, Anna is there waiting. As I push my trolley with my black suitcase round the corner, she comes towards me, smiling, her blonde streaked hair clipped on top of her head. She walks to the foot of my trolley, she hugs me and she says, 'You did it, didn't you?'

'Did what?'

'You ended it.'

'How do you know?'

'You don't need to be a rocket scientist, *cara mia*. I see it in your eyes.'

We walk out of the airport, our arms around each other. She is wearing a sleeveless grey T-shirt. The green butterfly tattoo on her right arm has faded a little. As always she is in jeans.

'You don't rip them any more.'

'Something has to change for me too.'

Night falls fast in southern Switzerland. The sky darkens, even as we drive for ten minutes uphill in her little grey Fiat, from the airport out of Lugano to her late father's house in the village of Muzzano. After New York and London, I am struck by the inky blackness of the country roads.

'You're too tired to talk about it tonight, aren't you?' she says.

'I suppose I am.'

Anna presses a button on the tape deck.

The deep late-night voice of an Italian singer says . . . *'Chissa, chissa, domani su che cosa meteremo le mani . . .'* We have no clue, no clue at all about tomorrow . . .

We are comfortable in silence, Anna and I, even though we have not seen each other for weeks. Because ours is one of those seamless friendships. One of those friendships that laughs at the idea that time creates distance. That distance over time creates barriers. And anyway it is the night before a heavy conference and we have learnt in the past not to speak of emotional things on those nights, because sleep is crucial. Because there is nothing worse than lying awake, stimulated by deep conversation, but begging for sleep, on the nights before a conference. When you know that if your mind is not rested the struggle for the right words the next day will be a physical one.

And so when we arrive at the house that I can barely see from the outside, Anna keeps the lights dim as she leads me to my room with its grey brick walls and wooden floors. She strikes a match and lights a candle for me at the small rosewood dressing-table where she has left me the papers for the next morning's conference. She brings me a hot chocolate in a dark green cup with gold edging and I sit down to look at the documents for a few minutes before I go to sleep.

'We'll talk about everything tomorrow,' she says. 'Dom . . . I'm so pleased you're here.'

'So am I.' And as she leaves the room I think to myself that throughout your life there are really no more than a handful of people with whom you feel truly safe. With whom you can be who you are.

'Oh I forgot to tell you,' she says, one foot already out of the room. 'You'll be in the booth with Marcus Schaller.'

Anna and I like to work in adjacent booths. I was afraid, always, at interpreting school when we worked together in the same booth, that she would make me laugh at a crucial moment. That, as on one occasion while I interpreted, she looked at me with a twinkle in her eye as if to say, 'What is this speaker on?' my voice would begin to shake with the threat of imminent laughter.

I have worked with Marcus Schaller before. Once in Zurich, just after I qualified. And I remember that he is a brilliant interpreter. That he picks up every note and nuance. That he has dark blue eyes and he is blind. There are a few blind interpreters in the profession but he is the only one I have ever worked with. When Anna and I arrive at the low modern steely-blue building of the congress centre the next morning and I pull open the cardboard door of the booth he is already sitting there waiting.

He turns round and I reach for his hand and say, 'Hello Marcus, Dominique Green. We worked together last year in Zurich.'

'Yes of course. I remember. How nice to see you again, Dominique.'

As I sit down next to him it strikes me that language caters only for the mainstream. That he is forced to use a word that never has, never can, never will correspond to his reality. But of course it is my thinking there in the tiny booth that is limited, because Schaller has turned the word '*see*' into a three-dimensional one. He has invested those three letters with the senses of sound, of smell and of touch. He has given them depth.

This is not, for once, a medical conference, but a sociological one. The delegates at this conference are historians and politicians. Here to discuss the Swiss immigration policy and the changes in attitude to foreigners over the last fifty years. In his darkness Schaller begins. He translates an octogenarian German-speaking woman, a Holocaust survivor who escaped across the Alps . . . a bent-over old woman with thick white hair who tells of how the Swiss let her in, but turned her family away. She has talked for half an hour and I turn to raise my eyebrows at Schaller to ask him if I should take over before I remember. And I am just about to tap him on the shoulder when I see him feel his watch. He turns to me and touches my arm. I close my eyes and begin to translate. The old woman is followed by an historian who says that whilst he sympathizes he feels that people forget that the Swiss, all those years ago, had a much more lenient policy towards refugees than any other country, that if they turned any away it could only have been because the country was bursting at the seams. I translate literally. I render each sentence as I should in its grammatical form. I open the relevant drawers in my brain for the most accurate phrase to convert his meanings from one language to another. I try to copy the cadence of the speaker's phrases as he says that no country can laud themselves in this respect as much as the Swiss. The speaker runs with his words. Had he talked a little more slowly I might have had time to remember the story I had heard once in the pink bathtub of how my great-aunt and uncle as teenagers on a freezing February day were almost allowed over the border in the Alps from Germany. Almost but not quite. But the speaker galloped and all that filtered through between words were the childhood images of ice and snow and begging at the border. And though, as I work, I am faithful in my translation, in my tone I am a traitor. I can feel how I wrap each word in irony. How I coat each sentence in cynicism.

We break for coffee. Before we get up Schaller turns to me, smiles and says, 'That is not the voice I heard last year.'

'Sorry?'

'You are a brilliant interpreter, but there'll come a point when our profession will no longer suit you, Dominique. You'll walk away from it.'

His words startle me. 'Why do you say that?'

He laughs. 'Oh I don't know. It's hard to explain . . . It's as if you've stopped merging with the speaker when you interpret. You're more than just an echo these days. You're Dominique translating other people's words.' He pushes back his chair. He puts his hand through his hair. He straightens his tie. 'Are you coming for a coffee?'

'I won't have one now, but I'll walk to the hall with you and then come back and cram in some of this vocab.'

I stand up and he says, 'You don't need to worry about

me. I know this place like the back of my hand. You stay here and do your stuff.'

He opens the door and then turns back.

'Is the light on in here?' he asks me.

'No.'

He reaches for the right-hand side of the desk and clicks the switch on the reading-lamp. 'You'll ruin your eyes without it,' he says and he walks out and leaves me alone in the booth.

Anna and I lunch with the delegates. The experience as always is a claustrophobic one, for you invariably find yourself stuck between a French and a German speaker, rotating your head from left to right translating the most inane of niceties. And so am I here at this long white table sandwiched between two ageing academics relaying vacuous comment on the clemency of the climate, between mouthfuls of trifle.

I look up. I see Anna refusing coffee. She catches my eye, smiles, and cocks her head to the side. The movement means 'let's get out of here.' We have half an hour left of our lunch break. We excuse ourselves and slink out of the dining-room, out of the conference hall, and turn left along a tree-lined street. We cross Lugano's cobbled central square, Piazza della Riforma, where, Parisian-style, people watch the world go by at outdoor cafés.

'Shall we?' she says, pointing to an empty table.

'No, I need to walk a bit,' I say. 'It was suffocating in there.'

We walk by the lake with the park's manicured lawns on one side and the still and sparkling water on the other.

'Schaller said some things that really troubled me.'

'What?'

'Later,' I say. Because I have looked at my watch. The

212

one whose strap has started to irritate the skin on my wrist. I have seen that we only have ten minutes and I need to empty my head of my personal thoughts before we go back, lest they should interfere with other people's words.

'Before dinner,' she says, 'I'm going to take you up there for a drink.' She gesticulates across the water, her tattooed arm outstretched towards a cleft between two mountains. 'It's called La Forca. The views are unbelievable . . . Apparently they hung people there till a couple of centuries ago.'

'Hanged,' I say, walking fast now.

'What?'

'They hanged people there. Hanged is the past of hung, if it's a neck in a noose, not a picture on a hook.'

And Anna, with her Eliza Doolittle English, smiles, amused that for once I have found a mistake to correct. 'I knew you'd get me one day,' she says as we quicken our pace in the heat, alike for once in our sleeveless dresses, by the water, through the gardens, back through the piazza to make it to the conference hall in time for the session that lasts till early evening.

She has not exaggerated the views from La Forca. High up. Hundreds and hundreds of feet above the lake. Opposite us the sheer sharp drop of mountains into the water. We are close to the white railing. 'Look,' she says, 'come here, Dom. Isn't it incredible?'

Incredible, yes. Even more so than the views from the plateau above Zurich. I feel the same sense of awe. But this place, I think, leaning against the railing next to Anna, could not be my oasis like the plateau above Zurich or the Frick in Manhattan. This place inspires *angst*, not peace. I feel not sheltered by its beauty, but exposed.

'I never knew I suffered from vertigo,' I say to Anna.

'You do?'

'It makes me dizzy to look down there. Imagine falling.'

'Imagine jumping,' she says. 'You know the literal meaning of vertigo, don't you?'

'Fear of heights,' I say, on familiar territory. Anna and I playing with words.

'No,' she says. 'Aha. Got you back for the hanged and the hung. Vertigo means fear of wanting to fall. I read it the other day,' she says, looking over the precipice.

'There's a long way to go. I think they tossed the prisoners over the side once they'd hanged them here.'

We sit down at a table close to the edge and she says, 'Tell me. Tell me everything.'

'No, you tell me about Mischa first.'

'I will,' she says with a fatalistic nod of the head. 'But I want to hear about you. About how you plucked up the courage to end it. My brave friend.'

She calls the waiter. She doesn't ask me what I want. She just orders for both of us. She asks for two bellinis. I smile, because now, when she speaks for me, I notice it.

'Delicious,' she says when they arrive.

I start to tell her about London. About those minutes outside the restaurant with my head over the gutter.

'Don't,' she says.

'Don't what?'

'You know, I don't want you getting miserable before the evening's started.'

'You're making rules.'

'Pardon?'

'About what we can talk about and what we can't talk about.'

But maybe it is better that Anna has made these rules, that she will not let me speak to her of Paul, because only in time does love's death come into focus. Only in time do you understand that the outgrowing of someone, the knowing that there is no oxygen left for the two of you together, still lends no meaning to the words, 'That part of my life is gone. Wiped out.' Over time you have moulded one another. He is not wiped out of you. Nor you of him. He is in your history and in the lines around your eyes. A part of what the next man loves.

Anna sips her drink. 'Nicholas,' she says. 'Tell me about Nicholas.'

Over the water the sky is turning orange. Amber almost. I see the streets of Manhattan. I see the dark brown pews of the church on Madison Avenue. I see him behind me in the booth.

'What are your plans?' she asks, smiling.

'What do you mean?'

'With Nicholas?'

I laugh. 'Anna, you sound like a Jewish grandmother.'

'Have you discussed it?'

'Not specifically. Not in so many words . . . I don't suppose one has to put everything into words.'

'No, not everything . . . but eventually you might have to . . . You're somehow more at peace though, aren't you?'

I raise my eyebrows.

'More than you were in Zurich.'

'With him, yes I suppose I am.' The white fizz of the bellini has loosened my tongue. 'But totally at peace? I don't know. Is anyone ever totally at peace? I'm not sure. I mean there are things on my mind. I tell him a lot. Most things. But not everything. Not absolutely everything.'

'So what dark secrets do you have to keep from him?' Anna asks laughing.

I lift my glass and drain the last drops. The sky is black now.

'Well there are some things I don't talk about,' I say.

'Like what?'

'Like . . . you know . . . confidential stuff. Stuff you overhear at conferences.'

'I've never overheard anything.'

'I did . . . once.'

'What?'

From inside the bar, they have switched on the lights. The glare of a bulb is on my face. Uncomfortable, I am forced to screw up my eyes.

'Months ago. At the beginning of the year. At the end of a conference at Landmark. Some hushed conversation about a whiz-kid who'd stumbled on an idea for treatment. Something about wanting to stop him from disclosing details for a while. I don't know. I didn't get it all.'

'Who were these people?'

'I don't know. I didn't see them.'

'What treatment were they talking about?'

'HIV, I think.'

I can't see her properly. My view is obscured by the light in my eyes, but I hear her say, 'You never told me.'

'No.'

'You told someone though, didn't you? What you had heard. You must have told someone at Landmark to get onto it. Didn't you, Dominique?'

'No.'

'What?'

'No . . . no, you know, confidentiality and all that stuff . . . I . . .'

Silence. Silence that grips you round the neck, winds

you, paralyses you. And then in the semi-blackness, almost in a whisper she says, 'You're not serious are you?'

'Anna . . . don't you remember what they drummed into us? Your vows are as solemn as the Hippocratic oath, as sacred as the nun's marriage to Jesus? What was I supposed to do?' I feel a black knot in the pit of my stomach. I feel the tears well up.

But it is Anna and not me who begins to sob. Loud angry sobs as she bangs her fist on the table. Sobs that are uncontrolled and uninhibited. 'You . . . don't have a clue . . . do you? Not a clue. You don't . . . understand,' she wails. 'Don't you have a voice?'

And it is on the word *voice* that the sound of splintering crosses the table as the tall thin glass crushes in her hand.

I hear the screech of her chair. I see the back of her moving fast and disappearing round the side of the bar. For a moment I am unable to move. And then I am up and running. And at nightfall, high up, in this place they once used as gallows I am calling after her. 'Anna, Anna, *dove sei* . . . where are you? Where are you?'

Inside the building, at the door of the ladies' toilets, I hear her gulping still. I see the streaks of blood against the white sink and Anna crouched down on the floor, her face in her hands.

They carried disinfectant and a bandage in their first-aid kit at the bar. The fright had stopped her sobs and she let me wash the blood from her hand and wrap the gauze around it. She let me drive her car down the mountain. We sat there, not now in stony silence, but in the silence that follows shock. And I was just about to ask her to direct me back to her house when she said, 'Take a right here.' The bend in the road is sharp. I turn the wheel, turn the corner and she says, 'Now a left. Keep going.'

For three or four minutes I keep going, fixed on the road ahead, unused to driving.

'It's just here on the left,' she says.

'What is?'

'The restaurant.'

'The restaurant?'

'We need to talk.'

'Don't you want to go home?'

'I'm fine.'

The typical Tessin restaurant is called a grotto. Underground in the one-time wine cellars of the old grey stone buildings with wooden beams, almost no light, and acoustics that lend themselves to hushed tones, you sit on benches at wooden tables. The austerity of the atmosphere is designed to focus your mind on your palate. I remember nothing of what we ate that night. I remember only saying to the waiter that yes, it was delicious, he shouldn't be offended that I hadn't really eaten. I didn't have much appetite.

Anna wants to know. She wants me to repeat the words that I heard months ago verbatim. She begs me. She takes my hands in her one good hand and shakes them as though they were linked to the nerve endings of my memory. I tell her. I tell her everything I remember of a conversation that lasted all of a minute. And I begin to explain why I said nothing to anyone. Why probably there was nothing to it. Why anyway, even if there was it is highly unlikely to have made a difference to Mischa. She stops me. Not angry now. Her tone more gentle now, but firm, and leaning across the table she looks me straight in the eye and she says, 'I want a promise from you.'

'What?'

'Tell me you'll say yes, whatever it is.'

'I'll say yes. I promise.'

'I want you to find out when you go back. I want you to find out if it was someone in Landmark and what they have. We have to know. You can't just let this go, Dominique . . . Promise me.'

I am silent for a moment.

'Dominique,' she says.

'I promise. But where do I start?'

'Ask Nicholas,' she says. 'He'll help you.'

Lugano to Zurich, August 1st

'Paradiso,' says Anna the next morning as she pulls up outside Lugano's pink station building.

'Pardon?'

'The name of the station . . . Paradiso,' she says, and points to the blue plaque on the pink wall that bears the words 'Stazione Lugano-Paradiso'. She is not taking the train to Zurich with me as we had planned. She says she has things to tidy up in her late father's house before she goes back. But I know she wants me to see Mischa alone. She thinks that will make me keep my promise. She hugs me when she says goodbye. Against my bare arm I feel the gauze of her bandage.

Everything changes in those three hours northwards from Lugano to Zurich. The south of Switzerland is a different world from the north. At first, through the outskirts of Lugano, Locarno, Bellinzona, I bathed my face in the hot sun that streamed through the half-open window. I closed my eyes and conjured up the beach at Amagansett the morning after the Landmark party. I hear a rustling and feel a touch on my arm. The fat woman in red opposite me has unfolded the silver paper of her salami sandwiches and is passing them around. I decline, close my eyes again, hear the chatter around me in Italian. For once freed from the need to listen I make no attempt to take in the words. I wallow instead in the sounds, in the music of the language.

Even with your eyes closed you can sense a change in the light. I knew as we entered the tunnel cut into the mountain range that separates north from south. I felt the rattle of the carriage and sensed without seeing that we were in darkness. I pulled my cardigan around me. It was cold suddenly and though it can have been no more than ten minutes, it seemed to me as though I was in darkness for much, much longer.

And I knew, too, when we moved out of the tunnel. The light touched my eyelids and though when I opened my eyes the fat woman in red with her salami sandwiches and her fellow-travellers had got up to leave, and though when I looked out of the window the blinding sunshine of the Tessin had been left behind, there was a beauty too in the sky that had replaced it. More still perhaps, less dazzling, but somehow more real.

Going back to where you used to live brings with it a strange feeling. Getting off at the bottom of the hill close to the university at the tram stop, I wanted to say to the driver, 'I'm not a tourist, you know. I used to live here. This tram stop used to be mine.'

I stepped onto the tree-lined street that I had been dragged along by Anna when I first arrived in Zurich. Mischa still lived in the same building as Peter and Karl, though not now in the same apartment. His surname, Eisner, is written next to the bottom bell. I ring and he buzzes me into the building. He lives on the ground floor now. He is lucky that the landlord was prepared to redecorate the two-room apartment and rent it to him. Close to Mischa's front door I walk past a silver stand that contains a green umbrella and a walking-stick.

The door is ajar. I hear him call, 'Come in, Dominique.' I push the door, step tentatively into the narrow sky-blue hallway.

'Mischa?'

'I'm in here. On your left.'

I walk into the lounge. He is sitting by a healthy yucca plant at the far side of the living-room. The shutters are half closed. He lifts his head. I suppress the gasp that threatens me. Stock-still, he looks at me, and I at him. Ten seconds. Maybe fifteen. Till I run across the room and throw my arms around him.

And so it is not while I am still looking at him from the other side of the room, but only while I hide my face with my forehead against his collarbone that I admit to myself what I have seen. A young man in a grey track suit with a shaven skull. A face that seems as though he is sucking in the sides of his cheeks. And across the skin that once was milky-white a purple patch that has crept its way from the side of his mouth to the corner of his right eye. And it is not while I am hugging him, but only as I draw back that I know I have felt the sharp fragility of his fading.

And now of course there is no escape. Neither for him, nor for me. In this high ceilinged room with walls that are painted an off-white oyster colour Mischa and I must look one another in the eye.

'Was it selfish of me to let you come, Dom?'

'What a ridiculous question. Have you lost your mind?'

'Not yet.'

A silence and then, 'Dom, you look fabulous.'

'Thank you . . . and you . . .'

I had no idea when I began my sentence how it would end. He interrupts me. He spares me the searching.

'What? I don't look too bad? I haven't changed that much in a few months? You're sure my skin will clear up with some ointment.'

'I wasn't going to say that, Mischa.'

He closes his eyes, lets out a sigh.

'I'm sorry, Dom. I didn't mean to . . .'

I hold up my hand. 'Forget it.'

'Dom, I really am very happy to see you. You know that don't you?'

I smile. I nod. I know he is speaking the truth.

'I have a surprise for you,' he says.

'What?'

And he reminds me that today is August 1 and every year on Swiss Independence Day, over the lake there is a firework display to music.

'You want to go?'

'I'd love to. But can you? I mean, are you . . . are you up to it?'

'We, my lovely Dominique,' he says between deliberate steps towards his walking-stick, 'are going to paint the town red.'

Huge wide red brush strokes that rocket upwards into the sky from the deck of a ship on the lake of Zurich. Pink and purple spirals that scrawl their celebration in the black air, as we watch sitting next to one another packed amongst people on a low stone wall. Green and gold concentric circles that burst one by one into the night. And as though he has timed it on purpose, between explosions, with the gasps and exclamations of pleasure from the crowds Mischa shouts, 'I experimented you know . . . with the drugs.'

Another burst of colour. Beautiful. Breathtaking.

'I left it too late to take them. Did my own medical research.'

And then everything together. The pink and the purple scrawls. The reds that rocket upwards. The gold and green explosions. Deafening as the echo in the dark of Mischa's name, as the all too brief display ricochets downwards towards the water, dissipates and drowns.

THIRTY

Nicholas

The Velvet Room in uptown Manhattan is a late-night place. In the orangey glow of the bar, the burgundies, the auburns and the dark greens of the sofas and the armchairs are plush and inviting. Dominique arrived back from Zurich in the early evening. A meeting kept me at Landmark till after nine and though I knew she would be at the Velvet Room before me, I walked slowly from work. I wanted the blocks between Fifty-Fourth and Seventy-First Street to underline my working day, to separate the frenzy and the fumes of midtown from my meeting with Dominique. The bar was full of people and the sounds of jazz after dark. She had chosen the left-hand corner of a low sofa to wait for me. She sat there, a pen in her hand, paper on her lap, a glass by her side. I watched amused as a man in jeans approached her, leant towards her, asking, hoping to sink into the low seat next to her. She gesticulated towards the door. She looked up and she saw me.

I realized then that some small part of this woman with the dark brown silk top that fell slightly off one shoulder and the deep brown silky hair that fell over the other, was still a stranger to me. The thought in no way troubled me. It excited me rather, not having seen her for some days, to stand at the other side of the room and watch her watch me in this late-night light.

I walked over to her, touched the velvet of the sofa with one hand, her face with the other. 'Dominique.'

'Nicholas.'

Her fingers on my lips and mine on hers. A tacit under-standing that tonight is not the night for me to ask and her to talk. That tonight we will tell little of the previous days. That there are other ways of speaking. Beside me, against me, she sips her brandy. I order one too. The music has changed. From jazz to classical.

'Bach,' she says.

'Bach's what?'

'His *Musical Offering*,' she says.

'I'm not convinced.'

'Excuse me waiter,' she says, 'do you know by any chance, what this tape is?'

He smiles, disappears, returns.

'Bach . . . *Musical Offering*.'

'Thank you.'

I laugh, defeated. She laughs, triumphant.

'I have Bach's *Musical Offering* at home somewhere. I should have known. By the way, Dom, I heard a piece of Schubert's piano music that made me think of you the other day.'

'What was it?'

'His *Wanderer Fantasy* . . . I have it in my apartment. I'll let you hear it later.'

'Your etchings,' she says.

'My what?' My English doesn't yet stretch to that level of idiom. She has to explain. We want to leave. Both of us.

The late-night summer rain is hot and heavy. The Velvet Room is uptown. My apartment is downtown. She sees a cab. I lift my hand to hail it. It drives past, splashing us. We begin to run. Hand in hand where we can. Letting go to circumvent the obstacles on the pavement.

The water makes it hard to hear. I have to shout almost.

'The wanderer,' I say, running home in the rain beside her.

'What did you say?'

'You're the wanderer.'

Sixty-Fifth Street. Sixty-Fourth. Another cab slows down next to us.

'Macdougal Street please.'

Up a flight of stairs to my apartment. Breathless.

Inside the front door. In our soaking clothes.

'You . . . are the wanderer . . . between countries and languages . . . Wait . . . I'll put it on.'

'No, the Bach. I want to hear the Bach from the Velvet Room. You said you had it.'

Though it is midsummer, I light the fire because the air is cooler now and we are both dripping wet. In the semi-darkness I look for the music she wants to hear. I am focused until I find it. I do not notice where she is, but as the notes of a lone violin fill the room, I turn round and she is standing by the door. For a moment we are both very still. She has never done this before. Framed by the doorway, a sculpture, an offering. And I, as a second strain of music joins the first, am still in my clothes. Half dry now in the heat. Half wet still. And for the few moments that it lasts she trusts the imbalance. She is unafraid of its vulnerability. She kneels down close to me. The violins of Bach's *Musical Offering* are met by deeper notes. A cello. They touch one another's sound. Mingle with her words. In my language and then hers. Her voice, that I have not heard like this before. At first a whisper. Stronger then. Though a little quieter than the music, that has slowed down, moving with the flames. Asking, telling. Where and when. Wanting now to be listened to. A new language I did not know she knew. As natural, when she is ready, as the others that she speaks. From somewhere a flute playing with the strings. Between them. Above them. Sounds that are faster now and sure. Confident that you are there, enveloped, caught up with them. Knowing where they are carrying you and taking you there. Both of you with the music, in a trance of heat and darkness. Louder though and freer. Cries that meet, abandoned as they join. Voices. Together. Hers and mine.

THIRTY-ONE

Dominique

He lifts first his shoulder, then his elbow. He brings his hand close to the right side of his face and moves it slowly downwards from his cheekbone to his jaw. Not that I can see his face, though he if he wanted could see mine. He must think I am still asleep or else he would have said '*Ciao bella.*' He would have come over to where I lie under the soft feathers of his navy duvet in his king-size bed. On his side of the bed so that I am almost directly opposite the bathroom door. So that I can watch him from behind in the light that filters through from the small bathroom window. So that I can imagine the alternate roughness and smoothness of his face. And I wish as I lie there, that it was Saturday or Sunday. That we could stroll through SoHo, buy the *New York Times*, find a place to brunch and sit reading snippets out loud to each other. Because I love to listen to him read to me in English with that accent. The way he has to blow to pronounce his h's, the way he rolls his r's a little like the pilot on the way to Lugano. But it is neither Saturday nor Sunday and this morning Nicholas is trying to be extra quiet because I am not working today and it is only 6.30 a.m.

6.30 in New York. 12.30 in Zurich. 12.30 still, according to my body clock.

'Good morning,' I call towards the bathroom, smiling.

He starts and turns around, one shaven stripe on his right cheek. So that when he faces me, I see little more than his nose and his black eyes.

'*Ciao bella*, I didn't mean to wake you. I'm sorry. I should have shut the bathroom door.' He walks towards me, leans over me, leaves a little of the white shaving foam on my lips. 'It's fine,' I say as I prop myself up against the pillows, warm, relaxed, lazy. Happy watching him back at the sink again now, sensing him looking in the mirror at my reflection in the shadow of the bedroom.

He laughs. 'You interpreters. In bed all day. *La bella vita* . . . and I'm late already. We have a 7.15 meeting. I have to get there on time.'

Perhaps it is the word *time* that jars, that jolts me, that reminds me of my promise.

'Nicholas.'

'Mmmmm,' he answers, distracted in the way one is when focusing at the same time on a physical activity.

'I need you to do me a favour.'

'Sure.'

'Do you know everything that goes on inside Landmark?'

'Not everything,' he says and then pauses. He has moved his arm further across. He must be shaving his upper lip now. 'Not everything, but lots. You get to hear what's happening in other departments.'

'D'you know anything about a new HIV treatment?'

In mid-stroke his arm freezes for a second. 'What?'

'Some discovery they haven't developed yet. Something someone's holding close to his chest.'

'Close to his chest?' he calls, without turning round.

I translate for him. '*Qualcosa che qualcuno si tiene stretta.*'

229

He runs the tap water now and I have to wait for an answer.

'Why d'you ask?'

'Long story but I need to know.'

'*Per che cosa?* . . . What for?' He has slipped into his mother tongue. One does that at difficult moments in the first years in a foreign country. But there is no reason why this moment should be a difficult one for Nicholas, apart of course from the fact that he is late and he's rushing and he has sensed that I'm tense.

'Nicholas, I need to know, because, because . . .'

I'm sitting up straight now, no longer propped up by the pillows. 'Because . . . can you just ask around a bit and see if you can find out?'

His blue razor still in his hand, he turns round, comes back over to the bed. The right side of his face is shaved now. The left still covered in foam. So that when he looks at me he reminds me of one of those clowns with the painted faces. Half laughing, half crying. Above his lip on the right side I notice a few tiny drops of blood. Next to the bed in his yellow towelling robe now he stands over me.

'What is this all about?'

A sharpness in his voice that I do not know. He's in a hurry of course. He hasn't finished shaving. I feel guilty for bringing it up now. Bad timing. All the same it is strange the first time you hear an edge in someone's voice. When you didn't know it was there. When you had never imagined that tone from his lips. Something twists inside you when you hear that for the first time. I take a deep breath. I put my hand on his neck under the back of his yellow towelling robe. His skin feels wet under my fingers.

'It can wait till later,' I say.

'Dominique. It can't. You can't give me half a story. I need you to talk to me.'

He reminds me of Anna when he says that. Of her taking my hands in hers in the grotto and saying, 'Dominique, tell me. You have to tell me.'

And here in the blue sheets under the soft feather duvet in Nicholas's bed after a night of passion, with him sitting on the edge now, wanting the whole story, I hear everything together in my head at once. The teacher at interpreting school yelling 'Confidentiality . . . Your vows are as solemn as the Hippocratic oath. Anna's voice in my head saying, 'Promise me one thing. Just promise me.' And Mischa between the purple spirals and the concentric gold circles of the fireworks calling, 'I experimented you know . . . with the drugs . . . I left it too late to take them.'

I hear those things but now there is no real dilemma. No choice to be made, because those hours with Mischa have made up my mind and I have promised Anna and anyway I trust Nicholas. He has gained my trust. Slowly over the months. And I know now he will not break it.

I sigh. I lean over. Put my head against his chest for a moment, move back and say, 'I'll tell you. But you can't say that it came from me.'

He says nothing.

'I heard it months ago at a conference.'

'You heard what?' he says stressing the 'what', his voice going up at the end of the sentence. 'Please Dominique.'

'I think . . . I'm not sure, but I think, someone's holding something back for whatever reason.'

'Holding what back?' The way he has closed his hand round the razor blade reminds me of Anna and the glass. I prize his fingers open. He hardly seems to notice.

He repeats himself, 'Holding back what?'

'Some new HIV treatment . . . Nicholas go and finish shaving.'

'Dominique. You heard what, where? Which conference?'

The shaven side of his face has changed colour.

'I heard two men whispering about plans to keep someone quiet about some discovery. To keep it from Landmark. To wait till the time was right and make a fortune with it. That's all I know.'

'How could you have heard that? It's impossible.'

The alarm clock next to the bed begins to ring. A loud ugly ring that reverberates in my head. I lean over to switch it off.

'What do you mean it's impossible?' I ask him.

'Who could you have heard?'

He is speaking as though in a trance, the lateness forgotten. The meeting abandoned. 'Who could have been speaking? Who could you have overheard?'

'Nicholas, do you know something about this?'

He turns to me, looks at me. And it is only in retrospect that I see on his face the expression of a man questioned about his fidelity. It is only in retrospect that I realize he answers my question with a question. 'This has something to do with Mischa, doesn't it?'

'I promised Anna I'd find out. She went crazy when she heard I'd kept my mouth shut all these months. She said it was wrong, awful if this was happening. If the development of a drug was being held back. And she's right. I know she's right.'

He sits up straight. He stands up. He tightens the cord of the yellow towelling robe around his waist. 'I'll see what I can find out,' he says.

'Promise me.'

'I promise.'

He goes into the bathroom to finish shaving and this time he shuts the door behind him.

THIRTY-TWO

Nicholas

In most of our lives there has been a journey that in retrospect remains a total blur. There has been a time when we have dropped everything and have rushed in blind panic to confront or avert disaster.

And a time much later when we have wondered about the details of that journey, about what we said or thought in our state of turmoil in the train or the taxi, on the plane or in the subway. But if at that later point we turn our heads in question, our memories may allow us no more than some dark, disquieting and sweaty sense of those movements between the moment of alert and the moment of arrival. And so I cannot tell you how on that morning I found myself, not sitting in that meeting at Landmark, but waiting instead in the lobby of a West Side high-rise on Columbus and Ninetieth. I imagine that in the thick of the morning traffic I competed for a cab on the corner of Macdougal and Bleeker Street. And I am sure as we crawled bumper to bumper uptown I must have agonized over whether I would arrive at his apartment before he left that day for Washington and that the speeches I rehearsed must have hurtled in my head against the sound of Dominique's voice saying, 'Do you know something about this, Nicholas? Do you know something about this?'

But that is only my imagination, for in truth the only

memory I have of the journey that morning between my home and Tom's, is the memory of panic. I do recall, though, running past the doorman to the elevator, pushing the button turning around and calling behind me, 'Tom Dewar. I'm going up to see Tom Dewar. Which floor is it?'

And I remember the doorman catching up with me and saying, 'Sorry sir. All guests must be announced. I'll call up to Mr Dewar and tell him you're here. Your name is?'

'Manzini. Nicholas Manzini.'

And I stood while he rang Tom's extension with my eyes fixed on one of his embossed gold buttons that hung precariously from a thread on his well-worn navy jacket. Close to the doorman, at the other end of the phone I heard the intonation of surprise in Tom's voice. 'Manzini? Here? Now?'

'Yes sir.'

'Right well . . . er . . . send him up.'

And I thought as I waited in the dark and narrow corridor in front of the grey door of his apartment on the fourteenth floor that this was hardly a building that warranted a doorman. That the man with the faded jacket and the falling gold button was a façade, suggestive of some lifestyle beyond the means of the inhabitants of these apartments. Tom comes to the door, his blond hair wet, his torso bare, a blood-red towel around his waist.

'Nick, what's going on?'

And me, standing there, awkward suddenly at the heavy prison-like door that he has not yet opened wide in welcome.

'Tom. I have to speak to you. I wanted to get you before you left for DC.'

'You just caught me,' he says opening the door wider

now, the question 'What on earth are you doing here?' in fluorescent lettering across his forehead.

'Come in,' he says. 'I was in the shower. I don't have much time Nick, but sit down for a minute,' and then 'what on earth is this about?'

The lounge is light, but box-like. Bare almost except for the huge grey leather sofa and armchair, the black coffee table and a large unfilled vase in a bookcase that is empty save for a few medical journals that lie on one shelf, a book on the New York Marathon and another entitled, *How to Make It Big in Business . . . Ten Easy Steps* that face me, propped up against the wall.

Tom fetches another smaller red towel, comes back, lifts one foot onto the edge of the sofa and begins to dry his calf.

'So Nick, old boy, what's up?'

'I had to talk to you. I remembered you were off to DC today. I had to speak to you before you left.'

'Yes?'

I lean forward. 'I want out, Tom. I don't want to join Zlack. I want out of the agreement.'

'What the hell are you talking about?'

'I don't feel right about it . . . I'd never thought about it like this before. But what I'm doing is wrong.'

'Wrong?'

'Immoral in some ways . . . waiting till I can get out of Landmark. Waiting till my . . . what's it called? Restriction . . . ?'

'Restrictive covenant,' he says, irritation in his voice.

'Till my restrictive covenant has expired and I'm allowed to work with you. Look, I'm not saying that what I've come up with is great. It might be nothing. But what if it is something? What if it might eventually improve some people's lives and here I am waiting till it's the right time for me, to begin to work on it. It just suddenly feels all wrong. Selfish. It's like someone just switched a light on.'

'Are you going soft on me Manzini? You know what, maybe you need to take a break. You need to get away from those cells you're so passionate about. Look at me. 5.30 every day and I'm out of there,' and he begins to dry his other leg.

'I'm serious about this, Tom.'

He looks at me, his expression blank. 'Nick, I hate to throw you out, but we'll have to talk some other time. I need to get dressed and go. My plane leaves at 9.30.'

'Where from?'

'La Guardia.'

'I'm coming with you.'

On his face astonishment. 'To DC?'

'No. To the airport. In the cab. We can talk on the way.'

A silence and then 'Up to you,' and he disappears into the next room.

I must have been in another world because back in the lounge, standing there in his short-sleeved red shirt and his jeans, his black overnight bag in one hand, his briefcase in the other, he startles me.

'OK,' he says, his voice expressionless. 'If you're coming let's go.'

Out of the air-conditioned building, past the doorman, on to the heat of the street. Tom throws his bag onto the back seat of the cab. He jumps in and I follow.

'La Guardia,' he says.

The driver turns around. 'What you say?'

'La Guardia. The airport.'

'OK. Airport.'

He speaks almost no English. He sounds Hispanic. I ask him in Italian if he has understood where we are going. I think of Dominique.

'Did he get it?' Tom asks.

'Yes.'

He leans back in his seat. 'So, what is all this nonsense Nick?'

'Look I made a mistake, Tom. People make mistakes. I should never have signed.'

'What is this crazy attitude all of a sudden?'

'I told you. I don't think it's right to delay the research till I'm free from Landmark.'

His tone changes. He shows a face he has not shown before. A face one doesn't expect from a friend. 'What about your poor little leukaemia babies?' he says. 'I thought you were so loath to leave them.'

'Maybe I can do both. I want to speak to Goldmann.'

'To Goldmann?'

We are on the freeway now. The cab is moving faster.

'I just want to tell him about it. I'll say I've kept it quiet for a while because I wanted to be sure I was onto something, but now I'm ready to work on it. I want to tell him that. Sorry Tom, but you'll do fine without me. You and Zlack will find other projects.'

'Hey, Nick, hang on a minute.' He's speaking very quietly now. 'Hang on a minute. You're tied with us, boy.'

'I told you, Tom. I'm sorry. Really I am. But I want to get out of it.'

He laughs. An empty cynical laugh. 'Get out of it! The opportunity of a lifetime. And you want to get out of it.'

'Tom, this Zlack thing won't work for me . . . And anyway,' I say as the cab lurches, 'you wouldn't want to

wait all these months to start work on the HIV stuff . . .
Somebody knows about it.'

The driver has accelerated again now. We are moving
dangerously fast.

'Don't talk rot.'

'I'm telling you the truth . . . Two guys were overheard
whispering about it at a conference.'

'Nicholas, you're insane. Nobody could possibly have
been whispering about it. Unless you've opened your
mouth. Nobody knows about it, except you and me and
Zlack.'

'Did *you* ever talk about it Tom?'

He doesn't have to think twice. 'Never.'

'Were you and Zlack ever at a Landmark conference
together?'

'Once . . . what the hell are you getting at?'

'And that once did the two of you have a conversation
about this thing?'

'For Christ's sake Nicholas, how the hell do I
remember?'

He's raised his voice now, here in the back of the hot
taxi, where there is not much space for the air or the anger
to circulate.

'Perhaps. Maybe. So what if I did?' he says. 'Are you
trying to turn this into some kind of spy story?'

I try to open my window further. The handle is stuck.

'It's claustrophobic in here.'

'Did anyone ask you to take this waste-of-time trip to
the airport?'

The cab-driver turns round.

'Delta? American?'

'Delta.'

Tom reaches into his pocket for cash. The cab

screeches to a halt. He pays the driver. Opens the door. We both get out and there on the pavement, his lips pursed, he grabs hold of my arm. Just enough for it to be more than jocular. Just too little for me to be sure of the menace in the gesture.

'Don't get any funny ideas,' he says.

And then as though aware of the dangerous ambiguity in his tone, a slap on the shoulder and, 'We're in this together.'

The word 'together' unlocks my anger. Anger that in the cab was stifled. Because, in truth, in Tom's tone there is now not so much as a hint of togetherness. As he picks up his bag from the pavement, slings it over his shoulder, and begins to walk into the airport building I hear myself suddenly shouting at his back. Still close enough to hear me he turns round, shakes his head and looks astonished. I think at first it is because I have lost my cool and it is not until he has disappeared inside the airport terminal that I realize that he has understood nothing of my swearing. For I have cursed him of course in Italian.

The journey back from La Guardia is not a total blur. I took the subway. Pressed in the neon glare against the sweaty rush-hour bodies. Squashed between a huge unwashed woman in lime-green shorts and a grey-faced commuter I am headed back to Landmark.

Out of the stinking subway into the sterility of my laboratory. Outside the door I put up the red ABSOLUTELY NO ENTRY sign. No coat. No gloves. No mask. Past the freezer and my microscopes. Straight for the telephone at the back of the laboratory. I dial 411.

'ATT. Which city?'

'Washington.'

'DC sir?'

'Yes.'

'Which name?'

'Zlack Enterprises.'

'Please hold for your number.'

The recorded voice of a nasal Southerner comes on the line.

'The number you require is . . . Please dial 1 to be connected.'

I am sure that if the recorded nasal woman had not shown me the kindness of offering to connect my call directly for an extra $1.50 and I had dialled the digits alone, somewhere between the first and the last I would have opted out.

'Zlack Enterprises. Mavis speaking.'

'Good morning. I'd like to speak to Mr Zlack please.'

'I'm sorry. I believe Mr Zlack is in a meeting. But I'll just check for you. Your name please.'

'Manzini. Nicholas Manzini.'

And while I wait, almost sure that I would not now speak to Zlack this morning, that I had been given time to choose the right words to renege, I hear, 'Nicholas. What a pleasant surprise. How are you?'

'I'm fine, but I really didn't want them to haul you out of a meeting for me.'

He laughs. A dry laugh. 'They always say I'm in a meeting, so I can vet who I speak to. Actually they got me on my cellphone. I'm in my car right now. On the way to meet Tom at the airport. Now to what do I owe the pleasure of this call?'

'Well, Tom'll probably tell you this, but I've er . . . I've been having second thoughts.'

Through the receiver I hear the car's engine. I hear the radio and its volume being suddenly lowered. 'Second thoughts, Nicholas. About what exactly?'

'I've decided to stay with Landmark sir.'

'None of this sir. I've told you to call me Walter,' he says coughing.

'I've decided to stay with Landmark, Walter.'

'I don't quite understand. Perhaps you could explain.'

'I'm not happy with my decision. It's been bothering me. I feel suddenly that it's wrong to wait with something potentially so important and . . . well there's no other way to put it. I'd like to opt out of our agreement.'

He laughs. A hard empty laugh. A nasty chilling laugh and he says, 'It doesn't quite work like that here, Nicholas.'

'I'm sorry?'

'Well, perhaps in a smaller place like Florence agreements are made to be broken, but in the US a handshake is a handshake. And of course, what is more important, a contract is a contract. And you and I, Nicholas, have signed on this.'

I take a deep breath. I wonder if I should continue this conversation, knowing all the while that he is driving. But it's too late now. I've started and I need to get it behind me.

'I'm sorry to have to let you down. But I've taken my decision. I really have decided to stay with Landmark and to work on my findings there.'

I hear the hooting of a horn. I imagine Zlack behind the wheel, stiff and upright, almost too tall to fit into the car, his head touching the roof.

'Nicholas.' He is speaking very quietly and I can no longer hear the engine. I wonder if perhaps he has pulled over to the side of the road. 'Nicholas. You will not be staying with Landmark. Because Landmark will not want you if they find out you have been hiding something all these months. Something they will say belongs to them.'

I lean back against a workbench. My legs feel weak.

'But . . . but Tom told me that in the States it would be considered my discovery. He said he looked it up in the Medical Law Library. And anyway Landmark don't know that this is not something I stumbled on yesterday.'

That laugh again and then without once raising his voice he says, 'No. They don't know. And they needn't ever know as long as you join Zlack Enterprises as agreed. You see we own your findings now, Nicholas. And it would be more than foolish for you to tamper with our agreement. If you even hint that you're going to go back on a deal in this country, your name can so easily be blackened. You can even be prevented from working in a research lab or a hospital again for the rest of your life and that would be a pity now wouldn't it? So forget these crazy ideas, Nicholas. You'll come to Zlack Enterprises as arranged and we'll develop this drug together. Now, if you'll excuse me, I don't want to be late for Tom. I look forward to seeing you soon,' and he revs his car engine and hangs up the phone.

THIRTY-THREE

Dominique

We ordered in that night. Or rather in Nicholas's apartment I ordered in for both of us. I had dozed on and off till midday after he left for Landmark. In his big navy bed with images of him and of Mischa that vied for my attention. Nicholas relaxed, leaning towards me in the Velvet Room. Mischa, his skin stained a reddish-purple, taking slow deliberate steps towards the door. Nicholas tensed standing over me in his yellow bathrobe. And as one language fights for its slot with another, as a painkiller fights for its place over pain, so borrowing me as their battleground those pictures of him and of Mischa pitted themselves against one another. Alternating slowly at first, building momentum, till sparring with the frenzied speed of fencers they roused me.

In search of nothing in particular I sauntered around the wide streets of SoHo in the hot sunshine that afternoon, my body unaware still of the time of day. In and out of modern art galleries and interior-design showrooms. In and out of trendy boutiques and scented bathroom shops and it was not till early evening, till I was on my way back to Nicholas's apartment that I gave into a few moments of heavy and overwhelming sadness. I noticed in the hours I had been out of the apartment that something had changed. A half-empty glass of water next to the sink. A white towel on the bed. And in the lounge on the table next to the titanium sculpture of the man and woman lying interlocked, a folded orange slip of paper.

I opened it and read, 'I came home to see you. I'll be back at 8.00.'

I put down the note and I translate. He came home in the middle of the day to tell me it's all over. He came to tell me that while I was away he found someone else. He didn't want to let me know the minute I got back, but he's going home to Florence. Last night by the fire with the Bach was fun but . . .

The air-conditioning unit rattles. A door slams. A siren sounds. I laugh at myself. Nicholas will soon be back.

And it was my choice last night that we listen to Bach's *Musical Offering* so now I walk over to the rack and search for the music that he had wanted to hear. And I remember it was called the *Wanderer Fantasy*. I hear him calling it out to me in the rain. But here in his rack I can't find it. And I reach instead for another piece of Schubert's music. His *Unfinished Symphony*. Dark, dramatic and threatening in parts. Though the darkness and the drama melt from time to time into more melodious sound that moves me, here, alone this time, in Nicholas's lounge and lulls me into a false sense of security. As though the menacing sounds will not return.

And so I order in from the Chinese on the corner. It's strange how one remembers the irrelevant details. Sesame toast. Seaweed. Sweet and sour prawns. Crispy duck with pancakes. Chicken with cashew nuts. And chopsticks.

And Nicholas sitting there opposite me at the table, pale in a navy shirt in the yellow kitchen, not really eating. Playing with his food. And something in the way he looks at me gives me confidence and I say, 'I thought you came back today to tell me it was over. That you'd had second thoughts while I was away.'

He puts down his chopsticks. He takes my face in his hands. He lets me know in silence that nothing could be further from the truth.

'But you might have second thoughts,' he says.

'Me?' I laugh. 'I can't imagine it. I'm too far gone for that.'

He smiles. A weak smile. Too weak and he lifts a pancake onto his plate.

'So why did you come home in the middle of the day?'

He fills a teaspoon with sauce and spreads it on the pancake.

'Sorry?'

'Why did you come home this afternoon?'

He reaches for the strips of cucumber.

'I needed to speak to you, Dominique.'

'About what?'

He places the pieces of duck on the pancake with the plum sauce and the strips of cucumber and still he says nothing.

'Nicholas. About what?'

He rolls the pancake till it is ready to eat and looks up.

'About this morning. About our conversation.'

He looks serious. As if he's going to say that he can't help me. He can't find out who if anyone is keeping their discovery under wraps.

He begins to speak and I am listening, but anticipating what he will say. Interpreters learn bad habits. They learn to finish the speaker's sentence before he does. To get inside his head and predict his train of thought. And usually we get it right. Usually but not always.

'You're going to tell me that you can't help me, aren't

you?' I say.

'I wanted to tell you that I know who's held back on the development of the drug all these months.'

'You do? You know already? You're a genius,' I say laughing now. 'How did you find out so fast?'

Again he says nothing. Just closes his eyes, takes a deep breath, opens them again.

'It's me,' he says.

'What?'

'It's me.'

And I am about to laugh again. To laugh and say, 'Yes, right Nicholas, of course. Now when you've finished with the jokes could you please tell me the truth.' But somewhere in my throat the laugh is broken and is strangled. And in my gut . . . a wrenching, a twisting, a tightening so that I have to put my hand to my stomach and hold it. And his face, ashen, anguished. And then a voice, that enters my head. My mother saying, 'Remember, Dominique, always remember, *c'est le ton qui fait la musique* . . . It's not just what you say. It's the way that you say it.' And in the music of his tone I know I have heard the truth.

'Why?' A whisper almost.

Silence.

'Why, Nicholas. Why?'

His face in his hands now. He shakes his head. And I want for a split second to touch him. To put my hand on his cheek. I want to. I move my hand forward. But I can't.

He uncovers his face. He slumps back in his chair and it is there in his yellow kitchen, in his apartment in downtown Manhattan without me having to ask again that I learn his story. It is there that he talks and talks. As though he, this time, were telling the story to himself as I told mine in Central Park. His contained excitement at his discovery. His impulsive revelations to Tom. His decision not to go to Goldmann in the heat of the moment, but later when he is sure his findings are more than just a figment of his imagination. His meeting in the Four Seasons with Zlack. His signature of the contract the next morning. Tom's betrayal of him. His phone call to Zlack.

And on the kitchen table his hands. The beautiful hands with long bony fingers. Hands, that now are tied.

A story that I might have interpreted in a very different way, were I coming from another place. Were there no history. No Anna. No Mischa.

And now as I sit and listen to him, not interrupting, unable to do so, unable at first even to steady my breathing, the battle of images from this morning rages anew. So that in my own world I do not notice that he has stopped speaking. Perhaps because with the sounds of the *Unfinished Symphony*, that has been playing again and again from the room next door, we are not in silence. Perhaps because I cannot look at him, while I use all my strength to wrestle with the feelings that well up in me and because I know suddenly, as they threaten to overtake me, that for the moment I must go the other way. I must force myself out of the fear and the falling into a state of unreal calm and I must lift my head instead and say, 'Nicholas, tell me what it is you think you've found?'

He doesn't hesitate. He doesn't question me. He offers me no preamble. Instead, his voice exhausted now, on another planet, not stopping to check if the details are beyond me he begins to explain.

He talks of a fourth therapy to complement the triple therapies. He talks not of a vaccine or a cure, but of a fourth mode to attack resistant virus. He talks of another route to prolong life.

248

And this time as he speaks I do not translate simultaneously in my head into French. Instead I concentrate hard on his words. On understanding them and on memorizing them. As though here in Nicholas's kitchen, I were preparing to stand up and regurgitate what I have heard. But this is different. No standard piece of consecutive interpreting, this. Because I have no pad and paper to jot down symbols to jog my memory and this time it is not there and then that I have to stand up and repeat what I have heard. This time it is for myself that I am listening.

He looks at me when he has finished, imprints the expression in his black eyes on my mind and says, 'I know what you think, Dominique, and you're right. But I never really thought of the delay. It was just a few months and I. . .'

He must have noticed my pallor, because he stops in mid-sentence. I unclench my fists. I notice the nail marks on my palms and not now making eye contact, though turned in his direction, so that I see the veins on the side of his neck where the skin is thin, I hear myself say, 'Not now Nicholas. I can't talk about it. Please not now.'

Standing up. My voice growing louder, higher. More choked. 'Give me time. I just need . . . some time.'

And Nicholas still there at the kitchen table with the untouched sesame toast, the seaweed, the sweet and sour prawns.

That is where I left him as I ran out of the kitchen, out of his apartment, into the night, with the drama of Schubert's *Unfinished Symphony* behind me.

THIRTY-FOUR

Nicholas

I ought to have learnt from my work that life makes more promises than it can keep. I ought to have understood that from the many times the parent of a newly diagnosed patient turned to me in disbelief and said of his still rosy-cheeked offspring, 'But Doctor, he looks so well.' I ought to have realized too that it is not just in sickness, not just in the proliferation of malignant cells that there is a hidden story that unfolds, a parallel story that runs its own course till its joining with yours becomes as inevitable as the confluence of two streams at a river.

But if these were not lessons I absorbed early enough from my profession, what I did learn was that once things have gone wrong you can only do so much. You can use all of your skills to attempt to change the course of events. You can chastise yourself for the part that you played and rewind the spool in your mind a thousand times, but then, however great the pain, you have to sit back and wait.

The morning after that night, without peace, without sleep, without Dominique, I went into Landmark, as though it were a normal day. On my way into the lab I passed Goldmann in the corridor. And though his greeting was no more or less cursory than usual, I imagined that his cool eyes rested on me for just a moment too long and that in that fragment of time, just by looking at me he knew it all.

I had called Dominique the night before. The first time I left a message on her answerphone. 'Dominique, please call me when you get in. Just to let me know you got home safely.'

She didn't call back of course. Long after she must have been home she hadn't called back and hours later, still at the kitchen table, I dialled her number again and listened to her recorded message. 'Hi, this is Dominique Green . . . Please leave a message after the tone,' and it struck me that a person could be dead and on their answerphone their voice would still be the same. They would sound still as though nothing was wrong.

I tried her again the next morning from the lab. 'Dominique, I know you said you needed time. I understand you. But please, please, we have to talk.'

With the modicum of reason that was left to me I forced myself to turn to matters practical, to find the Yellow Pages in the cupboard at the back of the lab where the dusky pink file was kept and to search for a legal practice that specialized in pharmaceutical law.

I found myself, within minutes, in conversation with a sympathetic Englishman at the end of the phone.

'May I ask you to tell me the nature of the problem, without going into too many details over the phone of course. Just so that I know if you should be dealing with me or with a colleague?'

'Yes . . . er . . . well I suppose it concerns a discovery I've made since I arrived in New York.'

'I see, and there's clearly some conflict involved. Is that right?'

'Well there is, or there was, though I don't suppose I really realized it . . . and now it looks as if I run the risk of losing it completely.'

'And this is something of significant importance, I take it.'

'Yes,' I said. 'Yes, it's of great importance. I've known that all along, but you know what it's like. Sometimes you don't realize quite how important it is till you risk losing it.'

The lawyer says, 'Yes, yes, I quite understand,' though in truth he sounds a little baffled, explains that he will be out of town for the next week, but that he can either schedule an appointment for his return or pass me on to a colleague and I, too fatigued and frazzled right there and then to be passed on to yet another stranger, take out my diary and pencil in an appointment for the following week.

I tried when I put down the phone to adopt my normal routine. To remove some blood cells from a Petri dish, to place them on a slide and to examine them under the microscope. I sat on my stool and I put my eye to the microscope's lenses. And usually for me that familiar action brings with it a comforting feeling. Like listening to a song whose words you know by heart. Like being on the last stretch of road on your way home, when your car knows its way so well that it drives for itself.

But that day I could see very little through my microscope. And though I was sure that I had left it on the right settings, my view was grey and hazy. I altered the angle of its neck. I fiddled with the buttons at its base and I put my face back to the lenses. And yes, that had worked. My manipulation had restored its focus. Because close to it, pressed against it, what I saw now for a few moments at least was sharp and clear. Instantly recognizable. A pinky-brown colour, a Cupid's-bow shape, moving, talking. And I watched. Mesmerized. Transfixed. Till the salt water that filled the lenses obliterated the picture from my view.

I sat up, wiped the lenses and remembered suddenly that Landmark was hosting a conference that day. Not a conference that was in any way relevant to me. Not one that I would normally have been expected or invited to attend. But I stood up then. I took off my gloves. I rushed to the sink and took off my protective clothing. I washed my hands, ran down the corridor, and down the stairs to the entrance of the building's conference hall. I slipped into a chair at the back. The session was in full swing. The speaker, a Frenchman, was in mid-sentence. The interpreters' booths were out of my line of vision. In front of me on the desk a set of headphones and the control panel on the black box switched already to the English channel. I put on the headphones and this time there is no searching as months before there was. Her voice is there in an instant. The deep voice. That voice that were she a singer would be a mezzo-soprano. And the words go over me, while the sounds go through me. I hear her that first time in the booth laughing by mistake. I hear her reading *Washington Square*. I hear her by the fire with the Bach. I hear her in my headphones long after she has stopped talking and her colleague has taken over. When the speech has ended and the session breaks for lunch I make my way to the back of the hall, to the English booth and a grey tight-lipped woman comes to the door and says, 'If you're looking for Ms Green, I'm afraid she's left. She won't be working this afternoon or tomorrow.'

And I think, as I walk away from the booth and out of the conference hall, that once things have gone wrong you can use all your skills to change the course of events, but then however great the pain there are times when you just have to sit back and wait.

THIRTY-FIVE

Dominique

The nights are the worst. The blackening grey that beckons, and falls as if to cover you, then smothers you instead in stifling silence and condemns you to the war of words inside your head.

On the first night, I broke the silence. I reached in the darkness for the button on my answering machine, and listened again and again to Nicholas's voice. 'Dominique, I know you said you needed time, but please, please, we have to talk.'

The second night, the same. And on the third night, or rather in the early hours, lying there, hot despite the air-conditioning, cold despite the covers, I reached for the telephone.

'I woke you didn't I? I ... I ... thought you might just have done the night programme,' I say. 'I'm sorry James. Of course I woke you. I just had to talk to someone. I ...'

A grunt and then, 'Dominique, what's wrong?'

'Nothing I ...'

'You don't normally call to shoot the shit at 3.00 in the morning.'

'I can't tell you. Not over the phone.'

'In the middle of the night you call to tell me you can't talk.'

'I just ... I don't know where to start. I had to hear a

friendly voice.'

'OK. I'm here. So get up, get dressed and I'll meet you.'

'Now? In the middle of the night?'

'This is New York City, kid. Remember? And it sounds like we've got to get you out of some kind of trouble.'

'Are you serious?'

'I'm pulling on my sweatpants as we speak. I suggest you do the same. I'll jump in a cab. See you on the corner of Fifty-Sixth and Second at the Plaza Diner in fifteen minutes. I'm just dying for some eggs and bacon. Been lying awake dreaming of eggs and bacon all night.'

And so I am waiting in the Plaza Diner at 3.20 in the morning. And though I have breakfast there every day I hardly recognize it. No smiles or nods as I walk in from faces that I know. No comforting porridge placed in front of me, even before I have to ask for it. Just a woman by the window, behind her fading foundation, tired from her night's work. Just unforgiving fluorescent tubes above the red plastic chairs and the grey Formica tables.

He walks over to me in green sweatpants and a white sweatshirt, brown sandals on his feet. He plants a kiss on my cheek, pulls out his chair, ruffles my hair.

'Dominique Green, what an unexpected pleasure,' he says, the cheeky grin on his face even at this hour.

'James, I'm sorry. I really am. To drag you out, like this in the middle of the night.'

The waiter comes over, dark stains on his jacket, deep pock-marks on his face. James says, 'Just a minute, I have some important business to attend to here. I'll have two fried eggs with bacon on white toast please.'

'Sunny side up?' says the waiter.

He has a strong foreign accent. A Greek accent. Close in intonation to the Italian.

'Yes please, sunny side up. And you, Dom? What will you have?'

'Nothing. I don't want anything.'

'Come on, you can't just sit here and watch me.'

'I'll have a pot of tea.'

'So I guess this has something to do with the coloured bubble?'

'Sort of.'

'Come on Dom, I need to see a smile. Just a little one. It can't be that bad. Nobody's dying.'

I say nothing. Just look down at the grey Formica table.

'OK. Let's hear the whole thing.'

I tell him as much of it as one can put into words here in the Plaza Diner in the middle of the night. The conference. Mischa. Barnes & Noble. Central Park. Amagansett. Zurich. Anna. Mischa. And Nicholas. His discovery. My dilemma. The nights. And Nicholas.

'And I can't speak to Anna,' I say. 'And I can't speak to Mischa. And I can't speak to Nicholas right now. I want to. But I can't. I just can't.'

'So you're speaking to me,' he says and he laughs. 'A last resort.'

I laugh too and he says, 'You see, I got you to smile.'

A brief smile though. A smile that feels out of place. As out of place, as unexpected as James's reaction.

'Tell me more about the discovery part.'

'Sorry?'

'Nicholas's findings. That bit. Tell me more about that.'

'Why?'

'Because it's relevant to your story.'

Too worn-out now, too spent to question or protest, three days after I have first heard it at Nicholas's wooden kitchen table, as though the symbols on my lined pad were in front of me to jog my memory I perform my party piece. A piece of consecutive interpreting. An almost verbatim repetition of Nicholas's story.

I look up and he is sitting there, his jaw open, excitement on his face.

'Dom, this is fantastic.'

'What?'

'I mean, from a journalistic point of view. What a coup.'

'I don't know what you're talking about.'

'For the current events programme. We could make some awesome radio out of it.'

He must have seen the horror on my face. He must have felt me freeze, because he checked himself, he leant across the table, put his hand on my shoulder and said, 'I'm sorry Dom. I really didn't mean to upset you. Just the investigative journalist in me firing on all cylinders.'

He takes a sip of coffee that must by now be cold. 'Listen, as for Nicholas. Only you can work that out. It depends just how strong it is, I guess. I suppose it would have to be some pretty earth-shattering feeling though, to conquer this one. I'd take a few days to think about it if I were you.'

As cars begin to hoot and day begins to break, he crosses Fifty-Sixth Street with me. 'I'll walk you back.'

'I'm fine. Honestly.'

'Are you sure?'

'Yes. Really. Thanks James. Thanks for coming out.'

I begin to walk towards home. He calls after me, 'Remember, day or night, you know where I am.' And then, 'Oh and if you decide you want to do that story.'

I walk towards Beekman Place, towards the indigo blue light that glows still outside my building.

Slowly up the splintered wooden stairs to my apartment. Up the first flight. Then the second so that I know by the time I have reached my front door, by the time I have put the key in the rusting lock, confiding in James has had its effect. So that I know, as I push open the door and the light of morning hits me, as I run the hot water over a flannel, as I lie down on my bed and place it over my eyes, that having told him I am more alone now than I was before.

I took James's advice though. I took my time. Four days without speaking to Nicholas. Five days. Six. On the sixth day I woke from a fitful night shivering, burning. I called Deborah at the agency. 'Sorry, I can't work,' I croaked.

'What's the matter sweetie?'

'My throat . . . closing up.'

'Try not to talk today,' she said.

And so I didn't talk. I didn't respond to my mother's message. My father's. Nicholas's. I told the doorman, if anyone came, to say I was away. And I just lay there, my heart racing at will. I didn't read. I didn't listen to music. I didn't do anything. All day I lay there, grateful despite the sweating and the swelling that the struggle had been passed from my mind to my body. And sometimes it is when you give in that the answer comes to you. When you cease the search, that you feel unequivocally what it is that you need. And I did. On the seventh day I woke, weak, washed-out though the fever was gone. And I knew, in my gut, where it was that I was destined to be in the end. And I would have dialled his number later that day. I would have gone to see him. I would have confronted Anna too. Said that I knew he'd done wrong, but there was so much more to him. I would have told her the truth and risked her wrath. Except that she called before I did.

I had given up screening my calls. Because today I knew where I was going, and what it was I wanted to say. And I was so sure, because I had waited till things had become clear in my head, that the outside world would reward me. So sure, as I reached over to my bedside table and I answered the phone, that the outside world would fall into place with my decisions. In my ear I hear the click of a long-distance connection. And as the inmates of the camps knew it in the click of a Nazi heel, so in that click at the end of the line I knew it all. It hit me even before I heard her voice. She didn't really speak though. She just made some sort of sound at the end of the line. Some attempt at 'Hello.'

'Anna?'

That sound again. As though she were trying to talk but couldn't.

'Anna, is that you?'

'Yes.' I hear her take a long deep breath and then she says, '*L'ha fatta finita.*'

She says it in Italian, slipping just like Nicholas did into his mother tongue, and then her voice higher this time she repeats herself.

'*L'ha fatta finita.*'

And though I had felt in my gut what was coming, the brutality of the words made it real. Too real to translate simultaneously. Too real to understand, to analyse and to absorb all at once. So that though I understood the horror of their sense, still it took a few moments to translate them in my head. And it took weeks, months, a year even to absorb the words that she repeated to me again on the phone, this time in English, in a voice that was lost and broken. 'He killed himself. He took an overdose . . . Dominique . . . Did you hear me? . . . He's dead.'

THIRTY-SIX

Dominique

Grabbing me by the wrist, numbing me and propelling me forward, grief had me in its grasp.

It began as I dressed and built up on the way there. The pins and the needles in my hands and in my fingers. In my wrists and my ankles. In my feet and my toes. And in the midtown midday heaviness I feared the onset of a bursting blinding migraine. I feared the pounding and the pain that would cause my vision to blur and my voice to slur. In the shadow of the skyscrapers, past the stressed and the sneakered, power-walking back to work. Past the suited and the skirted queuing outside sandwich bars, I turned off Thirtieth Street and onto Third Avenue. Not ready yet to go inside, I stood in front of the main entrance to the blue mirrored building. I ran my finger along the embossed letters of the copper plaque. And it was in that moment, as I touched the coolness of the plaque, that the pins and the needles began to drift. That they began to move and to merge, like the joining into paper chains of those questions that Nicholas had asked me in Central Park. So that in the elevator, by the time the red numbers lit up and announced the eleventh floor, the tightening and the tingling had spread to every inch of my body. Like an ink blot that seeps over what is written beneath. Like a local anaesthetic that obliterates not the knowledge of searing pain, but its sensation.

The ginger-haired girl who met me at the elevator wore ripped jeans and a lime-green tie-dye T-shirt and as we walked along the corridor it struck me that I, in my tailored black trouser suit and my white body, was dressed as if for television.

It struck James too, as he walked into the ante-room to the studio, dressed in sweatpants and a sweatshirt as he was in the Plaza Diner. He threw back his head and laughed. 'Dominique, you look very nice, but they can't see you on radio you know!'

And normally I would have been embarrassed by his observation that I was overdressed. Normally I would have wished for the ground to open up and swallow me, but the anaesthetic by now was in full force and I felt nothing. Nothing at all.

He asked, 'Did you bring your notes?'

I began to remove my backpack. Slowly. First one strap. Then the other. Free of its weight I moved my shoulders. I shrugged one. Then the other. I unzipped my bag and reached for the sheet of lemon-coloured lined paper and unfolded it. The first time I had looked at it since it had been written. I stared at the words in black ink on the page. No symbols this time. No neat little pictures to denote medication or microscope or money. But Nicholas's words in my handwriting. Words that can only have been committed to paper the night of the Chinese take-away. The night I ran out of his apartment into the darkness. I saw by the jagged edge at the top of the sheet that I must have ripped it off its pad and I saw by the slant of the script how it must have been written in a hurry. But as I sat there in that ante-room, I remembered not one second of the frantic half-hour it must have taken me to write. As a poet fails the next morning to recollect the creation of a poem penned in a burst of nocturnal activity, I was unable to conjure up the image of myself distraught but determined at my desk by the window.

Nor do I recollect much now of that ante-room at Riverside Studios. Nothing more than a mirror and a calendar opposite me that was turned to the page dated August 18 with a photograph of a chestnut horse, un-saddled, unbridled, in full gallop, his thick mane flowing behind him as he moved.

'Can you decipher them?' asked James, standing over me.

'Yes, I can. Just about.'

'Dominique,' he said, one hand on his blond head. 'I think this is great, just great. A fabulous story. But, um . . . what made you decide to do it in the end?'

'I'd rather not talk about it . . . if you don't mind. Let's just get it done.'

'Sure. Sorry. I was just being nosy. That's all. Look, this is the procedure. You sit here and write the script. We'll look at it together and then the libel lawyer will check it over with you before we go on air.'

'What do you mean *I* write the script? I've never written a radio script in my life.'

'Nothing to it. You just tell your story as simply as possible in a fifty-second slot.'

'A fifty-second slot?'

'You read it back to yourself, out loud, and you time it. I'll lend you my stopwatch.'

And he pulls a silver chain with a stopwatch from around his neck and hands it to me.

'Here.'

'Thanks . . . but em . . . what's the point of me timing

it? You might read it at a completely different pace on the radio.'

'I'm not going to be reading it.'

'What are you talking about?'

'I'm not reading it, Dom. You are.'

'Are you crazy?'

'Absolutely not. You've got a great voice. I want you to read it. You can do a couple of the other items as well. We've got plenty of time to practise. Now get writing, kid. I'll get them to bring you in some water. You've got forty minutes.' He turns round, pushes open the door and he is gone.

Alone now, and as though I were speaking to the audience in a conference hall I squeezed, I squashed and I summarized Nicholas's story. So that it would fit, all of it, into the fifty-second slot.

In the mirror for a brief moment I see the reflection of a colder, harder version of myself. The version I would surely become if life disappointed me again and again. I turn to the computer screen in front of me and as though I were talking of a stranger, I type his story, in black on white. Like a secretary detached from her task, an interpreter disconnected still from the essence of the words she speaks, I depress the keys and I stare straight ahead at the chestnut horse on the calendar with his flowing mane. And I hear a voice then reading the paragraphs out loud. A voice that can only be mine. I reach the last word and I press on the little silver knob at the top of the stopwatch. One minute and ten seconds.

As if he has sensed that I have finished James is at the door, with a tray and two cobalt blue bottles of fizzy water.

'Sorry it took so long Dom. I had to locate the lawyer.'

He puts the tray down next to me, ruffles my hair and says, 'Well, what have you got?'

'One minute and ten seconds.'

'You'll have to cut twenty. Timing is everything.'

I look down and I scan what I have written.

'I can't. There's nothing to cut.'

'Of course there is. Out of the way a minute.'

He takes my place at the computer. 'What about this? You see, Dom, part of this sentence here is entirely redundant. We can get rid of it.'

Over his shoulder I look at the text and I watch the words, 'Due to subtle coercion the medical researcher in question has not yet disclosed his findings,' as James presses the delete key and they disappear backwards off the screen.

'Who cares if it was subtle coercion?' he says. 'The important thing is the researcher didn't disclose his findings . . . This is great stuff, Dominique. Brilliant actually for a first attempt,' he adds, excitement in his voice. 'I'm proud of you.'

And still I feel nothing. None of the pride. Nor the excitement. Just a sense that I am here doing what I have to do.

The man with the kind eyes and the thick grey hair who walks into the room then holds out his hand. A hand that feels in mine a little like Livieu's, my piano teacher, and he says, 'I'm Steven . . . Steven Ryner. The station's lawyer. Good to meet you.'

'I'll leave you two alone for a bit,' says James.

Steven sits on the chair in front of the computer. He reads the words I have written, while I stand behind him. He turns round. He pats the chair next to him.

'Sit down Dominique . . . This is some story. Look, I'm

going to have to ask you a few pretty probing questions to make sure our backs are covered. Ours and yours. So please don't be offended. Don't think I'm insulting your intelligence. OK?'

His tone is calming, soothing. Like the tone of the surgeon who looked down at me in the operating theatre just before he took out my tonsils, just before he knew that the blood was going to pour and he said, 'It will soon be over. All over.'

'How did you find out about all this Dominique?'

'I first overheard snippets of it at a conference months ago. I'm a simultaneous interpreter.'

'I see. And then?'

'I was told the rest.'

'By whom?'

'By Nicholas Manzini. The medical researcher.'

In my right temple I feel a slight and fleeting pain. The first sign that the numbness in my body will not last for ever.

'Were you friends with Manzini? I mean, do you believe you can trust his story?'

'Yes. Yes. I can trust it 100 per cent . . . He is . . . I mean, he was my boyfriend.'

'I don't want to pry, but this is not about revenge, is it?'

'No. It isn't. Not at all.'

'James would kill me if he knew I was telling you this in case I put you off, but you need to know the implications of doing a story like this . . . There'll be a big investigation within Landmark. Your friend may well be thrown out for having kept his findings to himself and then offering them to another company and then . . .'

That fleeting pain again. I start to speak. I say, 'But he . . .'

'Whatever the circumstances, Dominique. He made these discoveries in Landmark's labs while he was in full employment, so it's all a bit tricky. Of course he has leverage. He has his knowledge to bargain with. Oh and then there's the wider ethical question of whether one should hold up something like this.'

'I don't think he meant to. He wanted to be sure of his ground. He wanted to . . .'

The lawyer puts his hand on my arm. 'Dominique, are you sure you want to do this?'

I don't answer. That pain in my temple is sharper now. It lasts a few seconds longer. The lawyer repeats himself. 'Are you sure?'

Still I am unable to answer. For a moment I imagine I feel a lump in my throat. I fight it. I swallow hard. The lawyer tries a different question.

'May I ask you why you want to do this, Dominique?'

'For my best friend. He just killed himself. He was dying of Aids. I'm doing this for him. If I don't I . . . I . . . won't be able to live with myself. It sounds crazy, I know, but I em . . . I won't be able to face him at his funeral . . . if you know what I mean.'

'I'm sorry,' he says and then one last time, 'so you're sure then?'

And I think again how amazing it is that you can change the course of your life and of someone else's, in a syllable.

'Yes,' I say. 'I'm sure I want to go ahead.'

Things move very fast once James comes back. We go into the studio next door. Dimly lit, just like the booth. Two chairs next to each other in front of a large desk with a control panel. Ahead of us a large round window through which you can see the producer in his box. James puts on his headphones. Points to mine. I slip them on. Familiar but different from the interpreter's headphones. Just as in the booth, but blacker. Heavier.

James moves my microphone closer to my mouth. I hear myself laugh.

'That's one thing I don't need help with.'

He laughs too. 'Sorry.' He hands me a script and though the instructions are written in bold letters on the white paper, James is clearly nervous.

'I'll nod and I'll tap you when it's your turn.'

We practise. We read the text through twice, three times, four times. He reads his bits about a murder trial, an adoption bill, an anti-fur riot. I read mine, about famine supplies, about an aircraft disaster, about US/ Soviet relations and about Nicholas.

Just like in the booth when the speakers have thought to provide us with a text beforehand I practise reading and I feel little of that occasional fleeting pain in my right temple.

In my ears I hear the producer say, 'It sounds good. Four minutes and we're on air.'

I'm tempted to translate into French. I'm tempted to say, '*Très bien. Quatre minutes et l'on y va.*' And I do translate, though only in my head. Just that one sentence over and over again because it takes up time and because on my left I can feel James looking at me.

The producer says, 'One minute and we're on air.'

James squeezes my hand. Too hard. I feel it. The numbness has begun to wear off. He waits for the countdown. Five. Four. Three. Two. One. He flicks up a switch and he begins to speak.

The adrenalin pumps. Just like in the booth. James reads his first item and I read mine. And these words about famine supplies and aircraft disaster are not yet my words. And it goes smoothly. Just like in the booth. That transition from one voice to the next. He taps my hand. As I begin my sentence the adrenalin surges, and the voice that I find this time, the voice though harder at first to recognize, comes from somewhere deep within me.

'A European medical researcher, based in New York, has stumbled upon the key to a potentially life-enhancing new Aids drug. The discovery made within Landmark US has been kept under wraps for several months, until the researcher, currently contractually bound by Landmark, can effect his move to a start-up company, an offshoot of the conglomerate Zlack Enterprises. To date, even the management of Landmark is unaware of these developments. The researcher, who made his discoveries while working on paediatric leukaemia, describes his findings as "Potentially a fourth way to complement the triple therapies and to combat the Aids virus."'

And it is with the last word that the numbness is gone. In my ears I hear the producer say, 'Fabulous voice, Dominique.'

The programme is over. James pulls off my headphones and says, 'You were amazing.'

I hear him, but I am gone. Out of the door, along the corridor, past the studios, not waiting for the elevator, down eleven flights of stone stairs on to the street. And then it begins. A cry that at first is small. A sob that grows louder, that hurts with the pain and the pounding that has started in my head. Sobbing that shakes me. All-encompassing. Uncontrollable, as I run alone through Manhattan. Sobbing that lasts for hours. Alone at first, and clutching Anna then. Sobbing together, both of us, bent over almost, as they lower Mischa into the ground.

THIRTY-SEVEN

Dominique

The grey stone sculptures stood around me, in the warmth and the breeze at the bottom of Rodin's walled gardens. They watched me, as I sat there, with such intensity that for a moment I imagined they just pretended to be mute. That like the toys in the *Nutcracker Suite* soon they would come alive and begin their dance between the shrubs, the wisteria and the weeping willows. I had wondered some-times during that year in Zurich, after New York, how it would feel here, in some hidden corner, in Paris, com-posing myself, before I went in, to wait for what might or might not be.

Opposite me, one sculpture stood out from the others. Darker than the rest, her face down, hidden in the crook of her arm, she covered her eyes and her lips, as though afraid to open her mouth. I stared at her and knew her from somewhere, and I sensed the emotional tug of stumbling on some forgotten photograph at the bottom of a tin. At the opposite side of the fountain, she stood again in lighter granite that sparkled here and there. Taller, a different version of herself, her head held high, her lips parted as if to speak.

I had known all along that I would be here. Between the waves of pain that twisted and contorted me, promising for a few days to recede, only then to tear and rip again. As soon as the heaviest of the fogs lifted and I remembered where and when, I knew that I would come. And if in my head there were questions, in my heart there were none. I told Anna, though I feared that I would hurt her. Two days before I took the train from Zurich to Paris, I went into the radio station early, I wrote my script, I found a presenter to stand in for me during the afternoon broadcast and I arranged to meet Anna outside at our usual place by the River Limmat.

As we sat on the wall, our legs swinging down to the ledge over the edge of the water, I noticed how the sun had highlighted the blonde streaks in her hair and how under her eyes the dark shadows of the autumn, the winter and the spring had begun to fade.

'You look well,' I said.

Even now, even after all these months it sounded offensive. As though saying it in some way mitigated her pain.

'Time,' she said. 'That old cliché. It'll be a year on Saturday, you know.'

'I know.'

'I think I'll go to the cemetery. Just to talk to him for a while. Sometimes it helps . . .' and then suddenly changing her tone, she took hold of my wrist, she turned to me and looked me straight in the eye. 'So my friend, what is it you want to talk about?'

I laughed. 'Why do you always know?'

'Because once upon a time you would never tell me.'

And so, on the grey stone wall, in our sunglasses now, looking out across the river at Zurich's old town, I told her how he had said when he first saw me that I reminded him of a piece of art. A sculpture called *Mignon* that stood in the Rodin museum in Paris. I told her all that I recalled of that brief exchange between us in the Frick in Manhattan a lifetime ago.

She listened and on her face I saw not anger or pain as I had expected, but something much more gentle. Much softer.

'How do you know he'll be there?'

'I don't.'

'Why don't you try to contact him at least?'

'I did. Once. A couple of months ago. He left no forwarding address.'

'I know.'

'What do you mean you know?'

'I tried myself once, a while ago. To get in touch with him.'

The wall felt slippery under my hands.

'What for?'

'For me,' she said, 'and for you. I wanted to know what, if anything had happened with the drug. And I wanted to tell him to come and see you. I felt somehow responsible.'

'Did you speak to anyone?'

'They put me onto some miserable guy called Goldmann. Professor Goldmann who said he wasn't at liberty to disclose scientific information to strangers. He said something about the matter having been resolved and that if Dr Manzini had wanted to leave a forwarding address he would have done . . .' She touched my arm. 'Dom, are you angry with me?'

'No, no I'm not . . . Maybe it's better that he didn't leave an address or a number.'

She looked at me, astonished. 'Why?'

I paused, trying to formulate the thought first in my mind.

'I suppose I don't want to speak on the phone. If he hasn't remembered then . . .'

'Then what?' she asked.

'Then this year hasn't been for him what it's been for me.'

'Dom, not everyone has your memory.'

'No, but if he doesn't remember this then . . .'

She smiled. She understood. In the end Anna always understood.

'And what,' she said, 'if he's not there?'

'Not there, not there, not there . . .' The words fell from her mouth and splashed hard into the river beneath us.

I didn't answer.

'Come,' Anna said, and as she swung herself round and off the wall, she pointed in the direction of the *Uetliberg*, and she said, 'It's been some climb hasn't it Dom?'

On the bench in Rodin's walled gardens, I looked at the white-faced gold-rimmed watch on my wrist. 11.40. I remembered the tricks I had used as an interpreter before I took the microphone. Slow deep breaths. Eyes closed. Images, shapes and colours in your mind but no words. The power to turn words into nothing for a few moments before you turned them into everything. When I opened my eyes a wiry man with a weathered face, a black beret and a thin roll-up cigarette in his hand had sat down at the other end of the bench.

He looked at me. '*Le coeur brisé?*' he asked. 'Broken heart?'

I smiled, stood up and walked between the lawns, along the paving-stones past Rodin's grave and his wife's that lay next to it, up the stone steps and round the side of the majestic yellow sandstone house. Past the massive bronze statue of *The Thinker*, his chin in his hands, and round to the front garden, bursting even in the height of summer with the pinks of geraniums, the purples of pansies, the whites of roses.

Inside the main door, a table on my left was piled high with black headphones and small black boxes containing taped recordings of guides around the museum.

'*Les écouteurs, madame?*' asked a small balding man in a pea-green uniform, handing me a set of headphones.

I can't have answered. I must have been in another world, because seconds later I heard him ask again.

'*Madame. Les écouteurs?*'

'*Oui, s'il vous plaît.*'

'*Anglais 1, Francais 2, Italien 3, Allemand 4.*'

'*Merci. Merci beaucoup.*'

And I noticed how my voice, when I thanked him, quivered just a little. How when I reached out to take the headphones from him in my right hand there was a slight tremor and I felt how my breathing now was shallow.

I walked along the light wooden floors, past the intricate wrought-iron balustrades of the sweeping staircase into the first room. A room with engraved walls and high ceilings. I put on the headphones, switched to the English channel, let the deep and learned voice of the historian attempt to distract me with the story of the white and frightening plaster sculpture that faced me.

'This piece,' he said, 'is part of a group called *Fugit Amor* . . . *Love Passes*. These lovers sitting back to back are tormented by some invisible force. They seem to be at once fleeing one another and stuck inexorably together.'

I shivered, silenced the art historian with the press of a button and moved away, my eye caught suddenly by a pair of grey stone hands, with long elegant fingers. Beautiful hands I couldn't help noticing. Eyes and hands were always the first things that attracted me to a man. I touched them and noticed as I got closer that they were not in fact one pair of hands, but two right hands. His instantly visible. Hers behind it. I turned again to the voice of the art historian. 'This assemblage,' he said, 'is called *The Secret.*'

Next to me a tall woman with a grey bun and a high-necked blouse is contemplating the same piece and I wonder as I turn away if I should apologize. If I should say, 'I'm sorry for the noise. I hope I'm not disturbing you.' For surely she could not be oblivious to a sound as deafening as my heart pounding as if to break my ribcage.

I walk away. Without stopping to look or to listen I move into the next room. A small room, flooded with light. And at the end, standing alone by the tall arched French windows, overlooking the gardens, I see her as he must have done before he met me.

In an instant even from the doorway I recognize her. A more beautiful, a more sculpted version of myself. Her hair longer and thicker, her nose more aristocratic, her lips a little fuller. A shaft of sunlight falling on her bronze head lends it a hue of red.

I look at my watch then. I can't help myself. 11.53. It was me and not him wasn't it, who had said midday, that day in that throwaway conversation in the Frick? Midday by *Mignon* if the worst should ever happen, thinking as one does how it never could. Never would.

I remember how he took my face in his hands when I said we should meet here, if we ever split up. A year later. A year to the day. And I remember him saying '*Sei proprio impazzita?* . . . Have you lost it, Dominique?'

And now standing here, remembering the chestnut horse on the calendar in James's studio, I am fighting with myself. Not wanting, not daring to hope too much.

Because the higher you go, the further you have to come down. And the adrenalin that pumps and pumps, that at the time makes you light-headed, leaves you later weak and exhausted.

The expression on the face of the sculpture shames me. She is serene, dignified, accepting of her fate. Just as in the opera by the same name. Mignon, the calm and carefree gypsy woman, knows in the end she will find her oasis. Quite by chance one day, sitting with colleagues from the radio station in some smoky café in Zurich I saw a poster for a performance of *Mignon* by some unknown opera company. Half on the wall, half off, stuck with Sellotape, someone had left the poster with the picture of the gypsy woman there as an afterthought. An afterthought that caused my stomach to lurch. I would go to the opera, of course. I decided that in a split second. And it crossed my mind how bizarre it is, the things we will do to get close to someone in our heads. Even if they know nothing about it. Even if they might never know.

And he, I was sure, would have told me if he'd known that *Mignon* was a traveller . . . a gypsy woman in an opera.

I took out a pen to write down the number of the box office, but as I looked more closely through the haze of smoke, I saw that the date of the performance was long since past. And I remember how that afternoon I trekked from one record shop to another to find a recording of the opera. Like the child who made bets with herself about not stepping on the lines of the paving-stones so I whispered to myself as I walked along, 'If I can find it then he'll be there.'

In shop after shop the answer was the same, 'It's a very minor opera. By Ambroise Thomas. I'm sorry but it's no longer available,' until in the last shop the assistant said,

'No we don't have it, but we have the main aria from it on a collection. It's quite beautiful.'

'I'll have it.'

And so night after night I listened to Mignon's warbling voice as she told her lover her idea of paradise.

'Do you know the land where the orange trees bloom?' she sang. *'The courtyard where one dances in the shade of a great tree and the clear lake on whose waters glide a thousand light boats just like birds? Do you know the hall with golden furnishings and statues that call me in the night and hold out their arms to me? . . .'*

I took it as a sign that he would remember. That he would come to where the statues are. Though my conviction then did nothing now to dispel my fear.

12.02. He was late. I had never known him to be late. He had never kept me waiting in Manhattan, except once at the Velvet Room. Unsteady on my feet now I have to lean against the window, facing out towards the gardens, my back to the room, because I can no longer bear to look.

And I feel myself begin to sink. One last look out of the window and I prepare to turn around and leave when I am aware of someone close to me. I shudder at first and am frozen, like an exhibit, to the spot. And then from behind me I hear a voice. A man's voice that I have heard before. I turn round and standing there, looking at me as if to say, 'Is it you?' is the small balding man in the pea-green museum uniform.

'Madame. Vous n'êtes pas par hasard Dominique Green?'

'Oui . . . Oui c'est moi.'

He smiles and explains how he has kept an eye out for me every day over the last week at this time in this spot. He tells me how lucky I am that he is on duty this time every day, because none of the other members of staff would have bothered.

'*Monsieur, je ne comprends pas . . .*'

He starts to speak in English, and I explain that it isn't his French that I don't understand, it's his reason for talking, it is how and why he knows my name.

He stretches out his hand and on his palm in front of me I see a white envelope. He tells me that he was given it a week ago by a gentleman. A tall dark man whose name he had now forgotten, though he did remember that he said he was supposed to meet a woman here by *Mignon* at 12.00. But that perhaps she had forgotten or got the wrong day or decided not to come, but anyway her name was Dominique Green. She was tall with long mahogany-coloured hair and if she did come any time over the next few days this is where she would wait for him. '*En tout cas il voulait que je vous donne ça . . .* In any case,' said the small balding man in the pea-green uniform. 'He said if I saw you could I please give you this and I should tell you if you asked that he had gone home. And so I've been watching out and I've found you,' he said and he smiled like the cat who had just got the cream.

My thank-you, I think, must have been all too cursory because within a moment he is gone and I turn the envelope over and over in my hand.

Back at the bottom of the gardens, by the fountain, by the granite statues I tear it open and remove from it, not a note or a letter, but a single black cassette. I fumble to open the Walkman, to remove the art historian and replace him with the black tape. Again I lift the head-phones that are hanging still around my neck, pull them up over my ears and trembling now I press the green start button.

To anyone else, to any of the other visitors wandering around Rodin's gardens this would have been just another piece of classical music. Had I handed them my head-phones, the woman in the mauve dress by the fountain or the man with the black beret still on the bench might have recognized Tchaikovsky's *Swan Lake* with the opening of the first phrases. They might have been carried away, as I was, by its gliding, its sinking and its soaring. But they could not have seen the pictures, floating over the sounds, as I saw them. They would not have felt the hands that I felt. Nor would they have read the words that I read as they weaved in and out of the score between the notes.

THIRTY-EIGHT

Nicholas

As I walk in the early mornings under the hospital's Renaissance arches, through its courtyard, past its graveyard, its chapel and its fading frescoes on rough rose-coloured walls, I wonder sometimes if seven hundred years ago it felt much the same to be a doctor at Santa Maria Nuova. The sense of mission, the sight of nuns in white cotton habits, the sounds of steps on terracotta stone floors and of voices echoing through corridors can surely not have been that different.

When New York became untenable, I could have chosen to return to the hospital on the outskirts of Florence where I had once practised. And I might, when I abandoned research, have thrown myself again into the familiar world of paediatrics. But to do the same as I had done before would have been to move backwards and, even at a time when light for me was obscured by darkness, I knew that sometime in the future I might come to regret that decision.

From the moment when I first went to be interviewed at Santa Maria Nuova in mid-February, in the ice and bitter winds that hit me one way and then another as I crossed the Ponte Vecchio, I felt myself drawn to the place.

The timing too was right. The hospital had just made

an opening for a specialist leukaemia consultant in its renowned oncology department and through the medical network I heard about the post before it was advertised. Professor Solas, newly appointed to the head of oncology, had been a tutor of mine at medical school and remembered me well.

I noticed as we sat and spoke that he had a kindness and a depth to him that made a welcome change from Goldmann's indifference. He talked at first a little about the hospital. He stood with me at the window of his study on the top floor of the building from where we could see the curved wine-coloured roof of the Duomo and he said, 'Did you know if you stand at the top of the Duomo, you can see that Santa Maria is built in the shape of a cross? I'm not a religious man but there's something very spiritual about this place. Sometimes I think it's almost as much a refuge for the doctors as it is for the patients.'

'A refuge in which way, Professor?'

'It's hard to explain,' he said, moving to sit down, ushering me to a seat at the other side of his age-old dark wooden desk. 'Even though there is pain here, both physical and psychological of course, it's a peaceful place. You have faith here . . . Perhaps it's all these Madonnas and children all over the walls.' He smiled.

He poured two glasses of water from an earthenware jug, handed one to me and said, 'I think I've done my public relations bit for the day. We need to talk about you.'

'Yes, I suppose we do.'

He pushed a pile of books and papers out of the way and leant forward across the desk. 'Tell me, what brought you back so quickly from New York?'

To make life easy, to make sure the job was mine I was

tempted for a moment to equivocate, to say that in the end New York became unbearable and research left me cold. But somewhere I knew that he would have felt my omission and that this professor with his white hair and his lined forehead was a listener. And I, only just emerging from under the blanket of black and isolating fog, was overcome all at once by the need to talk.

To my left, through the high mahogany-framed window, the piece of sky I could see turned from aqua, to red, to orange to black as I told him my story. And somewhere between the red and the orange, I saw from the expression on his face that his interest was as much human as professional.

For a long time he was silent. Listening. Looking. Nodding in the right places. When for a few seconds I stopped speaking, he said, 'I don't know much about the workings of pharmaceutical companies, Nicholas, but surely Landmark threatened to take some action against you? After all you made your findings on their premises in their time.'

'Yes, they did threaten at first,' I said, wondering briefly how much I should tell him, how wise it was to open up this way, yet unable now to stop myself. 'They said if they took legal action I could be struck off the medical register and that I'd never be allowed to work in the States again. They suspended me on paid leave and made me sit at home and wait for their calls to appear in front of a investigative disciplinary committee . . . I don't want to sound dramatic, but it gave me an inkling of what it must feel like to be interrogated under torture . . . It was . . . they were . . . the most humiliating months of my life. The threats, the press on my doorstep . . . they got wind of who it was.'

I felt my voice start to shake. '. . . I'm sorry, I em I haven't talked about this much . . . Not at all really. Apart from to the lawyers.'

He raised his hand in a gesture of understanding and said, 'So I take it they decided not to proceed with the action against you. It wouldn't have been worth their while. What they wanted from you was your brainpower. I imagine they did a complete turn-around in the end.'

'Yes, you're right,' I said, laughing slightly. An incongruous laugh. A laugh of relief that someone understood. 'Their main concerns of course were that Zlack Enterprises knew everything and the delay that would be caused by court proceedings. In the end rather than abandon the project Goldmann went to Zlack and agreed on a joint research venture . . . I was astonished.'

'And you?' he asked.

'Oh, they tried to make me stay. One minute both Goldmann and Zlack were both threatening me with breach of contract and professional misconduct and the next, they were both trying to hang on to me. I remember Goldmann's exact words. He said, "Manzini, this is your baby. If you leave it's like aborting a foetus and dumping it in a garbage can."'

Solas winced. 'But you're here,' he said.

'Yes. It wouldn't exactly have been much fun to work with them after that. I had to give them all my findings and sign papers handing all rights over to the joint project. Subtle blackmail I suppose. And I had to promise I would answer questions if they ever needed to consult me. I hear through someone in the Virology department that the research with it is going well and my old colleague Tom is still involved.'

Solas stood up, walked over to the window and looked

at me from there as if trying to gain a different perspective.

'How could you let it go though, Nicholas? It might have led you to great things.'

I didn't know at first how to respond. How to answer the question I had asked myself again and again before I made the decision to leave. 'It was as if . . . I don't quite know how to put it . . . as if the whole story had just slain my ambition . . . and well . . . all I could think of was getting out of New York.'

I looked up and thought at first that Solas had lost interest, that I had spoken for too long, that I had out-stayed my welcome here with Madonna and her child in powder blue staring down at me from above his head.

I was wrong. He must have been following closely, because he came back to sit down and as he pulled out his chair, quite suddenly he said, 'And the woman who leaked the information to the radio? The interpreter. Did you know her?'

'Yes.'

'Ah . . . all the more shocking, I suppose.'

It was very still in the room and from outside the sounds of phones and of voices had faded with the light.

'A colleague, then?'

He had not yet turned on the lamp. It helped not to be able to see his face clearly.

'She was um . . . we were . . . we were together.'

'I see . . . I understand.'

He switched on the light. 'You must have been very angry. Perhaps you still are.'

And for a moment with the dazzle of the bulb, with the word 'angry' it hits me. A dizzying, deafening flash, that had caused my knuckles to bleed as I pummelled the walls of my room and screamed into the emptiness, 'Why, why did you do it? Why? Why? Why didn't you warn me?' A sharp and sickening stab that caused me in those first days to begin to dial her number and slam down the receiver again and again and again. A blood-red rage as I ripped the charcoal portrait of her, shaking, calling out to her as I tore, 'But I loved you. You knew it. You knew it. You knew.' A blinding burning burst of anger as the statue of the man and woman interlocked fell and smashed into jagged fragments of memory.

And me later, day after day between bouts of white fury, lying on my bed in mid-afternoon, unwashed, unshaven, staring up at the ceiling, the shutters still unopened.

I looked at Solas. 'Yes, I was angry. Burning. Furious. And though I have some idea now of why she did it, I still don't understand fully. I don't think I ever will . . . She must have known what it would do to me.'

'Have you been in touch?' he asked.

'No.'

More than my words, my tone must have given so much away because he said, 'Anger and love are difficult to reconcile aren't they?'

'Sorry?'

'*Le coeur connaît des raisons que la raison ne connaît pas* . . . The heart knows reasons that reason cannot understand . . . some famous French philosopher said it.'

And neither the proverb, nor his words about anger and love registered then as they did over the subsequent days, weeks and months. Solas gave me no time. He glanced at his watch and he held out his hand.

'Santa Maria Nuova will be good for you.'

I was astounded. He knew me of old and had seen my credentials on paper, but we had hardly touched on the

284

role here at the hospital.

'We'll need to discuss your position here in detail of course. We can do that tomorrow and then we'll have to pass this through the panel, but I have a feeling you would work well in the department.'

'Thank you so much, Professor.'

'I'm glad,' he said, 'that you found your way here.'

And he was right. Santa Maria Nuova was a refuge, that began to calm and heal its doctors as well as its patients. And as in the old days in Florence I used often to slip into a church to sit in the darkness and the quiet, so now from time to time at the end of a day I would pull open the heavy door of the hospital chapel, walk past the flickering candles, past the patients as they prayed and I would slip into one of the pews just to sit and to be. And it was there on the hard benches that Solas's words began to resonate in my head, 'Anger and love are difficult to reconcile aren't they?' It was there that though it never for a moment left me, the anger shifted slightly to make room for the emptiness. An emptiness that despite my protestations filled itself with Dominique.

I tried for weeks on end to banish the pictures of her. In my head I fought hard to destroy them. With sharp and searing scissor-blades. With black and ugly stripes of paint.

In late-night bars I sought to drown them. At my patients' bedsides I struggled to submerge them. But pictures in your memory are harder to destroy than those on canvas. Oh, they would pretend to go of course. To leave me for an hour or two while I discussed a treatment. For half a day even while I conferred with colleagues on a diagnosis and then, like the worst of opportunists, the second they caught me alone they were back.

Perhaps if Santa Maria Nuova were not so brimming with works of art I might not have thought of the Frick Collection. Of the Rodin museum. Of *Mignon*. I might not have seen her face appearing veiled through the fog in my mind. Perhaps had it not been the week before my birthday I might have not have remembered the date of the last time I saw her, before she ran out of my apartment into the night.

And if I had fought hard to banish the pictures of her, so now with all my strength I wrestled with the crazy idea that had wormed its way into my consciousness. I told myself I was losing my mind, that the memory of those words, 'If we ever split up I'll meet you there a year to the day at midday,' were but the figment of imagination of a man who had been too much alone with his thoughts.

And I convinced myself when I lost the battle and knew that I would go to Paris, that what drove me was no more than curiosity and the need, now, for some sort of explanation should she too be there.

She wasn't there of course, and I, standing waiting by *Mignon* till long past midday, pretending through my headphones to be listening to the guide, laid my hand on the cold bronze of her hair. With my fingers I traced the outline of her face. Her high forehead, her eyelids, the bridge of her nose, the Cupid's bow of her lips.

When much later that day I came back, the museum was about to close its doors and shocked at my own behaviour I begged my way in to speak to the man at the entrance to *Mignon*'s room, with a cassette in my hand as though it were a matter of life and death.

In the week that followed Paris, I worked late at Santa Maria Nuova. Till I was sick with fatigue in the early hours of the morning I stayed in my office or on the wards.

I turned my eyes away from the faces of the Madonnas. I avoided the chapel. I spent almost no time at home alone. I ate little and drank cup after cup of black coffee.

But lack of sleep catches up with you. You can dodge its effects only for so long. Then night after night of five hours' rest, four, even three, begin to take their toll. And when a young woman with arms like sticks and protruding blue veins, waiting for a bone-marrow transplant turns to you and says, 'Doctor, you're the one who looks sick,' you know then that you have gone too far. You know that it is time to shake yourself, to turn your back on self-pity and move on.

And so that evening as soon as I had seen all my patients, I planned to return straight home and sleep. Coming out of the ward I took not a right towards my office but a left towards the reception desk. The corridors were busy. With day staff leaving and night staff arriving. With patients walking up and down on the arms of their visitors.

Sleep deprivation is known to break you down. To cause hallucinations. You imagine you are hearing things. You dream that you are seeing things. Between fantasy and reality the line begins to blur. And so now I am standing only a few steps away from the reception desk when I think I see the back of a thin man in brown corduroy. A foreigner. An American, frustrated, distraught, desperate to make himself understood to the receptionist who speaks only Italian. 'My wife,' he says. 'They brought her in yesterday. We're here on holiday. She collapsed. They told me they've changed her ward. I need to see her.'

The receptionist at first is perplexed, says in Italian that the man in brown corduroy cannot understand, that she will fetch someone to translate. And I am only a few steps away. I walk towards them. I can help of course. But there is no need. A tall woman in black has begun to speak. I think at least that she was in black. Your eyes play tricks on you when you have had so little sleep. She puts her hand on the arm of the man in brown corduroy and she says to the receptionist, '*Non si preoccupi. Traducco io* . . . Don't worry, I'll translate.' For a minute she moves her head back and forwards between the receptionist and the thin man so that I catch a glimpse of her profile. And though I pinch myself, sure that I am seeing things, even in my stupor, even as it rises and falls, as it wafts towards me and away from me, I know that voice. Even as I stand behind her, rooted to the spot, unable yet to speak, I know her voice.

THIRTY-NINE

Dominique

Once in my first months in New York, in Central Park walking near the lake with Nicholas, for no reason at all over and over again I had heard this one line of poetry in my head, *'Wild waters whose foamy waves defy yesterday's frivolity to all who pass by . . .'* and though I was unable to recall the name of the poet, the vision in my mind was clear. I saw Nicholas and myself close to the sea. A rough, black and threatening sea at high tide. A sea with waves that stung and smacked as they hit the layers beneath them. I saw the picture of our silhouettes against a darkening sky with such clarity, such certainty, that when we found ourselves there, after Manhattan, after Paris, after Florence, as the ocean rolled and raged I was afraid but not surprised.

In Florence Nicholas had been unable to open up or to ask me why. In Florence I had been unable to explain. And I had thought that despite the Rodin museum, despite *Mignon* and the cassette, we might be submerged by the murky waters beneath the bridge.

And the uncertainty stayed with me by the sea, as we walked in the evening in the blustery late-night summer winds. 'Because of Mischa,' I said. 'That's why I did it. Because he took his life. I did it because I had to.'

And I thought at first that my explanation would be lost in the current. That the sea and the wind, powerful

289

and mocking, would drown the sound of my words. So I repeated them. I shouted them over the water, over the wind, so that he would hear them, 'I did it because I had to. That's why.'

And he shouted back, the pain that he thought had gone still in his words. Anger still in his voice as he called out to me on the darkening beach. 'I didn't think I could look at you again.' Again, again, again . . . the sea dragged his voice with it that night. The spray tasted salty as tears on our cheeks.

But violent waves grow calm. The air grows warm. The winds abate. The water the next morning turns from black to turquoise. You can walk without fighting the noise or the weather and Nicholas asks, 'Why weren't you there when I was?'

'Because it wasn't the anniversary of the day we split up.'

'It was. It was a year to the day after you ran out of my apartment at night.'

I laughed and stumbled a little on the sand. We brushed shoulders. 'You got it wrong. Or maybe I did. I came a year to the day from the radio broadcast.'

'From the time you spoke your own words.'

'Maybe.'

The waves in the morning have not forgotten their battles of the night before. You can still hear them speak to one another, foamy white in the turquoise water. They move forward, their voices quieter now. Strong but remembering. In the light of morning they have found a new language.